"You know I care about you."

She held him a moment longer, then rose up on her tiptoes to press a soft kiss to his mouth.

The contact arced through him, setting all his nerve endings on fire. She met his eyes for a beat, then kissed him again.

He groaned and opened his mouth, giving her the access she sought. He wanted nothing more than to lose himself in her, let her take away the stress and worry and anxiety about everything.

It felt so good to be holding her, touching her, and yet.... He pulled back, framing Claire's face with his hands. "We should slow down," he said, in a voice too unsteady to be trusted.

"Let me do this for you," she whispered, kissing his chin. "Let me help you tonight."

"Are you sure? If we go much further, I won't want to stop."

"Who's asking you to?"

Dear Reader,

I probably shouldn't admit this, but I've had a crush on Thomas ever since he appeared in my first book, *Deadly Contact*. And what's not to like? He's charming, funny, handsome, smart, and he has a fierce protective streak. In short, he's the perfect romance hero.

Thomas was originally supposed to play a small role in *Deadly Contact,* but he very stubbornly tried to steal all his scenes. That's when I knew he had his own story to tell, and once I stopped fighting him and started listening to him, I realized he was more than just a pretty face.

I really enjoyed working on this book. It was a rollercoaster ride of ups and downs, and I hope I've done his story justice. Thomas and Claire both hold a special place in my heart, and I hope you enjoy getting to know them as much as I did!

Lara

FATAL
FALLOUT

—

Lara Lacombe

HARLEQUIN® ROMANTIC SUSPENSE

Recycling programs
for this product may
not exist in your area.

ISBN-13: 978-0-373-27884-8

FATAL FALLOUT

Copyright © 2014 by Lara Kingeter

All rights reserved. Except for use in any review, the reproduction or utilization of this work in whole or in part in any form by any electronic, mechanical or other means, now known or hereafter invented, including xerography, photocopying and recording, or in any information storage or retrieval system, is forbidden without the written permission of the publisher, Harlequin Enterprises Limited, 225 Duncan Mill Road, Don Mills, Ontario, Canada M3B 3K9.

This is a work of fiction. Names, characters, places and incidents are either the product of the author's imagination or are used fictitiously, and any resemblance to actual persons, living or dead, business establishments, events or locales is entirely coincidental.

This edition published by arrangement with Harlequin Books S.A.

For questions and comments about the quality of this book, please contact us at CustomerService@Harlequin.com.

® and TM are trademarks of Harlequin Enterprises Limited or its corporate affiliates. Trademarks indicated with ® are registered in the United States Patent and Trademark Office, the Canadian Intellectual Property Office and in other countries.

Printed in U.S.A.

www.Harlequin.com

Books by Lara Lacombe

Harlequin Romantic Suspense

Deadly Contact #1778
Fatal Fallout #1814

LARA LACOMBE

I earned my Ph.D. in microbiology and immunology and worked in several labs across the country before moving into the classroom. My day job as a college science professor gives me time to pursue my other love—writing fast-paced romantic suspense, with smart, nerdy heroines and dangerously attractive heroes. I love to hear from readers! Find me on the web, or contact me at laralacombewriter@gmail.com.

For the redheads in my life: Will, Josh and Toby.
Love you guys!

Many thanks to Rachel Burkot, Patience Bloom
and the team at Harlequin.
Thanks also to Jessica Alvarez. Y'all are the best!

Chapter 1

"Dr. Fleming, can you comment on the recent alarm at the Central Virginia nuclear reactor after Tuesday's earthquake?"

"Dr. Fleming, is nuclear power safe?"

"Is the public in any danger?"

Claire Fleming pasted on a smile as she turned to face the handful of reporters standing on the sidewalk outside the Nuclear Safety Group's building. She'd known these questions would be coming, but had hoped to at least get a cup of coffee first. Mornings were tough enough without facing a barrage of questions, and she didn't feel human without that first cup of java.

"I want to assure people that there was no accident at the Central Virginia nuclear plant. The reactor experienced a low-level alarm following the earthquake, but the emergency systems kicked in without a problem, and at no time was the public in danger. Nuclear power continues to be one of the safest options for meeting the growing energy needs of our country."

One of the reporters—a short, round woman sporting large glasses and a frown—finished scribbling and opened her mouth to ask a follow-up question. Claire held up a hand before she could speak, shooting her what she hoped was an apologetic smile. "We'll be having a press conference later today, and I'd appreciate it if you hold the rest of your questions until then."

The small group grumbled but began to disperse, freeing Claire to walk into the building. She waited until the elevator doors closed, then leaned back against the wall and rubbed her forehead. What a mess.

The minor earthquake the day before yesterday had been a wake-up call. Although it was only a four on the Richter scale, the tremors were strong enough to trigger emergency shutdown procedures at the Central Virginia plant. While things had gone off without a hitch, it was only a matter of time before an accident happened. The plant was one of the older ones in the region and needed constant updating, and given budget shortfalls, money was tight. Paradoxically, Central Virginia's stellar safety record put it at the bottom of the list for repairs—a fact that aggravated Claire to no end.

She strolled past the reception desk with a quick smile for Eva. "I left you a gift on your desk," the woman called out.

"Is it coffee?" Claire asked, unable to keep the note of desperation out of her voice.

Eva shot her a sly grin. "Maybe."

"Oh, you are a goddess."

Eva's laugh followed her down the hall. She stepped into her office and there, on the middle of the desk, sat the distinctive black-and-white cup from her favorite coffee shop. She dropped her bag on the floor and snatched it up, holding it under her nose for a second to inhale the blissful aroma. Taking a sip, she nearly groaned aloud as the rich brew hit her tongue. Maybe today wouldn't be so bad after all.

"Morning."

Jerry Witter stood in the doorway, his large frame leaving little room for anything else. "Hey Jerry, how's it going?"

He shrugged and stepped inside her office, rubbing a hand over his bushy goatee before replying. "All right, I suppose. Had to shoot me a dog last night."

She blinked, unsure she'd heard him correctly. "You shot a dog?" she repeated slowly, trying to understand. The lack of caffeine must be getting to her.

"Yep. There was a dog in my garage last night."

"I see. Did you know this dog?"

He shook his head. "Nope. Seemed mean though. Kept jumping up on the door, barking and snarling at me. I read his owner's number off the tag on his collar and called. They're out of town, told me to just send him home." He shook his head. "Can you believe that?"

She shook her head, sinking slowly into her chair. "So what did you do?"

"Well, I threw some hot dogs out there, but the dog kept coming back inside the garage before I could get the door shut. I can't have a vicious dog by my house— what if he hurts one of my girls?"

Claire nodded, not sure she wanted to hear the end of this story.

"So I got my gun and shot him."

She felt her jaw drop as she stared up at him. "Jerry, why didn't you just call animal control?"

"What for?" He looked genuinely confused, as if the idea had never occurred to him. "I took care of it."

"But…" She searched for something to say, trying hard to relate to a man whose first reaction to a problem was to pick up his gun. "You can't just kill people's pets when they annoy you!"

"I didn't kill him."

She frowned, confused. "You said you shot him." *I haven't had enough coffee for this.*

"Yeah, but I used rubber bullets. He took off like his tail was on fire," he said, chuckling at the memory.

She smiled weakly. "Sounds like quite the adventure."

"I 'spose so. Did you have a good night?"

She sighed, taking another sip of coffee. "Not bad. Prepping for damage control after this earthquake."

He snorted. "That wasn't an earthquake. That was barely a tremor."

"Yes, well." She pulled her laptop out of her bag, placing it on her desk along with a number of other papers. "The Central Virginia alarm went off, so it's news."

"Yeah. Let me know if I can help with anything."

"Thanks—I appreciate it." She powered on her computer, taking another sip of coffee as it booted up.

Jerry turned to go but stopped at her door, snapping his fingers. "Almost forgot. Dr. Reed wants to bring me in on the Russian cleanup project, and he told me to get some contact information from you."

"No problem. Give me just a second…." She typed as she spoke, pulling up her contact list. It would be good to have another person on this project. There were so many nuclear power plants in Russia, many crumbling and unsecured, making them prime targets for terrorists looking to steal radioactive materials. The NSG had teamed up with their Russian counterparts in the hopes of reducing the threat, but it was an uphill battle, and they needed all the help they could get.

The new-mail icon popped up at the lower right corner of her screen, signifying an unread message. She clicked out of habit, smiling when she saw the email was from Ivan Novikoff.

"Actually, Ivan just emailed me, so I'll forward this message to you and you'll have his information."

"Sounds good. Thanks." He walked out, his movements surprisingly quiet for such a large man.

She clicked to open the email, frowning as a picture began loading. That was strange. Ivan never sent images—he was hyperparanoid about security, not wanting to risk his messages being intercepted and used against him. Concerns regarding the safety of nuclear power already ran high, and there were many protest groups who would not hesitate to take images out of context and use them to needlessly scare people.

She reached for her coffee as she glanced at the screen, then gasped. The cup fell from her nerveless hands, hitting the floor and splashing the burning liquid on her legs. She ignored the stinging pain as she focused on the image in front of her, trying to process what she was seeing.

No.

She shook her head, putting a fist to her mouth to contain the scream that clawed up her throat. *No!*

Leaning over, she retched into the trash can next to her desk. Suddenly Jerry was there, his hand on her back, his voice a buzzing drone in her ears.

"Ivan…"

She knew when Jerry saw the image by his sharp intake of breath. He reached out a hand, slamming down the lid of her computer. "Don't look at that," he said, his voice gruff.

She nodded, but it was too late. The image was burned into her brain. All she had to do was close her eyes to see Ivan, her friend and collaborator, lying in a pool of his own blood, the horrible words painted in jagged red script across his chest.

You're next.

"Again!"

Thomas looked down into his niece's smiling face and couldn't help but grin in return. "Okay, but this is the last time."

Emily watched in wide-eyed fascination as he pulled out his badge and flashed it at her. "Freeze!" he said in his best tough-guy voice. She dissolved into a fit of giggles, nearly crumpling to the floor in hysterics. Her reaction would have worried a lesser man, Thomas mused as he bent to scoop her up. Still, as long as he didn't have to bust a five-year-old girl anytime soon, he was probably intimidating enough to do his job.

"Let's go, squirt. We're gonna be late."

She let out a dramatic sigh. "Fine," she said in the tone of a long-suffering victim.

He set her on the floor with a pat on the shoulder. "Go kiss your mom goodbye, but be quiet so you don't wake her."

Emily ran down the hall, slowing as she approached her mother's bedroom. She carefully pushed open the door and entered on tiptoe. Thomas smiled as he watched her golden ponytail disappear into the dark room, then turned to press a kiss to his mother's temple. "Have a good day, Ma."

"You, too, dear." She patted his cheek. "Be safe today."

"Always."

Emily reappeared, closing the door with exaggerated care. "I'm ready," she said as she approached Thomas.

He handed her the pink-sequined backpack, let her struggle into it on her own. He'd made the mistake of trying to help her once, and the resulting fit had drawn Jenny from her bedroom. His sister-in-law worked nights at the hospital and needed her sleep, and she hadn't been happy about being roused after only an hour of rest to calm down her hysterical daughter.

"Bye, Nana." She reached up to hug his mother, who bent with effort to wrap her arms around the girl. She was moving slower and slower these days, but she still insisted everything was fine. He supposed it didn't take much effort to watch Emily at night while Jenny worked, but even so, he worried about her health.

"Goodbye, sweet girl. Have a great day at school."

Emily let out another sigh. "I'll try." She reached

up to take Thomas's hand, leading him out of the apartment.

"Is everything okay at school, Em?" They walked down the stairs together, hand in hand, her eyes on the floor while she carefully navigated the steps.

"I guess."

"Is anyone bothering you?"

"No."

"Do you like your teacher?" he pressed. The FBI had courses on the best methods to use when interrogating children, but he hadn't taken any of them since most of his investigations focused on adults. Now, faced with a recalcitrant niece, he wondered if maybe he should sign up for the next session.

Emily shrugged as he opened the passenger door. "She's okay." She climbed into the car, wriggling out of her backpack and setting it on the floor before reaching for the seat belt.

He slid into the driver's seat and started the car. "It just seems like you don't want to go to school."

"Yeah."

"Do you want to tell me why?"

He pulled into traffic, giving her time to think about her response. The silence went on for so long that he was about to ask her again when she said quietly, "I miss my dad."

His heart clenched at the admission. He reached for her hand, gave it a squeeze. "I miss him, too, sweetie."

Roger, his brother, had died in a car accident six months ago, but the details of that horrible day were never far from his mind. The afternoon phone call from his mother. The frantic drive to the hospital. The stale waiting-room coffee as they huddled together, waiting to hear if the doctors had worked a miracle. Jenny's piercing scream when the surgical team walked over, eyes downcast and shoulders hunched. And Emily's pale, tear-streaked face after he told her the earth-shattering news.

Roger's death had left a gaping hole in Jenny and Emily's lives, one that Thomas had tried to patch, albeit with limited success. While he never wanted to replace her father, he did want Emily to have a male presence in her life, a man who loved her unreservedly and without question. He had begun taking her to school in the weeks after Roger's death, stepping into the role Roger had performed so well. At first, Emily had been reserved and tearful, but she'd gradually begun to warm up to seeing him more often, and he treasured their mornings and the routine they had built. It was a small but important step on the path of healing.

But it was a bumpy road, as evidenced by Emily's quivering lip. "All the other kids have dads," she said in a wobbly voice. "I don't understand why mine had to die."

"I don't either, love. Nobody understands it." He ached to pull her into his lap for a hug, but contented himself with holding her hand as he kept his focus on the road. From the corner of his eye, he could see her lips press together in a pale line and knew she was trying hard not to cry. *My sweet, brave girl.*

She was quiet for the rest of the drive. He didn't press her to talk—he wanted to be a safe place for her, and if he pestered her, she would withdraw from him.

He pulled up to the curb in front of the school, then turned to face her.

"Try to have a good day, Emmycakes." It was his pet nickname for her, a play on her name and patty-cake, her favorite game as a little one. The name never failed to make her smile, and it didn't disappoint now.

She grinned up at him, her earlier sadness cast off like a discarded coat. "I will. You, too, Uncle Thomas."

He smiled at her serious tone. "I'll do my best," he assured her.

She leaned over to press a kiss to his cheek, then climbed carefully out of the passenger seat. He watched while she made her way up the steps to her teacher. He gave the woman a wave as she collected Emily and guided her inside along with the other children, then merged back into traffic.

Must be nice, he mused, thinking how quickly she had gone from tears to smiles. Would that his own grief and sadness were as easy to shake.

Although he understood on a logical, rational level that his brother's death hadn't been his fault, he couldn't dismiss the guilt that plagued him at the thought of Roger.

I should have taken Mom....

After a late-winter storm had pounded the city, his mother had called needing a ride to a doctor's appointment. Buried at work, Thomas had asked Roger to cover for him. Since he was off duty at the time, Roger hadn't hesitated to hop in the car and head over to their mom's house. It should have been just another drive, a normal errand, nothing to write home about.

Except for the garbage truck that hit a patch of ice

and slammed into the car, crushing it and his brother in the blink of an eye.

For the first few weeks after the accident, Thomas had woken almost nightly, soaked with sweat and with a scream trapped in his throat. The nightmares were graphic and all too real, the accident playing out in horrible slow motion while Thomas stood on the sidewalk, helpless to do anything but watch as his brother disappeared into a pile of twisted metal.

The images had gradually faded, but the worst part was that Thomas still couldn't think about his brother without imagining Roger's last conscious moments as he lay trapped in the wreckage. His pain. His fear. His worry for Jenny and Emily. He hoped that one day, he would be able to remember Roger without recalling the accident, but for now, thoughts of Roger just left him feeling raw, like he'd taken a bath in acid.

So he tried not to think about it.

With a shake of his head, he reached for the dial, wanting some music to distract him for the rest of the drive. No sense in brooding over a past he couldn't change. In that way lay madness.

Before he could settle on a station, his phone rang. A quick glance at the lit display showed his boss calling, which was unusual. Agent Harper liked to keep track of the team, but he usually wasn't overbearing about it. For him to call now, minutes before Thomas was due to show up at the office, meant something was going on.

"Kincannon here."

"How close are you?"

Thomas bit back the urge to reply *Good morning to you, too*. Harper's brusque tone made it clear his sense of humor was on vacation, and since Thomas still didn't know him all that well, he decided to play it safe. "Five minutes, give or take a few."

"I need to see you when you get in. Right away."

"No problem," Thomas replied to the dial tone. Snapping the phone closed, he tucked it back into his jacket pocket and pressed on the accelerator to beat a yellow light.

It sounded like Harper had a new case for him, an idea that had his pulse quickening with anticipation. Forget music—work was the best distraction.

Harper's door was partially open, so Thomas gave it a perfunctory rap with his knuckles as he walked into the office. The older man looked up from his computer and gestured for Thomas to take a seat. He did, glancing about the room as Harper finished typing.

While Carmichael, his former boss, had been a bit of a pack rat, keeping papers and other bits of miscellany piled high on every flat surface, Harper was practically a monk by comparison. His desk was clear of everything but his computer, a cup of pens and pencils, a desk calendar and a single piece of paper. The filing cabinets were a new addition to the space, the neatly labeled drawers a testament to Harper's organizational prowess. Thomas thought briefly of his own desk, which fell somewhere in the middle of the two extremes. Even though he wasn't terribly messy, he had the fleeting thought that Harper would not approve of his filing system. Good thing the man stayed in his office most of the time.

"I have an assignment for you."

Thomas returned his focus to the man in front of him, belatedly realizing Harper had stopped typing and was staring at him.

"What's up?"

The older man winced slightly at his choice of words, and Thomas bit his lip to keep from smiling. He knew his casual speech bothered the buttoned-up man, and the small, rebellious part of him liked to poke the bear. One of these days it was going to come back and bite him in the ass, but he didn't care.

"Dr. Claire Fleming received a death threat this morning," Harper informed him, pushing the paper across the desk toward him.

Thomas picked it up and glanced over the dossier. Claire Fleming. Thirty-two years old. Scientist with the Nuclear Safety Group. The grainy black-and-white photo didn't do her any favors, but he could see she was pretty enough, with her light hair piled atop her head and slightly plump lips under a straight nose. She didn't look like the kind of person to inspire death threats, but there were a lot of unhinged people in the world.

"Why do we get the case?" Death threats usually stayed at the level of the local police, so there must be something more to the story.

"This particular threat came from Russia. Dr. Fleming's contact, Ivan Novikoff, was killed yesterday, and she received a picture of his body with the threat." Harper pressed a few keys, then flipped the monitor around so Thomas could see the gruesome photo.

"Has this been verified?" Ivan Novikoff lay sprawled in a puddle of blood, his open mouth an echo of the gaping wound in his neck. "You're next" was written on the man's white shirt, the reddish-brown of the letters a stark contrast to his pale skin.

"Yes. It's legitimate."

Thomas frowned. "Is State involved?"

Harper pressed his lips together, a sure sign of agitation. "They are…facilitating discussions with the Russians," he said delicately, leaving no doubt as to his opinion of their involvement. "We're hoping to hear more from our counterparts regarding the circumstances surrounding Dr. Novikoff's death."

"Well, it wasn't accidental, that much is clear."

"Quite."

Thomas set the paper back on Harper's desk and stretched out his legs. "What are we doing?"

The older man regarded him with a level gaze. "There is no 'we' at this point. There is 'you.' And you will act as our contact with Dr. Fleming. I want you to stick by her side and keep her safe until we figure out what is really going on here."

"You want me to act as her bodyguard?" Disbelief made the words come out a bit sharper than he intended, but Thomas didn't bother to apologize. No way was he going to take a babysitting job when he had other cases to work, other responsibilities that needed his attention.

"Is there a problem?"

"Yeah, there kind of is. I've got other cases—I can't just drop everything to hang out with this woman on the off chance someone tries to pull something."

Harper narrowed his gray eyes, the atmosphere in the office growing decidedly chilly. "Agent Kincannon," he began icily, "lest you forget, you are in a precarious position. After the debacle that was the Collins investigation, the suits upstairs want nothing more than to fire this entire unit. I am all that stands between you and the brass. You will go where I tell you, do what I tell you and take the assignments I give you without question, or you will find yourself without a job. Are we clear?"

Thomas felt his face heat but kept his mouth shut. Now was not the time to protest that they had all done the best they could with the limited information they'd had at the time. It wasn't their fault a crazy man had blown up part of the Smithsonian. Besides, the injuries had been minor and the group had brought in not one but two suspects. It really should have counted as a win, but the guys upstairs had no tolerance for deviations from the plan. In the end, Carmichael had fallen on his sword to protect the rest of the team, but it sounded like the big boys wanted more blood.

"Yes, sir," he bit out, trying to keep his voice level.

Harper leaned back with a nod. "Very good. Dr. Fleming is still at her office, along with the local police and someone from computer crimes. I suggest you meet her there and introduce yourself. You'll be spending a lot of time together in the coming days, so do try to be nice."

Recognizing a dismissal when he heard it, Thomas stood and turned to leave. His fingers itched to fire off a mocking salute, but he resisted the impulse, knowing it would likely send Harper over the edge.

He paused at the threshold. "You'll let me know as soon as you hear from the Russians?"

Harper nodded, already turning back to his computer. "Of course."

Thomas frowned. He knew in his gut that something else was going on but had no idea what. He left the office, rubbing a hand over the back of his neck to massage away the tingling sensation dancing across his skin. Was it any wonder his alarm bells were ringing? Russians, nuclear scientists and death threats. All the makings of a disaster.

Pausing to grab a notebook from his desk, he headed back out to the car, softly whistling the James Bond theme music as he went.

"So it's done?"

Victor rubbed the blade of his knife with a soft cloth, buffing the metal to a gleaming shine. "He's dead."

"Did you have any trouble?"

He held back the snort of laughter. Trouble? Of course not. Ivan Novikoff had been an easy mark, a soft, careless man. He hadn't known he was being followed, hadn't suspected a thing when Victor had appeared in his office. The man had even offered him coffee, for God's sake. He shook his head. A stupid mistake, and the last one Novikoff had made.

"No trouble. It was quick and easy."

"Not too quick, I hope." The man's voice took on a slight edge. Victor's lip curled up in disgust. He didn't torture people without reason. He prided himself on making a clean kill—to do anything else was a waste of time and talent. The only reason he'd written on the scientist's shirt was because his employer had demanded it, and he was being paid very well for his efforts.

"The message was delivered as you requested," he said, hoping to change the subject. The man on the other end of the line could be a bit stubborn, grabbing on to topics like a dog with a bone, and Victor wasn't in the mood to relate the precise details of the job. He was paid to kill, not to give a play-by-play after the work was done.

"Good. And the papers?"

He hesitated a beat, knowing his employer wouldn't react well to the news. "There were no papers."

There was a pause, and Victor could practically feel the man's anger build in the charged silence. Victor wasn't happy about the missing documents either, but there was nothing to be done at the moment.

"Look, the job isn't over yet," he pointed out, hoping to stave off an explosion.

"You're right, it is not." His voice was lethally quiet, the cultured accent making his words seem even more dangerous. "You still have to take out Fleming. I hope, for your sake, she knows where the papers are. Otherwise, I will take it out on you."

Victor sucked in a breath. He had known the threat was coming, but it still hit him like a fist to the gut.

"That won't be necessary. I think she has them."

"What makes you say that?"

He set the knife aside, smoothing out the cloth as he spoke. "I found a package receipt in Novikoff's office. He'd sent a collection of documents to her the day before I got there, if the customs form is to be believed."

"You should hope it is. I don't have to remind you what happens to associates who disappoint, do I?"

The images flashed through his mind, a horrific

movie reel of pain and blood and a final, merciful death. The Russian mafia wasted no time in meting out retribution in creatively gruesome ways, and Victor had no intention of experiencing it firsthand.

"No. I remember," he said, suppressing a shudder.

"You have three days."

Victor flipped the phone closed, carefully placed it next to the knife and smoothed his hands over his face. He was walking a tightrope, to be sure. Killing Novikoff had been easy enough, and while he didn't relish the thought of killing a woman, it had to be done. The papers were the real target—Novikoff and Fleming were just collateral damage. There was no guarantee Fleming would have the papers he needed, though, and he knew that if he didn't get them, his mission would be considered a failure.

Failure was not tolerated by the Bratva. Failure was punished. The greater the failure, the greater the punishment. It was that simple. And since he would not tolerate failure, would not give his employer the satisfaction of punishing him, he had only one option.

Kill the woman. Find the papers.

Survive.

Chapter 2

Claire sat on the sofa in the break room, arms wrapped tightly around herself in a vain attempt to control her shaking. Ivan was dead. Ivan, who had visited just two months ago, who had been so full of life and energy, tirelessly taking on the problems of safeguarding Russia's nuclear material, was gone. And not just dead, but murdered in a horrific fashion. She blinked furiously to clear the tears that threatened to fall.

No crying. Not now. There would be time for that later, when she was home and could fall apart in private. But it just didn't make sense. Who would want to kill Ivan? He was—*had been,* she corrected grimly—such a wonderful man. He had made it his mission to keep people safe, to ensure that the crumbling nuclear power plants in Russia were decommissioned safely, that their dangerous fuel sources were disposed of properly. He had been a force of nature, using humor, charm and sheer stubborn will to get the authorities to listen to him. He'd had his share of enemies, but in the years they'd worked together she'd seen that even those who disagreed with him respected him.

Or so she'd thought.

A uniformed police officer sat by the door, idly flipping through one of the Nuclear Safety Group's newsletters. She didn't understand why he had to stay with her—she'd much rather be alone right now to gather her thoughts—but the detectives had insisted on leaving someone here while they checked her office. They'd shooed her out the door, politely but firmly, giving her no choice but to retreat to the break room while they pored over her computer and files. Even though she didn't keep anything personal in her office, she still felt a bit disconcerted by the knowledge that her things were being scrutinized by strangers.

You're next.

Goose bumps broke out across her skin as the bloody image popped into her head again. Why? Who would want to target her? What had she done?

Her musings were interrupted by the arrival of a new face. A tall man stepped into the room, stopped to murmur something to the police officer who had looked up at his entrance, and then turned and walked over to the couch. He sat down, close but not crowding her, and gave her a small smile.

"Dr. Fleming, I presume?" His voice was deep and smooth, calming. She nodded.

"I'm Agent Thomas Kincannon, FBI." He removed a badge from his jacket and held it out. She took it, inspecting the gold shield and picture ID. He looked so young in the picture, a fresh-faced boy probably just out of the academy. She glanced at his face as she returned his identification. The long nose was the same, but his cheeks were a bit leaner, and faint lines bracketed his mouth and feathered from the corners of his bright blue eyes. It would seem Agent Kincannon had grown up a bit since this picture was taken.

"Claire." She relaxed her arms, stuck out a hand. Standing five foot eight, she'd never felt particularly small before, but when his large hand enfolded hers, she felt positively tiny. His skin was warm, and the brush of his fingertips against her wrist had tingles shooting up her arm.

What was she supposed to say to him? *Nice to meet you* was a lie, given the circumstances, but manners dictated she say something. He turned to glance at the officer by the door, and the light from the window caught Agent Kincannon's hair, highlighting the mix of red, gold, amber and copper strands in the tuft that fell across his forehead.

"Your hair—it's beautiful," she blurted out. He turned to face her, eyebrows lifted and mouth twitching, and she wished desperately for the couch to open up and swallow her whole.

Where the hell did that come from?

"I always wanted red hair," she muttered, knowing she sounded like a crazy person.

"Trust me, you don't. I burn within five minutes of stepping outside. It's like I'm a vampire or something."

"I stay inside most of the time anyway, so it wouldn't affect me." *Stop talking!*

He merely stared at her with a faint smile, as if trying to determine if she was just socially awkward or if she'd skipped a dose of medication. Desperate to fill the silence, she rushed ahead. "I'm sorry. It's just, I talk when I'm nervous, and I don't really know what's going on here. Ivan is dead, and I have no idea who killed him or why they would want to." She paused to swallow, hating the tightness of her throat. It felt like a fist was squeezing her neck, making it hard to breathe or speak. Needing a distraction, she dropped her eyes to Agent Kincannon's hands. His wrists were lightly dusted with red-gold hair, and a large silver watch peeked out from under his jacket sleeve. She focused on the blue watch face, tracking the second hand as it ticked around.

"And apparently someone is after me, too, but I don't know why. It's not logical. Why would anyone want to hurt me? I haven't done anything!" She shook her head, still trying to make sense of the morning's events. A small part of her hoped this was all a bad dream, that she'd wake up in her bed and start the day over again. Things would go back to normal. But as she raised her eyes back up to Agent Kincannon's face, his expression of pity made it clear her life would never be the same again.

"I know you've had quite a shock this morning," he said, his voice kind and soothing. "But right now I want you to let us worry about finding out the who and why of this situation."

She nodded, knowing she wasn't much help in that department. "Have you already talked to the other detectives? They may have found something on my computer—I think they were trying to trace the email."

He shifted a bit, giving her the impression he was uncomfortable with her question. "No," he said after a few seconds. "I haven't spoken with them. I'm actually here for you."

What? That doesn't make sense. "I don't understand," she said slowly. "Why would the FBI send an agent for me? Shouldn't you guys be looking for Ivan's killer?"

"Well, it's a bit more complicated than that," he said. "We can't interfere in the Russian investigation, which ties our hands a bit. Really, all we can do is wait and see if Ivan's killer comes after you."

Her stomach somersaulted as his words sank in. "So you're saying I'm bait?"

"I wouldn't put it that way," he assured her. "We're not actually trying to lure the killer in. We just want to make sure you're safe, on the off chance the threat to you does materialize."

He made it sound as if she wasn't in any danger, but his words did nothing to ease the leaden weight in her stomach. "I see."

He stood, looming over her briefly before taking a step back. "There's not really anything you can do here, so I can take you home or I can take you to my office. Your choice."

Apparently, whatever she chose, she was now going to have a shadow. It might be safer for her at his office, but the thought of home was too tempting to pass up. She could brew a cup of tea, sink into her favorite chair and try to forget the image of her murdered friend. She may even be able to ignore Agent Kincannon and crawl back into bed, where she could cry for Ivan in peace.

"I'd like to go home," she replied. Alone, preferably, but since that was not an option, she'd settle for his company.

Agent Kincannon nodded, holding out a hand to help her off the couch. "Let's go."

The drive to her apartment was quiet, with Claire speaking only to give him directions. It was just as well, because he didn't know what to say to her. *Sorry your friend is dead* seemed a bit insensitive, even to him. Fortunately, she didn't appear to be up for conversation, so he wasn't forced to make small talk.

She held herself carefully, as though she was in pain or would break if jostled. Her brows were drawn together, lips pressed into a thin white line, and her eyes shone with that thousand-yard stare of shock he'd seen all too often on the faces of people who had suffered a life-changing blow. It was the same expression she'd worn when he'd entered the break room and found her sitting on the couch, lost in her own thoughts. He hated seeing that look on a woman's face, hated the feeling of helplessness that rose up in him at the sight of her suffering. He was struck by the urge to act, to *do* something, but no amount of soothing words would fix what a killer had done to her.

Besides, it wasn't his job to comfort her. He was supposed to protect her, keep her safe from harm. Well, physical harm, anyway. He couldn't do anything about her emotional pain, and she likely wouldn't welcome any of his clumsy attempts to make her feel better. She didn't know him, he didn't know her, and it was easier for both of them if it stayed that way. He had his hands full helping Jenny, Emily and his mother deal with their grief. He wasn't sure he had it in him to help Dr. Fleming process hers, too.

She directed him to an apartment building on Wisconsin Avenue, along a residential stretch of the busy thoroughfare. A wide sidewalk ran alongside the street, punctuated every few yards with small trees, the city's attempt at beautification. It was a pleasant-looking neighborhood. The sidewalk was in good repair, if littered with fallen leaves, and a quick glance at the cars parked nearby confirmed his initial impression that this was a solidly middle-class area.

After taking a few steps into her apartment, Claire stopped and stared at the living room, shaking her head back and forth as if trying to figure out how and why she was there. Recognizing the signs of an imminent collapse, Thomas stepped forward, resting his hands lightly on her shoulders. "Why don't you lie down for a bit? We can talk once you've had some time to process everything."

She nodded but made no move to head for a bedroom. He gave her a gentle push to get her started, and she walked mechanically down the hall until they reached her bedroom. The room was cool and dark and smelled faintly of lavender. He wasn't surprised to find the bed neatly made, the pale yellow comforter spread smooth across the expanse of mattress. The quick glance he'd seen of her apartment had left the impression of a woman who liked organization, wanted everything kept in its place. Now that her life had been flipped upside down, the lack of control must be killing her.

He helped her pull the covers down, then knelt to tug off her shoes as she sat on the edge of the bed. The gesture was surprisingly intimate, and he felt a sudden flare of heat as he pulled off the sensible brown pump to reveal the graceful arch of her foot, the pretty pink of her toenails. He'd never considered himself a foot man before, but he couldn't deny the good doctor was lovely. What else was she hiding beneath her professional armor? The thought drew him up short and he reared back, almost falling onto his ass in the process. *Get it together, Kincannon. One look at her toes and you're drooling? Pathetic.*

He stood abruptly, hoping she didn't notice the blush he felt creeping across his cheeks. He glanced down at her and realized he could have paraded a brass band through her apartment without disturbing her—she was beginning to shut down, withdrawing further into her shell in a bid to block out the world. He recognized the impulse, having done the same thing after Roger's death.

Moving woodenly, as if every gesture required more effort than she could bear, Claire stretched out on the bed and turned to her side, giving him her back. Interpreting the gesture as a dismissal, he stepped toward her bedroom door but paused when he realized he still held her shoes. She probably wouldn't want them just dropped on the floor, so he arranged them carefully next to the hunter-green chair that sat in front of a mirrored dressing table.

"Thank you." The words were soft but distinct in

the silence of the room. He stopped in the doorway, turned back to the bed. She was so still, a pale statue that blended in with the light sheets.

"I'll be in the living room if you need anything." He pulled the door closed after him, leaving it slightly ajar, then made his way back down the hall. He stopped in the kitchen, noting the window above the sink before moving on to the main room. The large room was lined with windows along the far end, giving the apartment a bright, friendly air. He walked over and drew the blinds down, effectively shrouding the room in a muted gray light. He was probably being paranoid, but there was no sense in making it easy for someone to see in.

The front door was the only entrance, which wasn't ideal. He walked back into the kitchen and leaned forward to see out that window, nodding in satisfaction as he caught sight of the fire escape railing. He unlocked the window and gave an experimental shove, wincing when it shuddered up with a creaking protest. He briefly debated oiling the tracks. On the one hand, it would be tough to make a quiet escape this way, but it would also provide an excellent warning if someone was trying to get in. Deciding the advanced notice of an intruder outweighed the need for a stealthy exit, he pushed the window back down, locked it and drew the shade.

Opening the cabinet next to the sink, he was rewarded with the sight of rows of glasses lined up with military precision. He pulled one down and filled it with water, shaking his head. While his collection of glasses was a mixed bag of free cups and hand-me-downs from his mom or sister-in-law, Dr. Fleming's were clearly of a set, uniform in appearance and size and all spotlessly clean. Her underwear drawer was probably the same way—white cotton panties all neatly folded and stacked…

Whoa. Where the hell had that come from? He had no business thinking about Dr. Fleming's underwear, or her underwear drawer for that matter. Pushing the unsettling thought firmly out of his mind, he walked back into the main room, pausing before the book-shelves. There were a few photos on display, mostly of landscapes or landmarks from past trips. His eyes caught on a picture of Claire, smiling and happy as she sat beside Ivan Novikoff on the steps of the Lincoln Memorial. The older man had his head turned and was pressing a kiss to her hair as she grinned up at the camera. Interesting. Had they been an item? He was old enough to be her father, but maybe she preferred older men. It would certainly explain her shock at his death.

If Ivan Novikoff had gotten entangled in something dangerous or illegal, would he have told his lover? Not likely, Thomas mused as he moved to scan the other set of bookshelves. He'd probably wanted to keep her safe, and had thought that keeping her out of the loop would protect her. But protect her from what?

His position gave him access to lots of nuclear material, both spent fuel from aging reactors and potent radioactive fuel. There was quite a demand for radio-active supplies on the black market, and Ivan was the ideal supplier. As one of the people who kept track of nuclear material, it wouldn't be difficult for him to fudge the records, divert a little bit of fuel at a time in exchange for money or power. And if he'd been in the business of selling radioactive materials, the kind of unsavory characters who were buying wouldn't think twice about coming after his lover if he'd betrayed them.

If that was the case, the Russians wouldn't work too hard to find his killer. If Ivan was part of an underground, black market arms trade, it would be hugely embarrassing for the Russians to admit that the man they had entrusted with the safe disposal of nuclear fuel had been selling it to terrorists and rogue states.

No, better for them to characterize his death as a random, horrible act, brush it under the rug and move on. Which meant it would be that much harder to figure out who had targeted Dr. Fleming.

Running a hand through his hair, Thomas set his glass on the coffee table and reached for his phone. Just as he flipped it open to dial Harper, Claire's terrified scream rent the air.

Claire sat across from Ivan, enjoying his company as they drank coffee and talked. His daughter was a musician with the Moscow orchestra, and he was telling her about Anya's latest performance, his eyes glowing with fatherly pride as he bragged about her violin solo.

"She was so beautiful," he gushed, patting his pockets in search of something. "My phone—you must see the pictures."

Claire nodded, sipping her coffee as Ivan pulled out his cell phone. His head bent in absorption, he carefully pressed buttons on the keypad, his bushy eyebrows drawing together as he searched for the im-

ages. While he fought with his phone, she let her gaze drift past the table, frowning when she noticed a dark, amorphous mass creeping forward. What was that?

She shivered as the smoky cloud drifted closer. There was something about it that seemed...malicious. As it drew nearer, she could see sparkles in the black fog as it glided across the ground, glints of light winking off something solid and metallic inside. It moved with such purpose that she knew it was heading for their table, and her heart began to pound, alarm sending spikes of adrenaline shooting through her limbs.

Ivan remained oblivious to the threat, still searching for the pictures of his daughter. She tried to speak, to warn him, but her throat closed up and she couldn't get the words out. Ignoring her frantic gestures, Ivan merely sat while the shadowy mass enveloped him, hiding him from view. Suddenly, his pained shrieks pierced the fog. She strained forward, reaching out her arms to grab him, but came up with nothing. After a breathless moment, the shadow disappeared to reveal Ivan, slumped over the table, his normally pale skin coated in blood from the thousand shallow cuts that crisscrossed his face and hands.

Claire screamed, fighting against an unseen force that kept her from reaching him. He was still and unmoving, the red pool on the table growing steadily with each breath she took. "Ivan! Ivan!"

"Claire!" There were hands on her arms, shaking her, pulling her away from the table, away from Ivan. "Claire!"

She opened her eyes, breathing hard. "Ivan," she whimpered. "I have to help Ivan."

"I know." The voice was deep and soothing, and she was pulled into a warm chest while a hand stroked down her hair. "I know."

She sniffled into the starched shirt, her awareness gradually returning as strong arms rocked her back and forth and a deep voice rumbled, low and comforting, in her ear. Ivan was dead. Her friend, her mentor—the man she loved like a father—was gone.

She'd lost her adoptive father almost twenty years ago. While she thought of him every day, the loss was no longer as raw as it had once been. She'd learned to cope, moving through life with the assumption that she would never again experience that kind of relationship.

Until Ivan came along, slipping under her defenses and becoming so much more than a professional colleague. He shared his family with her, and she'd reveled in his stories, basking in the reflected glow of the love he felt for his family. His wife had embraced her, as well, in what had been a welcome surprise, given Claire's strained relationship with her adoptive mother. Dena had remarried shortly after her husband's death, and hadn't wasted any time in starting a "real" family, one that Claire was decidedly not a part of.

Ivan was—had been—such a good man. How could this have happened?

She pulled back to wipe her face, her gaze connecting with the bright blue eyes of the man who held her. Agent Kincannon, that was his name. He smoothed her hair back with a soft hand, then gently stroked her arm. He probably meant the touch to be reassuring, but one of his fingertips had a small callus, and the rough patch dragged across her skin with a tickling friction that shivered through her body.

She was suddenly very aware of the fact that they were in her bed, and she wanted nothing more than to lie back and pull him over her, to surrender to his weight. His lips were so close—she had only to tilt her head forward to touch her mouth to his…the urge was almost overwhelming. She could lose herself in sensation, postpone the need to think for a little while longer.

The wild impulse must have showed in her eyes, because he leaned away, putting more distance between them. The cooler air of the room replaced the heat of his body, making her miss his warmth. She almost raised her hand to pull him back but stopped before she embarrassed herself. It wouldn't be right for her to touch him; he was here to act as her bodyguard, not her boy toy. Besides, she shouldn't be having such inappropriate thoughts in the wake of her friend's death.

"What happened?" She remembered lying down to rest, him leaving with a promise that he'd be in the living room. Why was he here now?

"You screamed," he said, scooting back to give her even more space. His shirt was blotchy with wet spots from her tears, and she flushed in embarrassment.

"I'm sorry," she said, gesturing to his shirt. "For that, too. I'm quite a mess."

He looked down, shrugged. "Don't worry about it. This isn't the first time I've come to the rescue of a damsel in distress." He shot her a sly grin, and she couldn't help but smile in return. "Nightmare?"

The smile faded from her lips as she nodded. "A bad one."

"Want to talk about it?"

She shook her head. "No. I don't want to think about it." Those horrible images, both from the dream and the picture she'd been sent, were running through her mind, and she wanted nothing more than to stuff them into a box. Talking about them would only keep them fresh.

"Fair enough."

She moved to get out of bed, knowing she couldn't go back to sleep now, wondering if she'd ever sleep peacefully again. Would she be able to close her eyes and not see Ivan, lying dead in a pool of his own blood?

Agent Kincannon stood as she got up, stepping back to give her room. "Did you want to talk to me?" she asked.

"Yes, but we can wait if you're not up for it yet."

She shook her head. "Let's do it now. Just give me a minute to splash some water on my face. I'll meet you in the living room."

Her body ached as she moved stiffly into the bathroom, flipping on the light as she entered. She winced at her reflection, the bright lights revealing pale skin, mussed hair, tear-streaked cheeks and red-rimmed eyes. Not a pretty sight.

She turned on the faucet, holding her fingers under the stream as she waited for the water to warm up a bit. She had no idea what kind of information she could provide that would help catch Ivan's killer, but she wanted to get this over with as soon as possible.

Agent Kincannon seemed like a nice enough man, but she didn't like having a stranger in her home, especially not when she was grieving the loss of Ivan.

She wanted privacy so she could fall apart without fear of being overheard. The last thing she needed was for him to hold her again. She was hanging on to her self-control by a very thin thread, and further temptation would cause her to break, a reaction that would only make things worse.

After a few splashes of water, she patted her face dry and then quickly brushed her teeth. She ran a brush through her hair, pulling it back into a serviceable ponytail. Her shirt was hopelessly wrinkled, but she couldn't summon the energy to change it. She didn't really care how it looked anyway. Taking a deep breath, she turned to head out into the living room. *I can do this*.

She settled onto the sofa, tucking her legs up so she was curled into a ball. Agent Kincannon took the recliner, leaning forward to place a glass of water on the table next to her. She blinked back the sting of sudden tears, absurdly touched by his thoughtful gesture. Not wanting him to see her emotional reaction to such an ordinary event, she reached for the glass, taking a small sip of water to wet her throat. "So, Agent Kincannon, where do we start?"

"How about we start with you calling me Thomas? We'll be seeing a lot of each other for the foreseeable future, so I think we can dispense with the formalities, if that's all right with you?"

Keeping her fingers wrapped around the glass, Claire nodded. "Okay," she said carefully, feeling her way into this new conversational territory. "Where do we start, Thomas?"

He leaned forward, and she caught a whiff of his

soapy-starchy scent as he moved. He rested his elbows on his spread knees and clasped his hands together in a loose fist, expanding his imprint in the chair.

He's so big, she thought, taken aback by how much space he occupied. She wasn't used to having a man in her apartment, especially such a large man. Ivan had been slight of stature, whereas Thomas was tall and broad. She could reach out a hand and touch his shoulder without having to stretch. The room seemed to shrink around her as he focused on her face, the space collapsing until only the couch and chair remained.

"Why don't you tell me about your relationship with Ivan?" His tone was friendly, belying the intensity of his gaze.

"What do you want to know?"

"Were you two close?"

She nodded. "I think so. We worked together for several years, so we got to know each other pretty well."

He cocked his head to the side. "How well?"

She frowned, searching his face for a clue as to what he was really asking. His eyes were flat, expression-less—the blue of a quiet sea. No help there. "I'm not sure I know what you're asking."

He leaned back, crossing his arms across his broad chest as he cast a meaningful glance toward the book-shelf. She followed his gaze to the picture of herself and Ivan, taken two months ago during his last visit.

"I am so happy, milaya, *my dear girl!"* he'd said, using his favorite pet name for her. *"The project is going very well, and I have you to thank for it."*

She smiled up at him, enjoying the feel of the sun on

her face. "It seems like we're finally getting through to the government—they can't just leave these sites unattended and hope for the best."

"They are learning," he replied, patting her shoulder. "They listen when a pretty woman talks, eh?" He winked at her, and she couldn't help but laugh at his expression, as if he took personal credit for her successful presentation.

"Were you romantically involved with him?" Thomas's voice interrupted her memories, pulling her back to the room. He was watching her carefully, like a stalking cat, waiting to pounce on any weakness. *Focus.*

"No."

He raised a brow, his doubt plain.

"No," she said, this time with an edge. "We were not sleeping together."

Thomas stood and walked to the bookshelf, picking up the photograph and studying it as if seeing it for the first time. "You seemed rather close," he remarked, extending the frame to her, his tone oh-so-reasonable.

"He was my mentor," she bit out from between clenched teeth. "He was like a father to me, and I won't have you twisting that into something dirty, something it's not." Her hands tightened around the glass, fingers pressing into the sides so hard she could see the tips turn white as they flattened against the smooth, wet surface.

"Okay." He set the frame back on the shelf, turned and walked over to the recliner, settling himself into the chair again. "Tell me about it."

She shook her head, unsure of where to start. "We met five years ago. I had just started at the Nuclear

Safety Group, and one of my first assignments was to provide support to the international decommission team, Ivan's group."

"What does his group do?" His voice was soft and unobtrusive, steering the direction of her story without distracting her. She kept her eyes focused on the water glass, tracing the lines of condensation while she spoke.

"They advocate for the safe and effective disposal of nuclear material from decommissioned nuclear power plants. There are a lot of plants in Russia that are crumbling in the wake of the collapse of the Soviet Union, which is a huge security risk. In some places, it's so bad that anyone could walk in and steal radioactive fuel. Ivan's group pressed for greater security, tried to coordinate with the government to secure the money needed to provide it."

"And you worked with him?"

"Yes. The first time I met him was at an NSG dinner. He was in town to drum up U.S. support for the latest round of talks with the Russian government, and I was seated next to him at the table. He turned to me, looked me up and down, and said, 'My dear, you are too pretty for this job. No one will take you seriously. You should get out while you're still young, find yourself a husband.'" She smiled wryly at the memory. "He was so…charming about it that I couldn't get angry at him. Over the next few days, I sat in on the meetings and eventually convinced him that I knew what I was talking about. After that, he decided to take me under his wing and introduce me to his contacts in Russia."

She paused, glancing up to find Thomas watching

her, his gaze steady as he listened. He nodded encouragingly, so she took a deep breath and continued.

"That's how we started working together. He was always very kind to me, making sure I was comfortable and included. He went so far as to introduce me to his family, take me to his daughter's concerts, his wife's dinner parties. I returned the favor when he was stateside, showing him around D.C. and keeping him fed and entertained when we weren't in meetings. Not that kind of entertainment," she said darkly, seeing his brows rise slightly.

"I don't know what you mean," Thomas replied, eyes wide with false innocence. She glared at him, but he merely smiled in return. "Was there ever any indication he was involved in something…shady?"

She shook her head forcefully, denying the question before he'd even finished asking it. "No. No way. Ivan was a good man—he'd dedicated his life to keeping these dangerous materials out of the wrong hands, and there's no way he would have compromised that."

"Not even for money? It sounds like securing these sites takes a lot of cash. Is it possible he was selling a bit on the side, not enough to be suspicious, but enough to fund some other operations?"

Claire blinked at him, not following this line of thinking. Was he serious? "Why would he do that? Why would he sell off spent fuel, only to turn around and use the money to keep spent fuel from getting into the wrong hands?"

"Maybe he didn't think he was selling to the bad guys," Thomas said, shrugging a shoulder as if he didn't care either way.

"That's not logical," she pointed out, needing Agent Kincannon to understand the fallacy of his argument. "Anyone who wants spent fuel has questionable motives, and Ivan knew that better than most. He wouldn't do that."

Thomas leaned forward again, mouth drawn as he regarded her. "You have a bit more faith in Ivan than I do."

"It's got nothing to do with faith." Exasperation made her voice shrill, and she paused to swallow the emotions tightening her throat before continuing. "It's logic, plain and simple. Ivan wouldn't do something so unreasonable."

"You like things to be logical, don't you?"

Was she seeing things, or did the corner of his mouth twitch upward? She arched an eyebrow, sending him what she hoped was a cool look. "You say that like it's a bad thing."

Okay, that really was a twitch.

"Not at all. I'm just trying to play devil's advocate," he said.

"And this is funny to you?"

The hint of a smile vanished from his face. "Absolutely not. I just want you to consider the possibilities."

"But you're wrong."

He stared at her for a beat, then sighed, a teacher disappointed in his student. "You just told me that you and Ivan were close, that he took you under his wing and made you part of the family. Do you really think he would have included you in something like this?" When she didn't respond, he pressed a bit more. "Or would he have tried to protect you, keep you out of the loop because he knew that it was dangerous and he knew you wouldn't approve?"

Claire stared at her lap, her thoughts swirling like flakes in a snowstorm. Could he be right? If Ivan had been involved in something illegal, she knew he would have kept it from her. But…why would he do that? What would compel him to toss aside his values and morals and his entire career? He'd spent his whole professional life trying to keep this material out of the hands of people who would use it for evil, so why would he join forces with them now?

He'd been so excited during his last visit, so hopeful for the future. She refused to believe he'd been selling spent fuel on the side.

As if sensing her turmoil, Thomas leaned back in the chair, giving her space. He didn't speak, but she could feel his eyes on her, watching her face as she worked through his hypothetical scenario.

"I suppose what you say is possible," she allowed, knowing she had to at least acknowledge the chance he was right, even though in her heart she knew it wasn't true. "But I don't think that's what happened here."

Thomas nodded. "Fair enough. I just need you to consider the possibility that Ivan was not what he seemed."

Claire opened her mouth to respond, but Thomas cocked his head toward the door, holding up a hand to keep her quiet. Footsteps sounded in the hall, coming closer to her apartment. He rose silently from the chair and padded over to the door, sliding up to the peephole to watch. Claire shrank down into the couch, huddling into a small ball, her palms slick from sweat and condensation. Her heart thumped hard in her chest when the footsteps stopped outside her door. She jumped when the doorbell rang, eyes glued to Thomas's broad back as he stared out into the hall. Who was at the door? Someone dangerous? Why wasn't he moving?

She heard a faint beeping sound, then a thud. Whoever it was walked back down the hall, and as the sound faded, Thomas relaxed. He opened the door, bent down and turned back into the apartment, an express mail package in his hands. She sighed as she realized the visitor had been nothing more than a deliveryman, shaking her head at her over-the-top reaction.

"Are you expecting something?" He set the package on the table with a frown.

"No." She scooted forward to examine it, reluctant to touch it while Thomas regarded it with such open suspicion. "Oh!"

"What?" He held out an arm to keep her from getting too close, alarm evident in his voice.

"I know that handwriting." Ignoring his grunt of displeasure, she reached out to trace the letters of her name. She looked up at him, his face blurry as she blinked back tears. "This is from Ivan."

Chapter 3

What the hell?

After a few tense moments, Thomas had agreed to open the package. He'd insisted on doing the honors himself—no telling what it contained, and if there was some kind of chemical or biological agent inside, better for him to be exposed than her. It was his job to protect her, and somehow, he didn't think Harper would shed too many tears if he were to meet his untimely demise.

The envelope contained nothing more than a yellowing stack of papers, neatly clipped together in the upper left corner. Claire removed the paper clip and began to flip through the pages, her eyebrows drawing together as she looked them over. He could see they were covered in tiny rows of precise, dark script but couldn't make out the language at this distance. He sat next to her on the couch, leaning over her shoulder to get a better view.

She smelled like lavender, and the neck of her shirt gaped open enough to show the edge of her bra strap. A soft pink that matched the color on her toes, not white as he'd assumed earlier. *Cut it out,* he told himself sternly. *She's a job, not a woman.* Feeling disgusted with himself, he forced his eyes away from the enticing sight, focusing instead on the papers in her hand.

At this range, he could see the writing was Cyrillic. "Can you read this?"

She jerked at his question, and he realized she'd been so focused on the papers she hadn't known he was close. She shook her head. "No, I'm afraid not. I don't understand why Ivan would send these to me. He knows—" she swallowed hard "—knew I don't speak Russian or read Cyrillic."

"Maybe he knew he was under threat and sent them to you for safekeeping."

"Maybe," she said, still sounding doubtful.

He stood, reaching into his jacket for his phone. "We need to get them translated, the sooner the better," he said as he dialed. "If there's a message there for you, we need to know what it says."

She said nothing as he relayed this latest development to Harper, who agreed with the necessity of a rapid translation. "Bring them in," he said. "I'll get the translator lined up."

He turned to find her standing next to him, her eyes wide but her mouth set in a determined line. "We need to take these papers to headquarters," he told her, reaching out to take them from her. "My boss is lining up a translator for us."

"Fine. Just give me a minute. I need to change my shirt."

She walked down the hall, leaving him holding the papers. He busied himself tapping them into place and returning them to the envelope, anything to keep his thoughts from drifting to images of her without a shirt on, that pale pink bra on display....

He swallowed hard, running a hand through his hair. *Not an option.* Yes, she had a delicate beauty about her—the way her hair curled at the nape of her neck, the graceful lines of her jaw and brow—and right now, she did have the whole damsel-in-distress thing going on, which had his protective instincts flaring. It had felt good—too good—holding her as she woke from her nightmare. She had fit so perfectly in his arms, her head naturally tucking under his chin, as if she'd been made for that spot.

She had rallied quickly, though, and he knew underneath her tears and grief was a core of steel. He had to admire the way she'd held it together this morning, only letting her emotions out when she had surrendered to sleep. He could relate to that. He understood all too well what it cost to project an image of calm composure when grief and sadness and rage were boiling inside. God knew he'd done it often enough for Jenny, Emily and his mother.

Thomas shook his head and released a small sigh. Why was he having these feelings now, after months of apathy? Roger's death had left him reeling, and he'd had no desire to start a relationship. Of all the times for his libido to wake up...

His brain recognized he had no business thinking

about Claire outside the bounds of his professional responsibilities, but his body had felt her curves and wanted more.

"Not gonna happen," he muttered, taking a long sip from his glass of ice water. Probably would have been more effective to pour it down his pants, but this would have to do. Besides, he thought, trying to use logic to appeal to his baser nature, Claire was dealing with a huge shock. Even he wasn't so desperate as to hit on a woman who was in the throes of grief.

She won't be sad forever, whispered his inner sixteen-year-old.

Damn.

Claire stared blindly at the clothes hanging neatly in the closet, her mind back on the papers and the man in her living room. He was too much…everything, she decided, reaching up to pluck a white blouse off the hanger. Too tall, too broad, too warm, too hard. His arms had made her feel safe and secure, and the steady thump of his heart under her ear had been a comforting rhythm. And that smell—soapy, clean, with the faintest hint of starch from his shirt. She could get lost in that smell, stay pressed against his chest for days. It would be the perfect escape from the nightmare her life had become.

Except it wouldn't solve anything.

Shaking her head, she stripped off her wrinkled shirt and shrugged into the clean blouse. She had no business thinking of Thomas—*Agent Kincannon,* she corrected—as anything other than a man assigned to a case. A blanket of guilt settled over her shoulders as she remembered why he was here in the first place. Ivan was dead, and she was now a target.

But I'm not dead, a wicked little voice inside her head proclaimed. *And if I really am marked for death, why not enjoy the time I have left?*

Firmly shutting the door on that line of thought, she buttoned the blouse and tucked it into her slacks. She wished, now more than ever, she was the kind of woman who could have a no-holds-barred affair, to simply enjoy the physical pleasures of a relationship without letting her heart get involved. But she had tried that tack once before, and it had been a disaster. No, she thought, shaking her head as she smoothed a hand over her hair. Agent Kincannon might be quite nice to look at, and his touch might set her heart racing, but she knew all too well how things would end between them.

She didn't have the best track record when it came to the people in her life, starting with the death of her adoptive father when she was eleven. It hadn't been his fault, of course, but growing up, she'd harbored a lot of anger toward him for leaving her in the care of an adoptive mother who had never really wanted her to begin with. Dena had viewed her as a burden, something to be tolerated but never embraced. Her new husband had followed suit, and their apathy had turned to outright emotional neglect when they had a child of their own.

"Don't call her that," Dena had snapped when she overheard Claire refer to Amanda as "my sister." "You're not related to her."

Despite everything, she had still loved the woman, trying everything in her power to please her. Because Claire had been adopted as a baby, Dena had been the only mother she'd ever known, and her rejections had stung each and every time. Eventually, though, Claire had learned a valuable lesson—no one could hurt her if she didn't let them get close.

Now she made it a point to safeguard her heart, never granting anyone the power to hurt her. It was a safe, if sometimes lonely, way to live, but it kept her heart in one piece.

So, as much as she might enjoy his company, Agent Kincannon was not a risk worth taking. She consoled herself with the thought that he probably wasn't attracted to her anyway. After all, she hadn't exactly been at her best today. First she'd blurted out any number of awkward statements, making her sound like an escaped mental patient. Then she'd woken up screaming, another strong moment for her. Finally, she'd snotted all over his clean shirt and argued with him, all while looking like a hungover college student with wrinkled clothes and red-rimmed eyes. Oh yeah, she was quite the catch. He probably couldn't wait to hand her off to someone else and get back to his swimsuit-model girlfriend.

He was standing by the windows when she returned to the living room, his back to her as he peeked through a crack in the blinds. "Is everything okay?" *Had he seen something?*

"Yeah." He gave the street another quick scan, then turned to face her. "Everything is fine," he said with an absent smile. "Just checking to see if anything is out of the ordinary."

She felt the corner of her mouth lift, amused despite her resolve to keep him at arm's length. "And how would you know what 'ordinary' is for this neighborhood?"

He tapped his temple with his forefinger as he walked over, carrying the papers in his other hand. "My extensive training and lethal instincts allow me to spot danger before it has a chance to appear. Why do you think they chose me to protect you?"

"Because of your modest and humble nature?"

He grinned at her, dimples appearing on his lean cheeks. "That, too."

He passed her the papers as he walked to the door, checking the peephole before opening it. "Stay close, all right?" he instructed, all traces of teasing gone.

Suppressing a shudder, Claire hugged the papers to her chest and followed him into the hall.

Where the hell is the package?

Victor rummaged through another drawer, his patience running low as he pushed the contents aside in a desperate search for the papers. The deliveryman had confirmed the package had been dropped off, and since it was no longer on the welcome mat outside the door, she must have brought it inside. *Unless he was lying to me...*

He quickly dismissed the thought. He had been rather...convincing with his interrogation, and the man's screams and pathetic begging hadn't been faked. He wouldn't have considered lying, wouldn't have seen a reason to. The package had been delivered, all right, but it was now gone.

He stepped away from the desk, scanning the rest of the apartment as he considered his next move. He could wait here, but who knew when she'd be back? By now, she'd received his email and would know she was a target. Was she running scared, or would she go to ground? Probably the latter, he mused. Her dossier gave no indication she'd know how to evade him, so even if she was running, it wouldn't be hard to track her down.

He wandered into the kitchen, considering his options. He could hide here, attack her when she came home and grab the package then. Kill two birds with one stone, so to speak. That would be the easiest thing to do. But then his gaze snagged on the glasses in the sink, incongruous in the otherwise spotless kitchen. Two glasses. One for her, and one for someone else.

Damn. She had protection. He hadn't expected that so soon. He'd known it was a possibility, of course, had even suggested that to his employer. The icy voice on the other end of the line had told him in no uncertain terms that he was to do as he was told, no questions asked. They'd wanted Novikoff's image sent to her, so he had done it. Part of him wondered now if they had wanted to make this job more difficult for him, to give them a convenient excuse to dispose of him later.

A cold ball of anger settled in his stomach. He wouldn't give them the satisfaction.

Waiting in the apartment was out. She might come home with someone, and he needed to know what he was up against before making his move. Going back to the desk, he carefully rearranged the drawer, placing all the contents back in order. At first glance, she wouldn't suspect anything was different. He needed to keep the advantage of surprise for as long as possible. He cast an assessing look around the apartment, making sure he hadn't left anything out of place, then slipped out the door.

"I'll be back," he whispered, the promise hanging in the empty air.

Chapter 4

"I don't understand—it's just a list of words."

Claire stared at the stack of papers with a frown, comparing Ivan's handwritten notes to the translation. "Are you sure this is correct?"

The man arched an eyebrow at her as he rose from the table. "Quite sure, thank you very much." His tone was snippy, but she ignored it, focusing instead on the papers. She didn't have the time or the inclination to worry about hurting the feelings of a stranger right now.

Out of the corner of her eye, she saw Thomas—*Agent Kincannon,* she corrected again—give the man an apologetic smile and reach out to shake his hand. "Thanks for coming down on such short notice," he said, his tone warm and friendly. "We really appreciate it."

"No problem." Some of the ice had melted from the

translator's voice. "I hope you find what you're look-ing for." Claire noticed his slight emphasis on "you" and rolled her eyes. It seemed Agent Kincannon could charm the birds from the trees.

He came back to the table to stand next to her, look-ing down at the papers. She was uncomfortably aware of his warmth and shifted a bit, putting a little more distance between them. If he noticed the movement, he didn't react.

"Does this make any sense to you?"

She shook her head. "No. As best I can tell, it's just a list of nonsense words."

He made a low humming noise in his throat while he scanned the translation, reaching out to flip over the page before sitting next to her. More words. What did they mean?

They read through the pages in companionable si-lence, coming to the end quickly. He glanced over at her, his expression revealing his confusion. "What do you think this means?"

Claire let out a sigh, pushing a stray strand of hair behind her ear. His eyes followed the gesture, making her feel suddenly self-conscious. "I don't know," she admitted. "Maybe it's a code of some kind? A mes-sage? Or…" She trailed off, hating the direction of her thoughts.

"Or?" he prodded gently.

She sighed. "Or maybe he's lost it, and these are the scribblings of a man suffering dementia."

"Did he seem impaired when you spoke with him?"

"No, that's just it," she said, thinking back over their last conversation. He'd been very lucid, very deliberate. Not at all confused or emotional. "He seemed fine. Besides," she said, and flipped through the pages, pulling the first one to the top of the stack. The handwriting was the same, but the ink had faded over the years, and the page was yellow and crinkled compared to its fellows. "Look at how old this page is compared to the others. He must have been making this list for years."

"Does anything about this jump out at you?" Thomas asked, studying her carefully.

She shook her head, at a loss to explain what the list meant or why Ivan had sent it to her. Plainly, he thought she could do something with this information, but what?

"I'll get some people working on this," he said, standing as he placed the pages and translation in the envelope. "Hopefully we can figure out what these words mean and why Dr. Novikoff spent so much time writing them." He walked out, leaving Claire alone with her thoughts.

Why on earth would Ivan send her a list of random words? Did he think she would know what they meant? It must be a code of some kind, but where was the clue to help her decode it? It was almost as if Ivan had sent her a puzzle, but why bother to hide the information? Was it because it implicated him in some way? Her heart clenched at the thought that he'd been involved in some kind of illegal business, but the seed of doubt Thomas had planted was starting to sprout, and she couldn't deny the chance he was right.

If Ivan had sold depleted fuel, could she really blame him? She knew he had been in a precarious position, often dealing with disinterested or even hostile people who refused to listen to the warnings about unsecured nuclear plants. But why would he have undermined the very thing he'd spent his life trying to accomplish? To teach people a lesson?

Perhaps he'd sold spent fuel so that when the inevitable dirty bomb attack occurred, he could point to it as an example of why he'd been right all along. It just didn't ring true, though. Whatever his faults, Ivan had never seemed to be a vindictive man, and she couldn't imagine him sabotaging his life's work just to prove a point. That wasn't his style.

She looked up as Thomas poked his head back in the room. "I've got to make some calls to arrange for your protective detail tonight. Are you all right sitting here for a few more minutes?"

"Yes, I'm fine."

"Can I get you anything to drink first?"

"Coffee?" she asked hopefully.

He winced slightly. "Well, I don't know that I'd call it coffee, but you can't really expect much from the government." He returned a moment later with a steaming disposable cup and gently placed it in front of her, along with several packets of sugar and a few creamers.

"Thanks." She picked it up, took a sip, then set it down and reached for the sugar.

"I did warn you," he said, his tone simultaneously apologetic and reproving.

A small smile curved her lips. "It's not really that bad. Just stronger than I'm used to. Go make your phone calls. I'll be fine here."

He nodded. "I'll be just outside the door, so holler if you need anything."

* * *

Thomas slid into his chair with a nod to James Reynolds, who was on the phone. While he waited for his computer to boot up, the other agent finished his conversation and turned to him. "How's it going?"

"Not bad. Working a new case. You?"

James sighed, running a hand through his hair. "Chasing down some leads. This organization, or whoever it was behind the Collins thing, is extensive. I think we've only scratched the surface."

"Scary, isn't it?" Thomas muttered, clicking open the directory listing.

"No kidding. Say, what are you doing this weekend?"

"Working. Why?"

"Kelly and I are going to the hockey game, and we have a couple of extra tickets. Interested?"

Thomas shot him a look over the top of the monitor. "A couple of extra tickets?"

James had the grace to look sheepish. "One of her friends is coming along, too."

Thomas rolled his eyes. "Yeah, that's what I thought. No thanks."

"C'mon, man. We need to find you a girlfriend. You're too young to waste your life on work."

Thomas shook his head. "What is it about you newlyweds? Always going around trying to pair people up."

James grinned. "Being paired up has its perks. Besides, I think you'll like this one. Blonde, tall and beautiful—a real catch. Too good for you, if you ask me."

Thomas held up his middle finger as he typed with

the other hand, making James laugh. "What's one date? Just give her a chance."

The image of Claire Fleming passed through his mind, and he frowned. They weren't together, so why did he feel slightly guilty at the thought of going out with another woman? "Not interested," he said, pushing aside thoughts of the delicate woman sitting in the conference room twenty feet away.

James was silent for a moment, making Thomas think he had dropped it. Then he spoke again, his tone apologetic. "Oh, I get it. Look, man, I had no idea— you've always been so good with women, I just assumed...I really didn't mean to offend you. My cousin is gay, too, so I should have considered the possibility. I'm sorry."

Thomas looked down and closed his eyes, digging deep for patience. He considered lying for a split second to get James off his back, but the earnest look on the other man's face made him reconsider. "I'm not gay. I'm just not interested in a relationship right now."

James held his hands up, palms out. "No problem. If you change your mind, let me know. Kelly has a lot of nice friends. Of course, they're not as great as she is...." As if on cue, the mention of his wife's name put a goofy grin on James's face.

Thomas snorted, shaking his head. It was almost comical how the serious, impeccable agent softened at the mention of his wife. Kelly had been good for him, and a small part of Thomas was jealous of his friend. *I want that, too.*

Shaking off the errant thought, he made several calls to arrange for Claire's protection. A D.C. cop would stay in the apartment tonight, starting at eight, and he would relieve them tomorrow morning after dropping Emily off at school. Satisfied with the arrangements, he returned to the conference room to find Claire staring into the coffee, lost in thought.

"Ready to go?" he asked quietly, trying not to startle her.

She jumped at the sound of his voice and sent him an embarrassed smile. "I'm not sure why I'm so twitchy," she said, twin spots of color appearing on her pale cheeks as she walked over to him.

"You've had a rough day," he responded, placing a hand lightly on the small of her back to guide her through the room. The silk of her blouse was soft under his palm, making him wonder what the skin underneath felt like.

"Agent Kincannon, a word, please." Harper stood in the doorway to his office, frowning. Great. What did he want now?

Thomas nodded to Harper, then steered Claire over to his desk. "I'll be right back," he said, shooting a quick glance at James before he left. *Talk to her, will you?*

James gave him a subtle nod and hung up the phone. *On it.*

Thomas walked back to Harper's office, working to paste a neutral expression on his face. The older man shut the door behind him, walked around his desk and sat, gesturing for Thomas to do the same.

"What did the pages say?"

"It was a list of random words."

Harper narrowed his eyes. "That's it?" He sounded

suspicious, as if he thought Thomas was keeping something from him. Refusing to acknowledge the implicit challenge, Thomas kept his gaze level and his tone even.

"That's it. Just words."

Harper steepled his fingers together, pressing them to his lips. "What do you think it means?"

Thomas shrugged. "I have no idea. It could be anything—a coded message, a list of favorite things, his grocery list. Who knows?"

"But why would he send it to Dr. Fleming?"

"Insurance? Maybe he knew he was in deep and sent it to her for protection."

Harper made a small grunt as he considered Thomas's words. "Perhaps. Though it doesn't seem to have protected him, does it?"

Thomas inclined his head but didn't respond.

"What do you think Dr. Fleming knows?"

"I don't think she knows anything. She seemed just as puzzled by the package and its contents as we are."

"She could be lying."

Thomas shook his head. "I don't think so," he said thoughtfully. "She's too much of a straight arrow. She likes rules, she likes order, and she was very offended by my suggestion that Ivan had been selling spent fuel on the side. If there was something shady going on, I don't think she was a part of it or knew about it— she's too black-and-white to go along with something like that."

Harper stared at him, his gray eyes flat and almost reptilian. "She's quite pretty," he observed, almost off-handedly.

His stomach twisted at the thought of Harper noticing Claire as a woman, but he knew the other man was only trying to provoke him. Refusing to give him the satisfaction, Thomas tried to sound bored. "Is she? I hadn't noticed."

The corners of Harper's mouth twitched. "I'm sure you haven't," he said drily. "Still, no matter how innocent she may seem, I'd advise you to keep a wary eye on Dr. Fleming. She may not be as lily-white as you think."

Thomas gritted his teeth, resenting the implication he let his dick do the thinking for him. "Noted."

Harper nodded. "Good. Her protection for the night has been arranged?"

"Yes. The D.C. police will take over for tonight, and I'll relieve them in the morning."

"Keep me posted."

Thomas rose and left the office, resisting the urge to slam the door shut behind him. Where did Harper get off, suggesting he was attracted to Claire, and that it was clouding his judgment where the case was concerned? He was a professional, damn it. He never let his emotions get in the way of a case—he'd only taken off one day to attend his brother's funeral. And he hadn't talked about Roger with the team beyond the general announcement, not wanting the sympathy and awkward condolences. Emotions had no place at work, and he made sure to keep his locked away where they belonged. For Harper to suggest otherwise showed how out of touch the man was.

He wove his way back to his desk, drawing up short when he heard Claire's laugh. Full throated and rich, the warm sound washed over him, settling low in his belly. She was smiling at James, her eyes bright and cheeks pink. A hot spike of jealousy knifed through his chest. She'd never looked at him like that, never laughed at his jokes. What the hell was so great about James? And why was he flirting with another woman when he was so happily married to Kelly?

He approached the desk quietly until he stood behind her, glaring down at James. His friend looked up, his smile of amusement morphing into a smug, knowing grin as he took in Thomas's glower. Claire turned around, as well, so he made a concerted effort to soften his features. "Did Agent Reynolds keep you entertained while I was gone?"

She nodded. "Oh yes. He's quite the storyteller."

Thomas's eyes flicked back to James. "Is he? I guess marriage agrees with him."

James merely grinned at the barb. "It does," he replied.

"He showed me the wedding pictures," Claire said, looking back at James. "It looked like a beautiful ceremony, and your wife was stunning. Did you know they were married on the beach?" she asked Thomas.

"Yes," he gritted out. "I was the best man."

"Oh," she said. "I must have missed that. I was so focused on her dress."

James bit his lip to hold back a laugh, and Thomas indulged in a brief fantasy of reaching across the desk and punching the other man in the mouth. His thoughts must have shown on his face, because James let out a strangled sound that he tried to cover with a cough.

"Are you all right?" Claire asked.

"He's fine," Thomas said, placing a hand on her arm. "Ready to go?"

"Sure." She stood, her expression uncertain as she looked from Thomas to James. "It was nice to meet you," she offered, sticking out a hand for James to shake.

Thomas saw the wicked gleam in his eye, but before he could intervene, James bent over Claire's hand and pressed a kiss to the back. "My pleasure," he said gallantly. She blushed, smiling shyly. "Let me know if there's anything I can do to help."

"It's under control," Thomas said, just as Claire responded, "Thanks."

With a final glare at James, Thomas steered Claire to the elevators. As they stepped inside, the phone in his pocket vibrated, alerting him to a new message. He pulled it out, flipping open the screen to read the text from James. Not interested? Doesn't look that way to me.

Thomas quickly typed out a crude reply, then stuffed the phone back into his pocket. Glancing over, he noticed Claire standing near the wall of the elevator, arms wrapped around her torso. Great. He had probably scared her with his temper. "Everything okay?"

She looked at him, frowning slightly. "I'm fine. You just seemed grumpy, so I was going to leave you alone."

He thrust a hand into his hair, smoothing it back. "Sorry about that. Talking to my boss always seems to put me in a bad mood."

"He didn't look very friendly."

"He isn't. He's the new guy, and he's trying to make

his mark in the department. He's just going about it the wrong way, if you ask me."

She nodded. "And you don't get along."

"Not really."

"So that's why you got stuck babysitting me." It was more of a statement than a question, making him wonder what, exactly, James had said to her.

"What makes you say that?" he asked carefully.

"Oh, please," she said, spreading her arms out. "I'm not an important person, which means guard duty could have been foisted onto any rookie with a badge. The fact that a senior agent was assigned to my case is a bit odd, and now that I know your boss doesn't like you, it's easy enough to see that you're being punished for something. So, what'd you do?"

"Excuse me?"

"What did you do?" she repeated. "Why did you get stuck with me?"

He gaped at her, unsure how to respond. "I'm not stuck with you," he began, leading her out of the elevator when the doors opened.

"You don't have to sugarcoat it for me," she said.

He huffed out a small laugh. "No, I can see I don't," he muttered.

As they climbed into the car, he could tell by her expectant silence that she was waiting for additional information. "Look, our last operation went badly. I can't really go into details, but our superior officer was canned. Agent Harper is now in charge, and he's bent on cleaning house. He doesn't trust any of us, and he particularly doesn't care for me, because I'm not appropriately afraid of him."

"I see." Was that amusement he heard in her voice? He quickly glanced over, but her expression was neutral, giving no hint to her mood. "But make no mistake, you are in danger, and I will work to keep you safe."

She nodded, pressing her lips together. "I appreciate it," she said quietly.

He reached over, laying a hand on her arm for reassurance. "It's my job."

She placed her hand over his, holding it against her arm. Tingles raced up his fingertips at the contact, and he fought the urge to stroke his thumb over her skin. She gave him a small smile, her large gray eyes soft and warm, then withdrew her hand. He pulled back his own, realizing too late that he shouldn't have touched her. Now that he knew what the warm satin of her skin felt like, he wanted to do it again. And that was just her arm—how would she feel elsewhere?

The air in the car became charged, expectant. Claire seemed coiled, as if she was waiting for him to make a move. He reached up to loosen his collar, suddenly warm in the confined space. He cleared his throat. "It's getting late. Are you hungry?"

"A little. I have food at home. I can make us something, if you like."

That sounded a little too domestic for him. If she were to cook for him, it would be all too easy to imagine that they were connected, had some kind of relationship, when the reality couldn't be further from the truth.

"Why don't I just pick up some burgers instead?" he offered. "I don't want you to have to go to any trouble."

Twenty minutes later, they arrived back at her apartment, bags of hot, greasy food in hand. Claire went into the kitchen, grabbing napkins and place mats, then set a quick table while he locked the door and shrugged out of his jacket. As he passed by the desk, he paused. Something seemed off. He leaned over to get a closer look but didn't see anything unusual save a crooked pen. Reaching out a finger, he pushed the pen back into alignment with its fellows. He must have bumped it on his way out last time.

They ate quickly but quietly, then sat in silence for a bit. Finally, Claire let out a sigh. "What you said in the car…" She trailed off.

"Yes?"

"Do you really think I'm in danger?"

He nodded. "I think we have to assume you are, for now. Why?"

She moved restlessly on the chair, as if she was trying to find a comfortable position. "It just doesn't make sense! I keep going over Ivan's death—his murder— and I can't come up with a reason someone would have wanted to kill him. Or me, for that matter."

"Once we find out what the list means, I think we'll be closer to knowing what's going on and why you're a target."

"How long will that take?" Her eyes were pleading, and he wished he could say something, anything, to reassure her.

He wanted to touch her again but settled for crumpling his napkin into a ball. "I'm not sure. It's a priority though, which means people are working on it now. We should know something soon."

She nodded, eyes downcast while she tore her paper

napkin into strips. "I guess we'll just have to wait then, won't we?"

"For now." He glanced at his watch. "Speaking of waiting, my relief should be arriving soon."

"How will that work?" she asked. "I don't have a spare bedroom, so where is this person supposed to sleep?"

"They won't," he informed her. "Their job is to stay awake and make sure nothing happens to you while you're asleep. They'll probably just sit in the living room and watch TV, if that's okay with you."

One shoulder lifted in a shrug. "I suppose. Maybe I'll watch TV with them. I don't think I'll be getting much sleep tonight anyway."

He gave her an absent smile as he pulled out his phone. Had the officer called to say he was running late? But no, he hadn't missed any calls, had no new messages. What was keeping them?

"I'm going to run downstairs," he said, slipping the phone back into his pocket. "Make sure the officer isn't roaming around lost, or locked out of the building. Lock the door behind me, and don't open it for anyone but me, okay?"

"All right." She nodded.

He gave her what he hoped was a reassuring smile. "I'll be right back."

After locking the door behind Thomas, Claire busied herself with clearing the table, throwing away the trash from dinner and returning the place mats to their drawer. She was tired, so tired, but she didn't want to sleep. *I can't stand another nightmare.* She shuddered.

She wandered aimlessly through the living room, pausing here and there to run her fingers along a shelf or to pick up a picture, only to put it back down again without looking at it. Her thoughts raced, her mind whirring as she tried to figure out what the list of words meant, why Ivan had sent them to her. Was there a hidden message for her? *What do you want me to do, Ivan?* she silently pleaded.

Unsurprisingly, there was no answer to her question. The room was still and quiet, and it seemed somehow smaller without Thomas. Ironic, that, since he took up so much space. She'd grown used to his presence in the few hours she'd known him, and she missed him already, even though he'd only been gone for a few minutes.

Not good. She couldn't come to depend on him. He was going to leave after this assignment was completed, so she shouldn't start thinking about him as any kind of fixture in her life. She was having trouble keeping her emotions in check though. He was so charismatic she felt drawn to him, a powerful pull that was almost magnetic.

She absently rubbed the spot on her arm where he had touched her in the car, trying to recapture the tingle she'd felt when his palm had rested against her skin. His touch had sent zings of awareness up her arm to settle into her belly, making her feel something aside from the general horror of the day. She idly wondered what his hands would feel like elsewhere on her body but shook her head. No sense in wishing for things that would never happen. He was a professional, and she would only embarrass them both by coming on to him.

A knock at the door interrupted her thoughts. She glanced through the peephole to see a small, dark-haired man holding out a badge. "Dr. Fleming? DCPD."

She frowned slightly, considering. Thomas had said not to open the door to anyone but him, but the man did have a badge and was obviously the police. Maybe they had just missed each other in the elevators? She flipped the lock and opened the door, stepping back to let the officer inside.

He gave her a friendly smile as he entered the apartment, his hazel eyes darting around to take in his surroundings. "I'm Victor," he said, offering his hand.

She took it, returning his smile. "Claire. Did you happen to see Thomas? He's wandering around looking for you."

The smile faded from his mouth, and his eyes grew cold. Claire took a step back, alarm bells clanging in her head as the hair on the back of her neck stood up. *What have I done?*

"Tall guy? Red hair? Yeah, I took care of him," he said, taking a menacing step forward. She saw a glint in his hand just before he drew it up to her neck, but before she could register what that meant, a cold pressure appeared at her throat, making her freeze in place. *Don't move. Don't breathe.*

"Where is the package?"

Her throat felt impossibly tight, but a small moan escaped. Victor drew back a hand and slapped her, hard. Her eyes watered, and the metallic taste of blood filled her mouth. "Where is the package?" he repeated calmly.

"I—I don't have it," she stammered.

He considered her for a beat, then shrugged. "Fine. We'll do this your way." He pulled the knife from her neck and pressed the tip to her cheek, bracing a forearm across her shoulders to keep her in place. She pushed against him, but he pressed himself flush against her, trapping her hands between them.

"One last time—where is the package?"

Tears streamed down her face and her body shook, her knees threatening to give out. "I don't have it," she repeated, sobbing. "Please, the FBI has it."

"Wrong answer."

He drew the blade down her cheek in an arcing cut and she screamed, the salt from her tears making the wound sting and burn. Warm blood trickled down her face as he moved the knife to her other cheek.

"I can do this all day, sweetheart," he said in the tone of a man bored with life. "It's really up to you. Just tell me where the package is, and I'll stop."

She drew in a shaking breath. "I told you already— I don't have it!"

"And I don't believe you."

He was so matter-of-fact, no emotion in his voice at all. He watched her with a clinical detachment, un-moved by her tears, her pleading, her struggling. "You killed Ivan, didn't you?"

"Yes." He pressed the knife harder against her cheek but didn't cut yet. What was he waiting for?

"And Thomas?" Was he dead, too, lying in some abandoned stairwell in a pool of his own blood?

"Yes. And now I'm going to kill you." He moved the knife from her cheek to her neck, holding it just under her jaw.

"Why?"

"Because you're not much help to me alive right now, and it'll be easier to search your apartment after you're dead."

"Drop it." The deep voice came from the doorway, low and commanding. Claire sagged with relief. *Thomas.*

Victor shook his head, a wry smile curving his thin lips. "I knew I should have taken more time with you."

Claire glanced over, biting back a cry at the sight of Thomas. He was standing in the doorway with his gun drawn, one hand pressed to the wound on his neck. His shirt was soaked with blood, and she could see it was still seeping through his fingers, running down his neck in thin rivulets.

"Rookie mistake," Thomas commented. "Step away from her."

"You see, the problem is that you're too tall," Victor said conversationally. "I'm not used to having to reach up so high. Messed up my angle." He shrugged, as if it didn't really matter. "Next time."

"There won't be a next time." Thomas took a step forward, swaying slightly. Victor noticed it and smirked.

"I think you may be right. In fact, I think I'll just stay here, wait for you to bleed out, and then take care of the good doctor." He jerked his chin toward Claire. Thomas followed his movement, his jaw clenching as his eyes tracked over the wound on her face.

"Or maybe I'll shoot you first."

Victor shook his head. "No, you won't. I'm too close to her—you can't risk hitting her."

"Yes, he can." Claire spoke quietly, her eyes locked on Thomas. *Do it,* she silently urged him, wanting him to take the shot. If she was going to die, she'd rather be shot by Thomas than slowly carved up by a madman.

He stared at her, blue eyes blazing in his pale face. She could tell by the set of his jaw he was fighting to find another way, but with Victor holding a knife to her throat and Thomas bleeding out before her eyes, she didn't see any other options.

It's okay, she mouthed, wanting him to know she understood. He shook his head slightly, taking another step forward.

"That's close enough," Victor warned. He pulled her from the wall, holding her in front of him as a shield. The knife returned to her throat, forcing her head up and her gaze off Thomas.

"Let her go," Thomas said. "You can't win this. Do you hear those sirens? They're coming for you."

He was right; the sirens that she had dismissed as background noise before were now louder, converging on her building. She felt a flutter of hope in her stomach at the thought that backup had arrived.

"Called in the troops?" Victor said, his voice a sneer in her ear. "Didn't think you could take me on yourself?" He pulled her back into the kitchen, and she almost slipped as her stockinged feet met the tile. She grabbed on to his arm for support, terrified of falling on his knife.

"I don't work alone," Thomas replied. She heard a shuffle, figured he was following them. Was his voice getting weaker? *Please, no,* she thought. *If he falls, it's over.*

Victor pulled her back another step, then paused. "I can see that I've overstayed my welcome. I'll come back again another time. Soon," he whispered in her ear. He angled the knife across her neck in a chilling caress before shoving her violently forward. She had a brief glimpse of Thomas's shocked face just as she careened into him, knocking them both to the floor.

He pushed her off him, wrestling his gun hand free from the tangle of their limbs. "Freeze!" he called out, but it was too late. Victor had yanked up the window and jumped out onto the fire escape. The fading clang of his footsteps on the metal stairs was barely audible over the shrill symphony of sirens below.

Thomas struggled to his feet and stumbled to the sink. Bracing his hands on the counter, he tried to climb up, clearly intending to follow Victor.

"Thomas, no!" Claire reached out, snagging his shirt to stop him. "You're seriously injured—you have to sit down."

He tried to shrug off her hand but she held fast, pulling him away from the counter and guiding him to sit on the floor. "Stay here," she commanded. She grabbed a towel and pressed it to his neck, biting her lip at the sight of fresh blood leaking from the wound. He sat, arms splayed on either side of his lap; his eyes were twin blue flames focused intently on her face. "You're going to be fine," she ordered, hating the tremor in her voice.

"What about you?" he asked, his gaze tracing the cut on her cheek. She reached up, wincing as her fingers touched the raw slice.

"That's nothing."

"It is to me." The words were quiet, but she heard the emotion behind them. She cupped his cheek with her free hand, stroking her thumb over the arch of his cheekbone.

"I can't believe I let this happen," he muttered.

"It's not your fault," she told him. The elevator doors opened down the hall, and she heard footsteps and the beeps of walkie-talkies. "Agent Kincannon?" a voice called loudly.

"In here," she yelled. Seconds later, the apartment filled with police and paramedics. A pair of hands pulled her away from Thomas, leading her into the living room. She could see the EMTs swarm around him and nearly sagged with relief. He would be okay.

His gaze found hers through the crowd, and she tried to give him a reassuring smile. As the medics loaded him onto a stretcher, he reached out a hand. She grabbed it, squeezing hard.

"She comes with us."

A chorus of voices responded to his declaration, everyone talking over one another in a bid to be heard.

"I don't think so—"

"That's not necessary—"

"Impossible—"

In what had to be an incredibly painful move, Thomas cleared his throat, then spoke loudly. "She is under my protection, and I will not allow her out of my sight. She comes with us." In the strained silence that followed, he added, "She needs medical attention, too."

One of the paramedics cursed under his breath. "Let's go. We're wasting time."

Thomas kept a firm grip on her hand, practically

dragging her along as the gurney made its way down the hall and into the elevator. Once on the ground floor, the EMTs loaded him into the ambulance with practiced ease. One of the paramedics boosted her up into the back, pushing her along the bench until she sat by Thomas's head. He glanced over at her, a small smile curving his lips.

"Having fun yet?"

She huffed out a strangled laugh. "Loads," she replied, appreciating his desire to lighten the mood. "If it's all the same to you though, let's not do it again."

He reached for her hand as he closed his eyes. "Deal."

Chapter 5

Claire winced as the nurse gently blotted her cheek with an alcohol pad.

"Sorry. I know that stings." Her eyes were tired but kind, the dark smudges underneath were a testament to her fatigue. *It must be getting close to shift change,* Claire realized with a small shock. After everything that had happened today, she felt it should be much later.

She shrugged a shoulder, blinking to clear the tears from her eyes. "I'll survive."

The nurse applied a few more pats, then drew her hand back, eyeing the wound critically. "You're lucky," she proclaimed, reaching over to pluck a small tube off the stainless-steel tray next to the bed. "You won't need stitches, and I doubt you'll have a scar." She twisted the cap off the tube, set it aside, then leaned in to apply the liquid across the cut. It burned a little, but the pain was nothing compared to how badly the alcohol had hurt.

"What is that?" Claire asked, trying not to move her face too much.

"Medical superglue," the nurse responded, keeping her eyes on her task. "Seals it right up and helps keep the cut clean." She dropped the used tube on the tray, reached for a bandage. She pressed it down with gentle strokes, covering the wound completely.

"You're all set," she said, leaning back and pulling off her gloves with a snap.

"Thank you," Claire said. "Can I see Thomas now?"

The nurse nodded, gathering up the trash. "I think so. He's just a few bays down. Should be all stitched up by now." She stood, tossed the bandage wrappers and empty tube and drew back the curtain. "I'll take you to him."

Claire hopped off the bed, nearly tripping as she darted after the nurse. They had been separated after arriving at the E.R., him being taken off for immediate examination while she had been shunted into a curtained area and told to wait for the nurse. Not wanting to distract the doctors working on Thomas, she'd sat on the bed, biting off all her fingernails as she waited for news.

The nurse stopped in front of a closed door and knocked twice in announcement before pushing it open. "Feeling up for a visitor?" she asked. Thomas must have said yes, because she stepped aside to allow Claire to enter.

His color was coming back, she noticed as she stepped inside. His skin was no longer deathly pale, but the green hospital gown didn't do him any favors. He sent her a tired smile, the expression doing nothing to distract from the dark circles under his eyes or the way his skin was drawn tight across his cheekbones. She walked over to stand by the side of the bed, staring down at him and the neat white square that marked his neck. She couldn't take her eyes off that spot, compelled to look at it, as if keeping it in her sight would erase the image of him slumped on her kitchen floor, blood draining down his neck.

He was studying her, too. She could feel his eyes raking over her face, touching on one bruised cheek and then jumping to her own bandage.

"We're quite the pair, aren't we?" she asked, forcing her gaze up to meet his. She spoke without thinking, only registering that she'd used the word *we* after hearing it. When had she started thinking of herself as part of a *we?* When had Thomas become the other half of that equation?

Careful. She couldn't let herself form a connection to this man. He'd work her case and move on, leaving her behind. That was simply the nature of his job. It wouldn't do her any good to become attached. It would only lead to more heartache in the end.

Still, she couldn't deny that the attack had shaken her, making her feel even more vulnerable than before. It was hard not to turn to Thomas for reassurance, and the fact that he'd been injured while trying to protect her only strengthened his appeal. While she'd never want anyone to be hurt on her account, she couldn't deny that a small, primitively female part of her responded to his act of bravery on a deeply instinctive level. Her head might be listing the reasons she should keep her distance, but her body wasn't listening.

He held out a hand. She stared at it for the space of a heartbeat, then took his hand in her own. The feel of his palm sliding against her skin sent an electric tingle up her arm, an unexpected rush of pleasure that took root in her chest and sent tendrils of sensation spreading lazily through her limbs.

His touch was warm and reassuring. She felt the tension leave her muscles as her body relaxed, secure in the knowledge that they were safe, that Thomas wasn't going to die on her kitchen floor. Thomas apparently needed the contact, too, as he tugged gently to bring her closer to the bed. She pulled up a chair and sat by his head, and he folded their fingers together, laying their joined hands across his chest. He reached out with his other hand to lightly touch the marks on her face with his fingertips. "I'm so sorry," he whispered.

"It's not your fault," she said, just as quietly.

His mouth tightened, but his touch remained gentle. "Yes, it is. I suspected something was wrong. I shouldn't have left you alone like that. If I'd been there..." He broke off, shaking his head.

"No," she said, leaning forward. "I shouldn't have opened the door. You told me not to, but when I saw the badge I assumed it was all right. I shouldn't have been so gullible."

"I should have called you the minute I saw what he'd done to the night guard. If I had warned you, you would have never opened the door."

She studied him for a beat, saw the regret and self-disgust in his eyes. "You're determined to blame your-self, aren't you?"

He laughed, but there was no humor in it. "Why shouldn't I? It's the truth."

"I wish you wouldn't."

He shook his head in response, dropping his gaze to their folded hands.

"I don't blame you," she offered, hoping the assur-ance would lighten his burden of guilt. If he saw that she didn't hold him responsible, perhaps he would cut himself some slack.

"You should." He sounded almost sullen, as if he was disappointed in her for not seeing things his way.

"Are you trying to tell me what to do?" she teased. Maybe humor would help draw him out of his mood.

"You could have been killed!" She jerked back at the sudden shout, surprised by his vehemence. "Don't you see? You almost died tonight, and it's my fault. I let you down, I failed in my job, I—"

Not knowing what else to try, she leaned in and pressed her fingers to his lips. Shocked into silence, he stared up at her, his eyes gone wide and round in an expression that was almost comical. Feeling sheep-ish, Claire pulled her hand away, fingertips burning with the impression of his mouth. She made a fist on the bed, unsure of whether she was trying to erase or preserve the feeling.

Thomas watched her as she drew back, his eyes never leaving hers. The intensity of his stare made her uncomfortable, and she fought the urge to squirm like a scolded child. Then, in the space between heartbeats, his gaze turned, surprised amusement giving way to heat. His tongue darted out to flick across his lips, right at the spot where her fingers had touched him seconds before. Claire couldn't take her eyes off his mouth, watching in rapt fascination as his lips curled up in a dangerously sexy grin that was filled with promise.

It was more than her fragile self-control could handle. Her body responded to the invitation before she had a chance to think, and she leaned down to press her lips against his. Thomas hesitated at the contact, his mouth frozen, lips stiff and unyielding. She angled her mouth slightly, but his lack of response was unambiguous. A hot wave of embarrassment washed over her, along with a mortifying realization. *He doesn't want this—he doesn't want me.*

Just as she began to pull away, he let out a harsh moan and kissed her back, his lips softening and molding to hers. He reached up to cup the back of her head, anchoring her in place as he nipped and caressed her mouth. The quick change stunned her, and she sucked in a breath, her knees threatening to give out in the wake of the sensations flooding her system. She reached up, plunging her hands into the red-gold strands of his hair as she moved to press her breasts against his chest, half-lying across him in a bid to get closer.

With the barest flicker of movement, he licked teasingly, questioningly at the seam of her lips. She opened to him, darting her tongue out to meet his halfway. The warm, slippery slide of his tongue against hers had heat pooling low in her belly, and made the muscles of her thighs and stomach tighten in delicious anticipation of his touch.

Thomas drew back, running the tip of his tongue along her bottom lip, then moved to feather kisses lightly across her cheeks. She shuddered at the contact, overwhelmed by both the feel of his mouth on her skin and the tenderness of his ministrations as he caressed her injury. Needing to regain control of herself, she angled her head to take charge of their embrace and pressed her lips to his eyes, his nose, his chin. As she bent to nuzzle his neck he stiffened, his hand gripping her arm tightly.

Torn out of the moment, she pulled back, blinking away the fog of arousal. *Did I hurt him?* He didn't seem to be in pain, though. She glanced at his bandage, still a pristine white. "What—" she began, but he quickly shushed her.

Had he heard something? Was something wrong? A flock of butterflies took up residence in her stomach as he turned his head to stare at the door, the corners of his mouth turned down. She tried to lean back, but his grip on her arm kept her from going far. He glanced back at her, and she was surprised to see his expression was not one of alarm but one of resignation, the surrender of a man about to face the gallows.

"Brace yourself," he murmured, pressing a quick kiss to her forehead as he released his grip on her arm.

Before she could sit down, the door flew open, hitting the wall with a loud thump and ricocheting back. A short nurse stood in the doorway, her eyes wide and expression panicked as her gaze swept the room. When she saw Thomas, her face visibly relaxed for an instant before her features smoothed out, a mask of professional detachment dropping back into place.

"Hi, Jenny," Thomas said quietly. A grin tugged at the corners of his mouth. "Nice hat."

Keeping her eyes fixed on Thomas, the woman reached up to tug off the white bouffant cap, revealing a fall of shiny blond hair that landed around her shoulders. She was quite pretty, Claire noticed, her large blue eyes and sharp cheekbones giving her the look of a pixie. She walked over to the bed, then reached out and grabbed Thomas's chin, tugging his head to the side and peeling back his bandage so she could look closely at his neck.

Thomas glanced up at Claire, rolling his eyes at this examination. *Who was this woman?* She plainly knew Thomas, felt comfortable enough to manhandle him without preamble. Was she a friend? A girlfriend? Her stomach sank at the thought. Please, not a girlfriend. He didn't seem like the kind of man who would kiss another woman while in a relationship. But she had started it, and maybe he'd kissed her back because he'd felt sorry for her.

After a few seconds Thomas reached up to remove the woman's hand from his face. "What are you doing here? Shouldn't you be off delivering babies or something?" His question was teasing, but Claire could tell by the set of his mouth that whoever Jenny was, he wasn't happy to see her.

"Yeah, as a matter of fact, I should." She crushed the cap in her fist. "But when I got a phone call telling me you had gotten your throat cut and were in my E.R., I told the woman to cross her legs and raced down here."

Thomas chuckled, triggering an even fiercer glare from Jenny.

"You think this is funny? What the hell happened, Tommy? You could have died!" Her voice rose as she spoke, and Claire realized she was struggling to maintain control.

Thomas seemed to realize it as well. He squeezed the woman's hand, tugging her arm until she sat on the bed beside him. "There was no need for you to come running down here," he said gently. "As you can see, I'm fine."

"Not that bad? Have you seen it? A little bit to the right—" she held up her thumb and index finger impossibly close together "—or a little deeper, and you'd have bled out before you hit the floor. You have no idea how lucky you are to be alive right now."

"I'll admit, it was a bit close for comfort," he allowed, reaching up to gingerly touch the bandage she had reapplied. "But I'm fine, so there's no need to worry."

"Did they catch the guy who did this?" She sniffed, wiping a stray tear from her cheek.

He looked down, shifting a bit in the bed as if trying to find a comfortable position. "Not exactly, but we have some good leads."

Jenny's expression darkened. "You can't be safe. What if he comes back?"

"He's not interested in me," he assured her.

"Then who is he after?"

"Me," Claire said quietly. Jenny whipped her head around, blinking in surprise as if just now noticing someone else was in the room. Claire moved to sit in the chair, not knowing what to do with Jenny's attention now that she had it.

"Who are you?"

"Claire Fleming." She held Jenny's gaze while the woman considered her for the space of a few heart-beats, then dismissed her just as quickly, her eyes flicking back to Thomas.

"Get another assignment," she ordered, a note of desperation entering her voice.

"Jenny," he said, quietly but firmly. "You know it doesn't work that way."

"No job is worth getting killed!"

"I won't," he said softly.

"You don't know that!" She pulled her hand free, jumped up from the bed and began to pace, gesturing as she spoke. "After all we've been though, you're telling me you're willing to risk your life for a stranger? For a damn case?"

"This isn't about our family, and you know it." For the first time, his voice held an edge. Jenny stopped pacing and turned to face him. Their gazes locked as they waged a silent battle, Thomas's expression growing more resolved as Jenny's became pleading.

So she was related to him somehow. Claire felt the tightness in her chest ease and realized with a small shock that she was absurdly pleased by the news that Jenny was not competition. She shook herself mentally, amazed at her own reaction. Since when had she ever been jealous, and over a man she wasn't involved with, no less?

Since he kissed you senseless, she thought wryly.

Air. She needed fresh air to clear her head. Claire eased to her feet and began to make her way over to the door, trying desperately to be invisible. Thomas and

Jenny clearly had things to discuss, and she shouldn't be here while they did it. After all, Jenny was right; she was a stranger to him.

"Stop," Thomas commanded. She paused, looking back. He broke the stare with Jenny to fix his gaze on her. "I don't want you out of my sight until I've arranged for protection for you."

"I'll just be outside the door," she said, inching forward again. "You two need to talk, and you shouldn't have an audience."

"Claire," he bit out, flinging the blanket off his legs and pushing himself up.

"What the hell—"

"You need to stay in bed—"

"Am I interrupting something?" Everyone fell silent at the question, heads turning to identify the newcomer. James stood just inside the room, hands tucked into the pockets of his dark gray slacks as he leaned nonchalantly against the jamb. He glanced from Claire to Thomas to Jenny, then back to Claire. "There seems to be quite the party going on in here."

Thomas leaned back, and Jenny moved quickly to tuck the blanket around his legs as if to secure him to the bed. "I was just explaining to Claire that she can't go anywhere without protection."

James nodded. "Sounds reasonable." He looked at Claire. "Where are you wanting to go?"

She let out a breath, shooting a glare at Thomas before responding. "I wanted some fresh air. I was just going to stand outside the door so they could talk in private."

James turned to Jenny. "I see." He stepped forward, hand outstretched. "James Reynolds. Nice to meet you."

"Jenny Kincannon," she said, reluctantly taking his hand. Claire nodded, appreciating the confirmation of her hunch. They were indeed related.

"Now then," James said, clasping his hands behind his back as he addressed the three of them in turn. "I'm here to take custody of Dr. Fleming and escort her to the safe house. You," he said, and looked at Thomas, "are to check in tomorrow morning, if your doctor clears you to return to duty. You—" he faced Claire "—are to come with me so I can get you set up at a secure location. And you," he said as he glanced at Jenny, "well, I don't really have information for you. Do whatever you like, I suppose."

Thomas nodded, closing his eyes. "Good. I'll sleep better knowing she's safe. Who's on guard duty tonight?"

"Me and Natalie."

His eyes snapped open and he started to lean forward again, but Jenny's restraining hand on his shoulder kept him from getting far.

"You? That can't be right—Kelly would never allow it."

James shrugged. "She's out of town at a conference, so what she doesn't know won't hurt her. Besides, would you really trust anyone else?"

"No," Thomas said quietly. "Just take care of her, will you?"

"Excuse me?" Claire interrupted, bristling at being talked about like she wasn't there. "I am not a pet. I don't need someone to take care of me. I can take care of myself." Well, sort of. As long as there wasn't a knife-wielding assassin in the picture.

"No one doubts that," James assured her, placing a hand on her elbow. "But this is standard procedure in the wake an attack. Let's head out so we can get you set up in your new home. I imagine you're pretty tired."

As if his words had broken the dam she'd built to keep the events of the day away, a wave of fatigue washed over her, nearly making her stumble. "Yes." She turned back to face Thomas, wanting to tell him good-night. She could tell by the look on his face there were things he wanted to say to her, but based on the set of his jaw, she knew he wouldn't speak in front of James or Jenny.

"I'll see you tomorrow?" she asked. It seemed they had a lot to discuss.

He nodded, blue eyes steady on her face. "Count on it," he murmured.

She glanced at Jenny as she walked back to James. "It was nice to meet you," she offered, giving the other woman a nod.

"Yeah," Jenny replied absently, her eyes still on Thomas. "Take care."

James reached out to place a hand on Thomas's blanket-covered foot. "Rest easy, man. You've got my number if you need anything."

Thomas nodded. "Thanks. I'll see you tomorrow."

"I'm counting on it." James gestured for Claire to precede him. "After you, Doctor."

As they stepped out together, she glanced back in the room. Thomas was leaning back in the bed, his gaze focused on her and an expression of longing on his face. When their eyes met, he gave her a quick grin and a wink, which had warmth blooming in her stomach. He held her gaze until the door swung shut, and Claire smiled as she fell into step beside James.

Thomas was safe. She was safe.

It was enough for now.

Thomas watched Claire walk away with James, hating that he was stuck in this bed while she was off with someone else. He trusted James completely—there was no one better for the job—but that didn't mean he had to be happy about being sidelined. Besides, after that kiss, it was clear they needed to talk.

He leaned back against the pillow, his body relaxing as he recalled the feel of her lips against his own. Soft and supple one minute, fierce and demanding the next, the woman kissed with a fearless abandon that made his blood heat and his groin tighten. And if her kisses were so uninhibited, how would she be in bed?

He rubbed absently at his chest, his skin still tingling from the weight of her breasts. He should have reached up to cup them—would have, had they not been interrupted.

He stifled a sigh as he regarded Jenny. Although her entrance had been unwelcome, it was probably for the best. A few more minutes, and Thomas would have had Claire pinned beneath him, hospital bed be damned.

"I don't like her." Jenny stared down at him with her arms crossed, the very picture of disapproval.

"You don't have to like her," he said, proud of himself for keeping his tone even when his first impulse was to defend Claire.

"Please, Thomas." She sat on the bed, taking his hand in both of her own. "Please get another assignment."

"You know I can't. If I ask for another assignment, I may as well turn in my badge."

"Would that be such a bad thing?"

Anger flared, hot and fast, burning away the residual arousal from kissing Claire. He opened his mouth to respond, but the look on Jenny's face stopped him. She was terrified, scared almost to the breaking point. She stared down at him, her expression pleading. He could see the ghost of his brother in her eyes, knew she was thinking about Roger's death and was worried about losing him, too.

It was something he'd thought about a lot in the months after his brother's death. Was it fair of him to continue working in such a dangerous job, knowing that if he were killed, it would destroy his family? His mother had already lost one son. Could he really ask her to survive the death of another? How would Emily respond, losing another link to her father? And Jenny, left alone to raise her daughter and care for her ailing mother-in-law.

On the face of it, his decision to remain with the bureau seemed a selfish choice. After all, he was willingly putting his safety at risk on a regular basis. Some would say it was only a matter of time until the risks caught up with him. Perhaps they already had. He absently ran his finger over the bandage on his neck, the gauze a small reminder of his mortality.

In the end, though, he couldn't walk away from a job that meant so much to him. His family was important, but deep down, he was afraid that if he quit to spare them the stress of his occupation, he'd grow to resent them. *That* was a risk he wasn't willing to take. Besides, he knew all too well that there were no guarantees in life. He could have the safest job in the world and still get hit by a bus.

He knew his mother and Jenny had a hard time accepting his decision to stay with the bureau. They had repeatedly suggested he transfer to another division, one that was more desk oriented and would keep him out of harm's way. Each time, he'd refused to consider it, knowing that such a move would not suit him. Each time, they'd dropped the subject when it was clear he wasn't going to change his mind. He'd thought they had accepted his choice, but in the wake of Jenny's request, he realized the issue was far from settled.

Even though he was not in the mood for this conversation, it was hard to stay angry with Jenny. It was obvious that her heightened worry over his safety was driven by a desire to protect the family she had left. He understood the instinct, and realized too that if he hadn't wound up in the E.R. tonight, the topic of his leaving the bureau would have stayed safely buried. Still, he was getting tired of defending his choices over and over again to the people he looked to for support. Just once, he would like to have a conversation that didn't end with him feeling guilty.

"I don't want to discuss this right now. Don't you have to get back to your patients?"

Jenny nodded, worrying her bottom lip as she looked at him thoughtfully. "I do, but I don't want to leave you alone."

Thomas resisted the urge to roll his eyes. He was lying in a hospital bed, for crying out loud. What could possibly happen? "I'll be fine," he said, trying to soften his tone. "I don't need a babysitter."

She arched her brow, letting him know his sarcasm was not appreciated. "Wouldn't you like some company? Mom is staying with Emily, but I could call Tanya—she'd be happy to come sit with you."

"God, no!" The last thing he needed was his ex-girlfriend to complicate an already tangled situation. Jenny's eyes widened, and he realized his rejection had been a little too enthusiastic.

"What's wrong with Tanya?" she asked, cocking her head to the side as she studied him. Her scrutiny made him feel like a suspect under interrogation, and he wanted nothing more than for her to leave.

"Nothing's wrong with her," he hedged, trying to come up with a plausible explanation for his knee-jerk negative response. "I just don't feel like company right now."

Jenny nodded, apparently satisfied. "Fair enough. But if you change your mind, I'd be happy to call her. You two were such a cute couple." She smiled, a dreamy look in her eyes. "In fact, I think she still has feelings for you."

Thomas didn't respond, unsure of what to say. He and Tanya had dated a few years ago, right around the time Roger and Jenny had gotten married. The two couples had spent a lot of time together, and Jenny and Tanya had become friends. It made sense that Jenny would look back on those days with nostalgia, since she and Roger had been so happy.

What Jenny didn't know was that Tanya had cheated on him with one of her coworkers. He closed his eyes, the image of her face as she confessed the affair still as fresh as ever. She'd been all tears and apologies, and he'd stood there in silent shock, his insides turning hollow, feeling like someone had just cut him off at the knees. He'd walked away from her without a word, and a few days later she'd moved to Chicago. He'd never told Roger and Jenny why they had broken up, and until recently, he'd never seen a reason to explain it.

But now Tanya was back, and she and Jenny had resumed their friendship. He didn't begrudge Jenny her friends—she definitely needed a support system, now more than ever—but he wasn't happy that Tanya had returned to his life, even if she was only on the fringes. He wanted nothing to do with her, and he especially didn't want her trying to worm her way back into his good graces through Jenny.

When this was over, he was going to have to sit down with Jenny and explain why he and Tanya hadn't worked out. She was welcome to count the other woman as a friend, but his relationship with Tanya was a thing of the past, never to be repeated.

"I hope you're not encouraging her," he said, holding her gaze so she would know he was serious. "I'm not interested in a relationship." *Except with Claire,* he silently amended. That was one woman he wanted to get to know better, in many ways.

"Of course I'm not," she said, a little too casually. "You're an adult. You can find your own girlfriends."

"Jenny," he said, drawing out her name in warning.

"I really should get back. I've been gone too long.

Have them page me if you need anything." She dropped
a kiss to his forehead, then turned and practically ran
out of the room. Thomas glared at the door, frustration mounting. It would be a cold day in hell before
he'd let Tanya back into his life, and the sooner Jenny
understood that, the better.

He dropped his head to the pillow and stared up at
the ceiling tiles, forcibly pushing Tanya from his mind.
He'd had a rough day, and he wasn't going to waste another minute thinking about his ex-girlfriend.

Better to think about Claire, and his current case.
His emotions settled as he sifted through the facts,
organizing his thoughts, the exercise as soothing as
meditation. It was clear Claire Fleming was in danger.
She hadn't been able to provide them with any leads
so far, but maybe the attack could give them one. The
man may have said something to her when they'd been
alone, something that had her reevaluating her previous
interactions with Novikoff. He made a mental note to
ask her about their conversation before he'd stumbled
into the room. There was a reason the assassin hadn't
killed her right away, and he wanted to know why.

He also needed to find out who they were dealing with. The man knew his way around a knife, that
much was clear. He was obviously a professional,
which meant there might be a file on him somewhere.

He spied the plastic hospital bag containing his personal effects on the chair in the corner of the room. He
sat up, wanting to retrieve his phone to make a quick
call to the office.

Whoa. The sudden wave of dizziness brought on
by his change in position hit him hard, and he closed

his eyes and swayed a bit, sucking in air as he fought against the urge to vomit.

After a moment, his own personal Tilt-A-Whirl came to a stop. Moving with a healthy regard for his balance, Thomas eased himself off the bed and made his way over to the chair, his legs and the IV pole providing a shaky support. Gritting his teeth, he retrieved his phone and began the long trek back, stepping with exaggerated care to stay upright. *Don't fall.* He'd never hear the end of it if he did.

He climbed back into the bed with a sigh, realizing for the first time just how badly he'd been injured tonight. In the heat of the moment, with his adrenaline pumping, he had underestimated the severity of his wound. Now, exhausted after making a round-trip of roughly six feet, he recognized just how lucky he'd been. Goose bumps broke out on his skin as he recalled Jenny's words. *A little bit to the right...*

Shaking off the memory, he gave the bag of blood hanging from the IV pole a salute. "Does a body good," he murmured, flipping open his phone and dialing in. He quickly relayed his recollections and impressions of the assassin, instructing the agent on the other end of the line to start combing the records and international databases immediately. The case wasn't going to stop just because he was in the hospital, not when the danger to Claire was still fresh.

Satisfied he'd done all he could from his sickbed, Thomas hung up and leaned back against the stiff pillow. His vertigo returned when he closed his eyes, but it was a pleasant, swirling sensation, nothing at all like the sickening whirlpool he'd been caught in earlier.

He pressed his fingertips to his lips, and drifted into the eddy with the image of Claire in his mind.

The house was nondescript, but she supposed that was how a safe house should look. The beige brick and brown wood trim blended in nicely with the rest of the neighborhood, making it just one more in a long line of cookie-cutter houses.

She was surprised the neighborhood was so close to the city. For some reason, she'd heard the words *safe house* and had immediately pictured a lonely cabin out in the woods, fortified by fences and alarm systems and guard dogs. This place was smack-dab in the middle of a neighborhood; the discarded bicycles parked under trees and sidewalks covered in chalk were a testament to the fact that families lived here, children played here. The thought of being surrounded by innocent people wasn't soothing, though—it was distressing.

"Is it safe?" she asked as James pulled into the garage, shutting the door behind them before unlocking the car doors.

"Sure is. It doesn't look like much, but it's got top-of-the-line security."

"I meant for them." At his blank look, she pointed at the garage door, indicating the houses beyond. "The neighbors. What if Victor comes back? I don't want anybody getting hurt because they were in the wrong place at the wrong time."

"That won't happen," he assured her. "In fact, having a lot of people around works to our advantage." He unlocked the door and stepped into the house, disarming the alarm and scanning the interior before gesturing her inside.

"How so?" She walked into the kitchen, glanced around. It was a bit on the small side, not much larger than the kitchen in her apartment. It was better equipped, however, she noticed, eyeing the Sub-Zero fridge, electric range and double ovens. All new appliances, from the looks of them. She relaxed somewhat. If they had taken such care with the kitchen appliances, the security had to be even better, right?

James popped back into the room, sliding his gun into its holster as he walked over to her. "The more people who are around, the more reluctant Victor will be to engage, even if he does find out where you are. Witnesses are always inconvenient, especially to a man in his line of work."

A sudden chill of fear skittered across her skin, making her shudder. James was right. This was Victor's job. Just as she took pride in her work, wanted to do her best, so did Victor. And that meant he wasn't going to stop until she was dead.

James noticed the gesture. "You've had a long day," he said kindly. "Are you hungry? I can fix you something to eat."

"No, thanks." Her stomach was already a bit queasy, and she didn't think food would help. "You mentioned another agent's name at the hospital—Natalie?"

He nodded, filling a glass of water and handing it to her. She took it, grateful to have something to hold. "Yes. Natalie is picking up some things from your apartment right now, like clothes and toiletries.

There are a few T-shirts and sweats in your room now, but we figured you'd prefer to have your own things."

"Thank you."

"You don't have to thank us, Dr. Fleming. It's what we do."

Yes, and that was the problem, wasn't it? These men and women put themselves in danger every day, and although most of the time they emerged unscathed, every once in a while someone got hurt. Someone like Thomas, who was lying alone in a hospital bed, lucky to be alive.

All because of her.

And now, other agents were in danger.

Exhaustion and emotion pulled at her, made her limbs heavy and clumsy. With shaking hands, she set the glass of water down on the counter. "If it's all right with you, I'm going to take a shower and head to bed. I'll meet Natalie in the morning."

"Of course. Let me show you to your room."

He led her down the hall to a small square room in the back corner of the house. At first glance, she thought it was windowless, but closer examination revealed a small opening, high up in the wall. It would let in light, but prevent people from seeing into the room.

"It's barred," James said, following the direction of her gaze. "And armed with several sensors. You don't need to worry about anyone trying to come through there."

He pulled open the top drawers of the oak dresser and showed her the collection of shirts and sweats. Then he guided her to the bathroom and retrieved a few towels from the upper cabinet. He placed them on the counter, turning to face her.

"I'll be in the living room if you need anything," he said. "Natalie should be arriving soon, so don't be alarmed if you hear another voice when you get out of the shower. We'll be up all night, which means you shouldn't be afraid to fall asleep, okay?"

She nodded, blinking back tears at his kindness. "Thank you."

He turned to go, stopping in the doorway when she spoke again. "Your wife is very lucky, Agent Reynolds."

He smiled at her, the expression transforming his face from simply handsome to beautiful. "I tell her that every day," he said, laughter lacing his voice.

Claire shook her head in mock dismay. "What is it with you FBI agents? Have you no humility at all?"

"I assume you're referring to Thomas?" At her nod, he groaned. "Oh please, my ego is nothing compared to his. We keep having to move his desk farther and farther away from the group because his ego crowds out everyone else. Eventually, he's going to have to sit in the lobby."

She giggled at that, then slapped a hand over her mouth, shocked at the sound. James sent her a gentle smile and reached for the door. "Try to get some rest," he said, closing it with a soft click.

She stood there for a moment, not wanting to face the mirror and confront her reflection. Her cheeks ached from their earlier abuse, and she briefly considered ducking back into the kitchen to make an ice pack. The desire for bed was stronger though, so she stripped off her clothes, forming a neat, folded pile on the counter. Then, taking a deep breath, she looked up.

Oh, man. Her face was a livid mass of bruises, swirls of purple and red and blue painting her skin. *Is that—?* She leaned closer, turning her head to the side to get a better look at her cheek. Yes, just there—finger marks where Victor's hand had slapped her. The sight made her blood run cold. *Bastard.*

She turned her face to the other side and gently peeled off the bandage. She studied the red slash critically. It wasn't as bad as she'd thought. It was smaller than she'd expected. Based on the amount of pain it had caused, she'd been steeling herself for something much bigger, much longer. She was relieved to see the nurse was right—it didn't appear to be too deep. She wasn't terribly vain, but the thought of walking around with Victor's mark on her face for the rest of her life had made her throat tighten and her heart pound. Seeing now that there would not be a scar eased some of that anxiety.

For the first time that night, she felt she had some degree of control. She wasn't hurt as badly as she'd thought, which was something she could take back from Victor. It wasn't much, she knew—after all, armed FBI agents were just a few feet away, so how much control did she really have?—but if she closed her eyes, she could pretend that this was just the end of another long day at work. She'd take a quick shower, throw on a ratty old T-shirt and climb into bed.

A quick search of the bathroom drawers turned up sample bottles of shampoo and bath gel, and she stepped under the warm spray with a sigh. The water did wonders for her aching body, so she stood there for a few moments, letting the hot water sluice down her arms and legs. Then, not wanting to fall asleep in the shower, she quickly washed her hair and body, taking care not to get her glued-together cheek too wet.

The bathroom was like a sauna when she stepped out, the mirror fogged with steam and the counter damp. The heat of the room made her feel drugged, made every movement and gesture a chore. She quickly finished up and stepped out into the hall, goose bumps popping up along her shoulders and legs as the cooler air hit the skin not covered by her towel.

She heard the low murmur of voices before she shut the bedroom door. The other agent must have arrived, but something was a bit…off. The deeper voice was definitely James, but the other voice hadn't sounded very feminine; it had been in the lower registers as well.

Maybe she's a smoker, she thought numbly, too tired to really care as she dropped the towel and pulled on a shirt. Not even bothering with the light, she tugged back the covers and slid into the bed, surrendering to the comforting embrace of sleep as a pair of deep blue eyes flickered across her mind.

They really needed to work on their security, Victor mused, pausing in his search to take a long pull from the beer bottle. They put so much information out in the public domain, he didn't even have to hack into their system to find a list of FBI agents, complete with photographs and phone numbers. It was child's play to scan the pictures, pick out the redhead who had refused to die. It was almost as if they *wanted* him to find the man.

He studied the picture, memorizing the image, matching it against the man from last night. He was much younger here, the perfect Norman Rockwellian Boy Scout, full of idealism and hope. His smile was so eager it made his teeth hurt to look at it. *Not so young now, are you, pretty boy?*

His eyes dropped to the bottom of the screen to read the name. Thomas Kincannon. A good Irish name, to go along with that horrible ginger hair. A few keystrokes and he was in the system, checking out Kincannon's jacket. A solid, dedicated agent, according to his record. Good case-closure rate, worked well with others—by all accounts, an ideal Fed. He'd emerged relatively unscathed from the disaster that was Caleb's operation a few months ago, no mean feat given the magnitude of that screwup. Even though he'd never met the man, the reverberations from that little operation had rippled through his circle of fellow operatives, made them all sit up and take notice.

He toggled back over to the file he'd amassed on Dr. Fleming. She was another straight arrow, and there was no indication she'd been involved in any illegal activities. The only reason she was a target now was due to her relationship with Dr. Novikoff. He shook his head as he pulled up her picture. So pretty. She'd felt nice pressed up against him, but he knew there was no chance she'd sleep with him. Not willingly, anyway. He was used to paying for his pleasure and knew that if he had enough time he'd find her price, but things were moving too fast now for that.

Had she been telling the truth about the file? He mentally replayed the events of last night, focusing on her panicked voice and wide eyes. She hadn't looked like she'd been lying, and in his experience, most people couldn't wait to give him information once he started hurting them. Not her. She'd stuck to her story, which made him think she was telling the truth. He felt a brief flash of regret at having marred her pretty face for nothing, but shrugged it off. She was going to die anyway, so in the end, it didn't really matter.

He leaned back in the chair and took another sip, considering. If she'd given the FBI the files, she would have passed them to Kincannon first. Which meant he knew where they were, how many copies were floating around, who had access to them now. It all seemed to come back to him…

He clicked back to Kincannon's page. He was the key to getting the file back. Dr. Fleming was still a target, of course. He couldn't let her live, not when his employers were so keen to see her dead. But perhaps he could take his time with that. It was the file they really wanted, and if he delivered that, they might be willing to give him some time to track down the good doctor. Hell, they might even decide to let her live, if he could convince them of her innocence in all of this. Maybe she'd feel grateful to him for saving her life. He indulged in a brief fantasy of tangled limbs and bare skin, breathless moans and slick mouths. Yes, that would be very nice…he and Dr. Fleming—*Claire,* he thought, deciding he'd earned the right to use her name—would get to know each other very well.

After a moment, he focused back on the screen.

What to do, what to do? He narrowed his eyes in thought as he considered his options. Special Agent Do-Good had probably whisked Dr. Fleming off to a safe house somewhere, which meant she was out of the picture for now. That was fine; he needed the file more than anything. But how to get it?

He performed a quick search on Thomas Kincannon, which resulted in several hits. Most of the articles were clearly about other people, but there, toward the bottom of the page, was a link to an obituary. One Roger Kincannon had been killed in a car accident six months ago, and was survived by his wife, Jenny, his daughter, Emily, his mother, Diana, and his brother, Thomas Kincannon. How tragic. How depressing, that a man was cut down in the prime of his life, leaving behind such a young family.

How perfect.

Adrenaline had his fingers flying across the keyboard as he dug deeper, made the connections between Thomas and Jenny. She was listed as his emergency contact, worked as a nurse in the labor and delivery department at George Washington hospital.

He clicked on Jenny's social network profile, tutting with mock disappointment when he saw she had no privacy settings in place. "You make this too easy," he murmured, scanning her page, opening her photo albums. A young girl sporting a blond ponytail grinned up at the camera with a gap-toothed smile, her brown eyes warm and sparkling. The next picture was a view of her riding piggyback, her lanky frame wrapped around the torso of a tall man as she clung to his shoulders. Although his face was turned away from the camera, that trademark flaming hair gave him away. Agent Kincannon.

Victor leaned back, a satisfied smile curving his lips as he continued to click through the images. A plan began to form, crystallizing as he focused on picture after picture of the man's weakness. It would be risky, he knew, but the payoff would be high. He'd come out on top, emerge with both the file and Claire. He'd win.

And that was all that mattered.

Chapter 6

"What have you got for me?"

Ignoring the look of shock on Agent Shannon Mitchell's face, Thomas rounded the desk and pulled over a chair, leaning in close to get a better look at the computer screen.

"Shouldn't you be lying down or something?" the young woman asked, skepticism weighing her words. "Are you sure you're cleared to come back to work?" Her eyes drifted over to his neck and the bandage he still wore, her doubt regarding his fitness for duty evident in her expression.

"Just keep it clean," the doctor had said this morning, typing madly on his tablet as he spoke. "Any abnormal redness, oozing or fever, come back. Otherwise, see your regular doctor next week to get the stitches out."

Thomas shuddered slightly at the word *ooze,* trying hard not to think about the implications of having a wound that did something so disgusting. It even *sounded* undignified, for crying out loud.

Release papers in hand, Thomas had quickly dressed and headed to the office before Jenny's shift ended and she figured out a way to have him admitted for another day. He hadn't bothered to stop at his own desk before coming over to see what Agent Mitchell had found out about last night's attack, and he still held the hospital forms in a death grip. Waving these at her now, he brushed away her concerns.

"I'm fine, and yes, I have my doctor's note. Now, if you're done acting like my boss and my mother, I'd like a report on the information I gave you last night. Have you found anything?"

Rolling her eyes, Shannon turned back to the computer with a muttered "Touchy," her fingers flying across the keyboard as she pulled up several files.

Thomas shifted, feeling slightly guilty at having snapped at her. She was only trying to be nice. He opened his mouth to reply, but the information on the screen snagged his attention, and the apology died on his lips.

"Based on your description," Shannon said, clicking on one page to bring it to the forefront, "I narrowed down the search parameters. Is this by any chance the man who attacked you?" She pulled up a grainy photograph, the image imperfect but the face clear enough. It was him.

Thomas nodded. "You got him," he said, letting his amazement come through in his voice. He hadn't given her much to go on, but Shannon was excellent at what she did, as evidenced by her finding this needle in a haystack.

She smiled a little smugly and turned back to the computer, tapping away to bring up another file. "His name is Victor Banner. Arrested ten years ago for aggravated robbery." A dated mug shot came up, confirming Thomas's identification. This was definitely the guy.

Shannon clicked again. "Did his time, got out. Seemed to be keeping his nose clean, but then he turned up on a surveillance tape and was a suspect in a murder five years ago. The cops were sure they had their guy, but he walked on a technicality." She clicked back to the photo she'd first showed him. "Since then, he's dropped off the face of the earth."

"I doubt that," Thomas said.

"So did I," Shannon replied. "So I did a search, looking for unsolved murders in the last five years."

Thomas raised a brow. "I bet that got some hits."

She nodded, the corner of her mouth quirking up. "A few. I narrowed the parameters, looking for cases where the murder weapon was a knife. And I found this." She pulled up a new file and scanned through a series of crime-scene photos, black-and-white images of blood-soaked death frozen in time.

"He does like to use a knife," Thomas murmured, reaching up to finger the gauze taped to his neck as he recalled the feel of the blade, a sudden, cold pressure that had morphed into a burning pain with one quick slice.

"True," Shannon agreed, studying the photos with

a clinical eye. "Even his early work is skilled. See the marks here and here?" She pointed to the screen as she spoke, moving from one body to the next. "Not the usual hesitation strokes we see with young killers. This guy is a professional, has been for a long time. Either we missed his early hits, or he got his practice in somewhere else."

"Could be a bit of both," Thomas said, leaning back in the chair. "What do we know about the victims? How do we know they're his?"

Shannon clicked through to another file. "The vics are all over the map. Geographically, racially, economically—no commonalities jump out. That's why I think he's a hired gun. Take these three, for example." She pulled up a few pictures as she spoke. "What we know is that they got involved in a drug-smuggling operation, and things went south when one of them was arrested. He made bail, but the next day, he and his two friends were dead."

"Retribution."

She nodded. "Probably. We don't know who hired him, but the message was pretty obvious. The locals didn't find any leads, and they weren't too keen on wasting resources on a case that was going nowhere. Besides, nobody missed three low-life dealers who'd gotten in with the wrong crowd."

Thomas frowned. "That's pretty thin. Got anything else to implicate him in these deaths?"

Shannon grinned. "I thought you'd never ask." She returned to the case file from the original five-year-old murder. "See this?" She zoomed in on a photo taken during the autopsy. It was a close-up of the victim's leg, showing a crude heart carved into the skin of the thigh.

"This mark is a big reason why the cops suspected Banner in the first place. See how it forms his initials? V and B." She traced the screen as she spoke, outlining the letters that made up the heart.

Thomas nodded, feeling a tingle of excitement dance across the back of his neck. "Tell me the dealers have the same mark."

"They do, indeed." She brought up the pictures, arranged them side by side. The marks were identical.

"Do the other bodies have connections like that?"

Shannon shrugged. "Don't know yet. I just started digging."

"Fair enough. Let's assume that he is an assassin. How did he wind up in Russia?" Victor was only part of the problem, the tip of a very large iceberg. Even if he was able to take care of this particular threat, until Thomas knew who wanted Claire dead, she'd never be safe.

"Can I get back to you on that?" Shannon asked, turning to face him with a wince. "Like I said, I'm still digging."

He placed a hand on her shoulder, squeezing gently as he stood. "You've done a great job so far. Keep it up."

"Can I take a nap first?" she asked hopefully. "I've been working on this since you called last night." She yawned for emphasis, releasing an exaggerated sigh to complete the picture.

"Naps are for winners," Thomas replied, giving her a wink while pulling the chair he'd used away from her desk. "When you find my Russian connection, then you can sleep."

"Whatever," she said, shooting him a mock glare before turning back to the computer.

"I believe in you," he said teasingly as he headed over to Harper's office.

Shannon's mumbled reply was lost when he rapped on Harper's door.

"Enter," came the soft reply.

Steeling himself for another argument about his fitness for duty, Thomas let out a silent sigh before pushing open the door. Harper glanced up from his desk, his eyes widening before his usual professional mask dropped back into place. "Kincannon. Good to see you." His gaze fixed on Thomas's neck, and Thomas resisted the urge to touch the bandage, vowing to throw it away at the first opportunity. The stitches underneath would make him look like Frankenstein's monster, but that had to be better than wearing this white flag that advertised just how close he'd come to getting his throat cut.

"You had quite the scare last night."

"Things got a little hairy," Thomas conceded. Hard to deny when Harper had yet to take his gaze off the proof of it.

"Ready to come back?"

"Absolutely."

Harper's eyes shifted, meeting his own. Thomas tensed, waiting for his boss to protest, but after a beat the older man broke the impromptu staring contest to look down at the papers on his desk.

"Good. What's happening with the case?"

That's it? No suggestion that I'm not ready to come back to work? Surprised by Harper's ready acceptance of his return, Thomas gaped at the man, his respect for his superior agent rising a few notches. No one wanted to be treated like a child, and Thomas appreciated the fact that Harper took him at his word when it came to his readiness for duty. *Maybe he's not so bad after all....*

"Kincannon," Harper said, drawing him out of his thoughts. "Your case?"

Thomas shook his head slightly, mildly embarrassed by the delay in his reply. Nothing like awkward conversational pauses to convince the boss you really were ready to come back to work. "Uh, Shannon has made good progress on identifying last night's attacker."

Harper leaned back in his chair and laced his fingers behind his head. "And? Anyone we know?"

Thomas shrugged. "Maybe. It looks like a guy named Victor Banner. He may be a pro—she's still digging."

"What's his connection to Dr. Fleming?"

"Still unknown. She's my next stop. I need to talk to her about last night, find out if he said anything to her before…well, before."

Harper nodded. "There's got to be something else at play here. Why didn't he just kill her when he had the chance? Why keep her alive?"

"He wants something."

"She told James he wanted the papers."

Thomas nodded, Harper's words confirming his hunch. "That's pretty much what I figured."

Harper frowned. "But we had the papers translated. It's just a list of nonsense words."

"Nonsense to us," Thomas said, "but what if it's a code?"

Harper waved his hand, dismissing the thought. "We've had cryptography examine the pages, and they haven't found anything. If it is a code, it's damn near uncrackable."

"Not to Claire."

Harper opened his mouth to respond, but Thomas cut him off. "Think about it—why would Novikoff send these papers to Claire in the first place?"

"Safekeeping? Maybe he meant to retrieve them later but was murdered before that could happen."

"Maybe. But you have to admit the timing is suspicious. He just happens to mail her a package of mysterious papers the day of his murder? I don't buy it. From all accounts, he was a smart guy. He had to know something was up."

"All right. That still doesn't explain why Dr. Fleming would be able to decode this message, if there even is one."

"He could have sent those papers to any number of people if it was just a matter of keeping them out of the wrong hands. But he sent them to Claire. He had to have a reason for that, and I think it's because she's the key to understanding them."

Harper studied him for a long moment, his expression impassive as he considered Thomas's argument. *Don't ever play poker with this guy.* Thomas brushed the errant thought aside, trying to keep his own expression neutral. If he appeared too enthusiastic, Harper might write him off as a conspiracy nut and refuse to entertain any more of his ideas.

"What do you propose?"

Thomas let his breath out slowly, sensing he was close to victory. *Don't blow it now....*

"I'd like to take copies of the papers to Dr. Fleming and let her spend some time with them. Maybe something will catch her eye, or she'll recall a previous conversation with Novikoff that will shed some light on the investigation."

"And if she doesn't?"

Thomas shrugged. "Then I've wasted an afternoon."

Harper narrowed his eyes at that, but then nodded. "Fine. Probably best for you to take it easy today anyway." He looked back down at the papers on his desk, a gesture that Thomas recognized as his cue to leave. "Get a copy of the translations from Alan. Let me know if you learn anything new."

"Will do."

Thomas stepped into the hall, shaking his head. Maybe he was still feeling light-headed from the loss of blood, but Harper had seemed almost pleasant. While the man would never be the warm, fuzzy type, he had lost the prickly edge that had characterized the majority of their conversations. *Maybe I should get hurt more often.*

Feeling a spurt of excitement that had nothing to do with the progress he hoped to make on the case, Thomas let his thoughts drift to Claire as he collected the documents and left the office. According to his watch, it had been only a few hours since he'd last seen her, but it certainly didn't feel that way. Time slowed to a crawl when she wasn't near, a realization that should have bothered him more than it did. He was anxious to have her look at the documents and to ask her about last night's attack, but more than that, he just wanted to be near her again.

She had a calming way about her, he mused, recalling the way she'd kept him from chasing after their attacker. She'd certainly distracted him in the hospital. He smiled at the memory of her kiss, a thrill of anticipation in his belly as he imagined kissing her again. And he would. Now that he'd tasted her, he wouldn't be satisfied with just one kiss. He needed more.

But he would have to wait.

First things first. Eliminate the threat to Claire. Then he could focus on getting up close and personal with the sexy scientist.

The sun was bright and cheerful, warming Claire as she stood at the window cradling a cup of coffee. It looked like the perfect fall day; the sky was the clear, vibrant blue of a robin's egg, and a slight wind stirred the red-and-gold leaves in the trees, sending a few drifting lazily down with each gentle gust. She glanced wistfully outside, wishing for the umpteenth time she could go for a walk or at least sit on the porch. She could hear the dim shouts of children as they played in the neighboring yards, their bicycle bells ringing while they rode in front of the house. The whole neighborhood was outside, it seemed, making her feel even more isolated. *Probably too chilly,* she told herself, drawing little comfort from the thought.

She turned away and walked to the table, setting down the mug before reaching up to rub her gritty eyes. She hadn't slept well. Though she knew on an intellectual level that she was safe, her emotions were still raw from the attack. Every noise, from the gust of wind rattling the tree branches outside to the low hum of the heater cranking on, had made her jump, her heart pounding into her throat as she was jerked awake. After a few minutes, she would doze off only to be startled by the next unfamiliar sound, a seemingly endless cycle that had left her more exhausted than she'd been before going to bed.

A discreet cough behind her drew her attention, and she turned to find Agent Reynolds standing by the kitchen counter. "Good morning," he said, pouring himself a cup of coffee. "How'd you sleep?"

"Okay," she lied, offering him a small smile.

He glanced at her as he stirred sugar into his cup. "Uh-huh. That's why you have such dark circles under your eyes."

Claire shrugged, dismissing the observation. "I'll be fine. I used to pull all-nighters in college. I just need a little caffeine." She gestured to the mug on the table and sat as James walked over to join her.

"Forgive me for saying this, but you were a bit younger in those days. It might take a little more than caffeine to bounce back now."

"I suppose you're right," she acknowledged, staring down at the mug cupped between her hands. "I just can't turn my brain off, which makes it impossible to sleep."

"Still thinking about last night's attack?"

She nodded. "That, and Ivan, and…" She trailed off, considering. Agent Reynolds and Thomas seemed to be friends, which meant he probably knew how Thomas was doing this morning, if he'd been released from the hospital. While she was worried about Thomas, she didn't want any of his coworkers to think their relationship was anything other than professional. If word got out they had kissed, it could be a disaster for his career. But surely she could ask about him without raising too much suspicion?

She glanced up to find James watching her, his expression kind. Yes, she could ask this man. She'd just have to be careful about it, keep her tone neutral and her face guarded so she didn't give anything away.

"Do you know how Agent Kincannon is doing today? Is he still okay?" That sounded good—concerned but not overly so. Perfect.

"He's doing fine. In fact, he'll be here in a bit to take over for me while Natalie gets some rest."

Her hand jerked, sloshing coffee over the rim of the mug. *Damn. So much for cool and collected.* She glanced up to see if he had noticed, but he was already fetching a paper towel, which he handed to her with a wry smile. Of course he'd seen. And now he probably suspected her interest in Thomas's condition wasn't just a matter of common courtesy.

She dabbed at the small puddle of coffee. "Oh, really?" she said, hating that her voice sounded so high. "That's good. That he's okay," she rushed to add, feeling her face heat as she finished mopping up her mess. "I know he said he was fine last night, but I'm glad to hear he didn't have any trouble during the night."

"Me, too," James said, plucking the wet paper towel from her hand and walking over to deposit it in the trash. "He almost got himself killed."

"It wasn't his fault," Claire shot back, her temper flaring in defense of Thomas. He'd done a damn fine job keeping her safe last night, and Agent Reynolds had no right to criticize him, even if they were friends.

He regarded her quizzically. "Didn't say it was," he said mildly.

"Oh." The fight went out of her at that, and Claire slumped back into her chair, feeling oddly deflated.

The man studied her for a long moment while he sipped his coffee. Claire fought the urge to fidget under his scrutiny, unsure of what he was looking for. The silence stretched between them, growing awkward, and she cast about for something to say. The ringing of his phone saved her from making a comment about the weather, and she sighed quietly as he shifted his attention away from her.

Had it really been only yesterday that this nightmare had started? She shook her head, still having trouble processing everything that had happened since that horrible email. A small part of her wanted to crawl into bed and sleep so she could wake up to find this had all been a terrible dream, the product of an overactive imagination and too much TV crime drama before bed. She'd open her eyes to find Ivan still alive, her life back to normal.

Except her life would never be normal again.

And as much as she wanted to hide under the blankets, that was the coward's way out. Denying her new reality wasn't going to make it go away, and the quicker she adapted to it, the better off she'd be. While she wanted nothing more than to rest, to let Thomas take care of her and protect her, she couldn't let herself depend on him. She was used to taking care of herself and fixing her own problems, a lesson she had learned from her adoptive mother years ago.

Frank Fleming had been the glue that held their little family together, and after his death, her mother had pulled away. Claire had always suspected her adoption was driven by her father, not her mother, a fact that Dena Fleming had confirmed years later. Dena wasn't cut out to be a mother, and any affection she'd felt for Claire had turned to resentment when faced with the realities of raising a child alone.

Why are you so needy all the time?

Why can't you just take care of yourself?

Why won't you leave me alone?

Stop bothering me!

While Dena had never been physically abusive, her neglect and outright hostility toward Claire had left painful scars. She could see now that Dena had been battling her own demons, but she couldn't bring herself to forgive, and she couldn't allow herself to forget. She hadn't spoken to Dena in years, not since the day she'd graduated high school. The older woman had been visibly relieved that Claire had finished school, and to celebrate, she'd given her a stack of cardboard boxes.

"You're an adult now. It's time for you to move out."

And so Claire had packed her things and left, staying on a friend's couch until college started in the fall. She'd begged, borrowed and worked her fingers to the bone as a waitress to pay for school, and not once had she asked Dena for anything. She'd vowed that she would never again grow to depend on another person, knowing that if she didn't need anyone, they couldn't turn her life upside down on a whim. It was a plan that had served her well.

Until Ivan came along and breached her defenses.

And now that he was gone, Thomas was quickly patching up the gaps in her heart.

James snapped his phone closed and turned back to her with a polite smile. "That was Agent Kincannon. He's about five minutes out. If you'll excuse me…" He poured the remainder of his coffee in the sink, rinsed the mug and placed it on the counter. "I have a few things to take care of before he gets here."

Claire offered him a weak smile and a nod. The news that Thomas was so close sent nervous zings of electric anticipation through her limbs, and she placed a hand on the table in a vain attempt to ground herself. Kissing him last night had been wonderfully distracting, but she'd been pulled away before they'd had a chance to talk. What if he hadn't felt anything? Or worse, what if he'd only kissed her back because he felt sorry for her? Was there anything worse than a pity kiss?

Restlessness pushed her to her feet. She paced a few steps, turned and walked back to the table. She picked up the coffee mug and took a sip, frowning at the lukewarm temperature. *Maybe another cup would help….*

She dumped out the dregs and poured a fresh cup, added sugar and stirred. She took her time with the ritual, using it to get her nerves under control. So she was going to see him again—she'd known it would happen. After all, he was assigned to her case, so that meant she'd have to interact with him as long as there *was* a case. She'd just have to keep things professional from here on out. If she didn't mention the kiss, perhaps he wouldn't either. An implicit rejection was certainly preferable to having him tell her outright that he wasn't interested. She shuddered at the thought. Her emotions were so close to the surface right now she was sure she'd start crying if he came in here and tried to let her down easy.

So don't let him.

Distraction was key. All she had to do was steer the conversation away from any topics that came even remotely close to being personal, and she'd be fine. It wouldn't be that hard. She did it at work all the time.

But she'd never kissed her coworkers. And none of them had bright blue eyes and a smile that kindled a warm glow inside her chest. She didn't feel at peace around them, didn't enjoy that curious lightness she felt around Thomas, as if his presence somehow lessened gravity's pull.

And none of her coworkers had ever saved her life.

It would be so easy to fall in—

No. She wasn't going to say it. The only L-word she was willing to consider was *like*. Anything else was far too risky.

I like him, she told herself firmly, emphasizing the word so her heart would know she meant business. Liking Thomas was acceptable. Loving him was not. For crying out loud, she had only met him yesterday! It simply wasn't possible to go from *nice to meet you* to *I love you* in the space of a few hours. That was the stuff of Hollywood movies, not real life.

Although, to be fair, armed assassins weren't generally the stuff of real life either.

It was the stress of her situation, she decided, determined to be sensible. Thomas had prevented her attacker from hurting her, and had gotten injured himself in the process. His actions had inspired her to cast him in the part of the hero, and she'd built him up in her mind, making him out to be bigger, braver, stronger, *better* than he was in real life. Her attraction to him was a natural extension of her imaginings. Once he arrived, she'd see that he was just a man, and her emotions would settle back into place.

Claire picked up the mug and blew across the surface of the steaming liquid, pleased to have that sorted out. She would stay here until Thomas showed up, and once she'd seen him again and proved that her feelings were based on adrenaline, she could turn her focus to other things.

She didn't have to wait long. She was a few sips into her coffee when he arrived. The low hum of male voices drifted in from the next room, and she closed her eyes, letting the comforting timbre wash over her, even as the sound of him made her stomach flip-flop.

Footsteps sounded in the hall and she turned away, presenting her back to the door. It was cowardly of her, but she didn't want him to know how eager she was to see him.

"Claire?"

Oh, God. That voice. It rumbled through her, thrummed along her skin like a caress. Just like that, she was back in the hospital room, her mouth pressed to his and her body crying out for more. She took a deep breath to dispel the sudden jolt of lust and swallowed hard before turning around, hoping her face wouldn't give away the effect he had on her.

"Hello," she said quietly.

He looked good, she noted, relief making her feel almost giddy. She hadn't expected him to be at death's door, but seeing him now, wearing dark gray slacks and a navy blue polo that darkened his eyes to the color of lapis, he was the very picture of health. If it weren't for the bandage on his neck and a subtle, lingering paleness in his lips and cheeks, she could easily pretend last night had never happened.

He walked forward, stopping a few steps away to study her. "How are you?"

She tried to smile. "I've been better."

His gaze traced her cheek and she lifted her hand, placing her fingertips on the slightly raised edge of the cut. "Does it hurt?" he asked, his own hand coming to rest on his neck in a sympathetic echo of her gesture.

"Not really. More annoying than anything. What about you?"

He smiled down at her, and the combination of his dimples and the sparkle in his eyes made her catch her breath. "The same. I have to go back next week to get the stitches out, but other than that it's no big deal."

"That's good." She winced inwardly, feeling suddenly awkward. Why did he have to stand so close? That starchy, soapy smell she would forever associate with him was having an unwelcome effect on her emotions, making her want to close the distance between them and press her nose to the hollow of his throat.

"Listen, Claire, I was hoping we could talk."

No. Absolutely not. No talking. No discussion of

feelings, of that kiss. Talking would only make her want him more, and she'd already decided there was no future for her down that road. She couldn't let him distract her now.

Claire looked down, casting about for something to say that would change the subject before Agent Kincannon asked her about last night's kiss. Her gaze caught on the papers in his hand, and she seized on the excuse with the relief of a drowning man who has reached the shore.

"What are those?"

He frowned slightly as he followed her gaze down to the pages. "Oh," he said, as if just now remembering he held them. "That's part of what I wanted to talk to you about. They're the decoded pages that Dr. Novikoff sent you. I thought you could have another look at them, see if anything jumped out at you."

Claire reached out and took them from him, excitement and anticipation flaring as she flipped through the papers. Finally, something else to concentrate on! Looking for a hidden message among the seemingly random collection of words would provide a wonderful distraction from thinking about her own situation. Even better, focusing on the papers meant she could no longer focus on Thomas and her confusing reaction to his continued presence in her life.

She returned to the table and sat, spreading the pages out so she could see all of them at once. Maybe they had to be read in a certain order....

Annoyance sparked as Thomas sat down across from her, but he remained silent, his own attention on

the papers. She was uncomfortably aware of his near-
ness, but a second set of eyes wouldn't hurt.

Soon she was completely oblivious to his presence. She read the words over and over, arranging the
pages in different patterns and trying every combination she could think of to tease out a hidden message.
So far, nothing had worked. Still, the more she studied the words, the more convinced she became that
they were not the random scribblings of a delusional
mind—there was a meaning here, a pattern, and she
just had to find it.

Please, Ivan. Help me understand.

Something was off.

It was clear when he'd walked into the room that
Claire was uncomfortable. What he couldn't figure
out was why.

Was she scared? James had said they'd passed a
quiet night, but he hadn't actually been in the bedroom with her. Maybe she hadn't slept well; maybe
she'd been too shaken to close her eyes. Not that he
could blame her. It wasn't every day she was attacked
by a knife-wielding sicko, and given the earlier shock
of Novikoff's death, she had to be on edge.

Still, something about her demeanor made him
think this wasn't totally about fear. It was the way she
avoided his eyes, the way she'd abruptly changed the
subject when he'd said he wanted to talk to her. She'd
looked almost panicked at the thought of having a conversation with him. He wouldn't have been surprised
if she'd actually bolted from the room. She probably
would have, too, if she hadn't seen the papers.

He studied her now, her head bent in absorption as she pored over the documents. Every now and then she'd tilt her head to the side, her blond hair turning a warm gold in the afternoon sunlight. Normally he'd be a bit more covert about his surveillance, but Claire was so totally focused that he could watch her freely, with no fear of being caught staring. She hadn't looked up when he'd brought her a fresh cup of coffee earlier, and he realized that she had no idea it was there. She had the enviable ability to concentrate so intently on one task that the world around her disappeared.

He idly wondered if she ever used that laserlike focus in bed and immediately quashed the thought before he got himself into trouble. Too late, though. He had a sudden, vivid image of her with her head thrown back and her eyes screwed shut as she moved over him, her lips parted on a gasp....

He shifted, casting a glance in her direction as he discreetly adjusted his pants. Thankfully, she hadn't noticed.

The image of her mouth brought another possibility to mind. Was she upset with him for the kiss last night? Although technically she had kissed him, he certainly hadn't held back. Perhaps he'd come on too strong, and she was afraid to be alone with him. The thought made his stomach cramp. The last thing he wanted was for her to be afraid of him. He'd never deliberately hurt her; in fact, he would do everything in his power to keep her safe. But how could she know that?

Christ, he thought, running a hand through his hair. She'd kissed him last night, and instead of recognizing it as the gesture of a woman who was overwhelmed, scared past all reason and seeking reassurance, he'd seen it as an invitation. He'd yanked her on top of him and plunged his tongue into her mouth, too caught up in his own arousal to recognize her hesitance. No wonder she didn't want to see him today. He'd been a first-class ass, and she probably figured he was more interested in bedding her than protecting her.

The realization hit a little too close to home, making him wince. *Way to make an impression, Kincannon.*

Not for the first time, he wished Roger were here. His brother would know what to do, how to apologize to Claire. Roger had always had a way with words. Even when they were kids, his fast-talking had frequently come to the rescue, saving them from several well-deserved punishments. The two of them had been quite the handful growing up. It was a wonder their mother had survived.

"Me?" Diana had said incredulously, when Roger had brought it up last Christmas. "It's a wonder you boys survived! There were plenty of times I wanted to lock you out of the house, or drive you to the middle of Rock Creek Park and turn you loose." She shook her head, her mouth curving in a smile as she stared at them affectionately. "But I suppose I'm glad I didn't, now that you're both grown and useful." She reached up to pat them gently on the cheeks.

"Gee, thanks, Mom," Thomas replied, rolling his eyes.

"What do you mean, useful?" Roger asked, affecting mock indignation.

"Well, you're very good at carrying heavy things," Diana offered. "And you've given me grandchildren.

At least, *one* of you has," she said, with a sidelong glance at Thomas.

Thomas raised his hands in surrender and backed away. "Hey, don't look at me. I'm not the one who's married. Talk to him."

Roger laughed and threw an arm around Thomas's neck, pulling him closer. "Don't worry, little brother. Your time will come. In fact, I bet you a round of golf at Congressional that you'll have a girlfriend by spring."

"You're on," Thomas said, offering his hand to seal the deal. "Loser also springs for lunch at the club."

"You'd better save your money," Roger taunted, a sly grin spreading across his face. "I'm going to be hungry."

As it turned out, Thomas had won the bet, but he'd never had a chance to collect. By the time spring rolled around, Roger was gone, leaving a hole in Thomas's soul that he didn't think would ever fully heal.

It should have been me.

Thomas shook his head as old, familiar irritation surged anew at the thought. Even if he lived to be a hundred years old, he would never understand why his brother, a family man and absolute good guy, had been killed that day, while he, a single guy married to his job, was still here. It really should have been the other way around. And sure, his mother would miss him if he were gone, but at least his brother's family would still be intact.

Claire moved again, shifting as if trying to find a more comfortable position. He watched her finger trace the words on the page, her lips moving as she silently read to herself. She was lovely to look at, especially now when her expression was unguarded and her features relaxed. More than that, though, she was a good person. He knew from her dossier that she was heavily involved in nuclear safety. He'd read several articles detailing her role in securing radioactive fuel from decaying reactors in unstable areas. She was, essentially, trying to save the world, one spent fuel rod at a time. And he admired her for it.

Maybe, just maybe, *she* was the reason he was here. He'd read enough popular science articles to know that a butterfly flapping its wings in Chile could trigger a monsoon in India. Maybe his initial choice to ask Roger to take their mother that day had set off a chain of events that had resulted not only in his brother's death, but also in Thomas being here, at this moment, keeping Claire safe so she could protect the rest of the world.

He found the thought oddly comforting, although part of him wanted to dismiss it as outright bunk, the product of blood loss and lack of sleep. He wasn't sure he believed in fate—it was a bit too convenient as far as explanations went. Even though Roger's death had demonstrated once and for all that he couldn't control everything, Thomas didn't like to dwell on the knowledge that there were things beyond his influence, events and circumstances that he couldn't affect. Still, despite his rejection of fate, he couldn't deny that the idea he might serve a greater good by protecting Claire made the loss of Roger a bit easier to bear.

At least for today.

Casting covert glances from under her lashes, Claire watched in fascination as an array of expressions paraded across Thomas's face. Suspicion gave way to amusement and then to pain, before something like resignation settled over his features. She was used to seeing humor on him—he always seemed to have a smile lurking just under the surface—but pain was something different altogether. It wasn't the look he'd worn last night, when he was physically hurting from his injuries. No, this was the expression of a man who had experienced a soul-deep loss. She recognized the look, as it was the same one she wore in her heart where the memories of her father lived.

What loss haunted him?

Against her better judgment, she found herself wanting to comfort him. It bothered her to see him like this, subdued and hurting. She wanted to see him return to his old self, the confident, joking agent who had protected her, made her feel safe and secure. Not the man in the hospital bed who had blamed himself for their attack, or the man in front of her now, lost in remembered pain. She didn't know what ghosts plagued him, but she did know that he deserved better.

She made a show of gathering the pages together, tapping them into a neat stack with a loud sigh. When she looked at him again, she found he was watching her, all traces of sadness gone, his lips curving up slightly to form a muted version of the smile she already knew so well.

"Any luck?"

Claire shook her head. "No. Maybe." She shrugged, trying to ease some of the tension in her shoulders. "It's like the answer is right there, staring me in the face, but I just can't see it." She rested a hand on the pages, as if physical contact would induce them to reveal their secrets. "Do you ever feel like a word is on the tip of your tongue, but you just can't say it?"

Thomas nodded, leaning back in his chair as he regarded her. "Sure. It's annoying as hell."

"Exactly!" She let out her breath and slumped forward, fatigue and defeat getting the better of her. "That's how I feel right now. Impotent and completely useless."

"Hey now," he said, a wicked grin spreading across his face. "I didn't say I know what it feels like to be impotent."

Claire couldn't help but laugh, shaking her head at his audacity. "Perish the thought," she replied, batting her eyes at him in an exaggerated tease.

He winked back, and something deep in her belly flared to life. It must have shown on her face, because in the next instant, Thomas's expression went from good-natured fun to absorbed attention, his blue eyes twin flames of need.

She felt her body tighten in response, her skin tingling in anticipation of his touch. She already knew what his mouth felt like—what would his hands do to her? She dropped her gaze to the table where his large hands rested, fingers relaxed and gently curled. Did he have calluses on his palms? How would they feel, dragging across the sensitive skin of her thighs, her breasts? The thought made her shiver, and she swallowed hard, forcing her gaze up to his face.

He stared at her, the silence between them growing heavy and charged. The unspoken question hung in the air, and Claire knew, without a doubt, that she had only to nod and Thomas would be all too happy to demonstrate the truth behind his earlier statement.

She was sorely tempted to let him.

Even though she knew it was dangerous, Claire ran the tip of her tongue along her bottom lip. Thomas's gaze tracked the movement, sharpening as he watched her. His eyes were predatory now, and an electric tingle skittered through her limbs at being the focus of his attention.

He sat forward slowly, his muscles tense with leashed power. She couldn't take her eyes off the shifting fabric of his shirt as it molded to his broad shoulders and chest when he moved. With his laid-back disposition and ready smile, it was all too easy to forget that Thomas was a physically powerful man. Seeing that power on display now called to something feminine inside her and served to further weaken her earlier resolve to keep her distance.

She felt herself soften, as if in preparation for an encounter with the hard planes of his body. Without conscious thought, she leaned forward as well, needing to get closer to him, to feel his warmth. A flicker of what might have been satisfaction flared in his eyes, but it was gone before she could be sure.

He stood with casual grace, unfolding himself from the chair with fluid movements that made her think of a panther on the prowl. Then he stalked toward her, his eyes never leaving her face as he approached. Claire felt trapped in his gaze, frozen in delicious terror with the knowledge that this man wanted her.

And she was going to give herself to him.

She stood on shaky legs, bracing her hands on the

table for support. Thomas stopped a few inches away from her, but the heat of his body washed over her like a caress. She felt drawn to him, her body like a compass needle that had found true north. She held his eyes while she raised her hand and placed it gently on his chest.

His heartbeat was strong against her palm, and she curled her fingers into the fabric of his shirt, wanting to have an anchor when she kissed him. The first time she'd felt his mouth on hers, she'd been leaning over him with no chance of falling. Now, standing upright, she wasn't sure she'd be able to keep her balance at the next touch of his lips.

Slowly, so slowly, Thomas leaned down to bring his mouth to hers. She rose on tiptoes to meet him halfway, her heart picking up speed as the distance between them shrank. Claire closed her eyes as his breath drifted across her lips, savoring the sensation. *Oh, yes…*

The shrill ring of a phone made her jump, startling her out of the moment. She opened her eyes to see Thomas staring down at her, regret and disappointment mixed in his eyes. "Damn," he muttered, casting one last look at her before stepping away to pull the phone from his pocket. "Damn it all to hell."

Her body agreed with the sentiment, even as her mind was rapidly coming back online. Thomas turned away to take the call, evidently wanting some privacy. She let out her breath in a heavy sigh as her personal space returned. What had she been thinking? Only a few hours ago, she'd made a conscious decision to stay away from Thomas, to avoid the temptation he represented. All it took was a sad expression on his face and she was falling over herself to make him feel better, and in the process, breaking her own rules about getting involved with him. For all she knew, he was upset that his favorite sports team had lost their game last night. Her reaction was totally inappropriate, and she had to rein in her emotions before she really lost control. Next time, she might not be saved by a well-timed phone call.

But she knew, deep down, that Thomas truly had been upset. And though she was angry at herself for her reaction, she did want to offer him comfort. Just not of a physical kind.

Her body still tingled with the lingering sensation of having him so near. She'd been so ready to kiss him, to be kissed, that the interruption had left her feeling unsatisfied and edgy. Seeking a distraction, she turned back to the pages of words. The text was cold comfort to her libido, but she needed to figure out why Ivan had sent her these documents, and kissing Thomas wasn't going to get the job done.

Though it would have been a hell of a way to recharge.

It was time.

He'd spent the morning learning her routine, watching her every move. She'd been oblivious, of course. Children were always easy to spy on, as they were such self-absorbed little creatures. He had to admit, though, she was better behaved than most of her classmates. She didn't run or push others down or talk back to the teacher like some he'd seen. She was quiet, almost reserved, a fact that pleased him greatly. Hopefully she wouldn't be too much trouble.

She was standing a bit apart from the gaggle of other children, her head turned to the side, obviously looking for her grandmother. According to the neighbors, the woman usually walked from the metro to meet Emily after school, and the two would set off together, sometimes stopping at McDonald's for an after-school snack. It was a sweet little ritual, a nice bonding time between grandmother and granddaughter.

Too bad Grandma wasn't coming for her today.

With a last glance in the rearview mirror, Victor stepped out of the car and trekked across the street to the steps of the school. Ignoring Emily for the moment, he approached her teacher. "Ms. Patterson?"

The woman glanced over at him, then returned her attention to the group of children, her eyes sweeping back and forth over their little heads as she made sure they all stayed together. "Yes?"

"I'm Special Agent Victor Banner," he said, pulling out his badge and holding it up for her inspection. Her eyes widened as she glanced from his face to the badge, then back again. He felt a small spurt of satisfaction as he tucked the counterfeit identification back into his pocket. *Fooled another one.*

"I work with Thomas Kincannon, and he sent me to pick up his niece, Emily."

She frowned a bit at that, eyeing him dubiously before glancing back to the children. "Her grandmother usually picks her up."

"Yes, well. She's had a bit of an accident."

Her eyebrows shot up, a look of concern replacing the suspicion. "Is she all right?"

"She will be. She took a fall, may have broken her hip. Thomas and Emily's mom are at the hospital with her now, so they sent me."

"I see." Her tone was friendly but still guarded. This woman wasn't a fool.

Not wanting to spend more time with her, he reached into his jacket pocket for his ace in the hole. He pulled out the folded paper, opening it for her to read. "They sent this along, if that helps any."

"This" was the official form listing who was authorized to pick up Emily from school. There were only three names on the list: Jenny Kincannon, Diana Kincannon and Thomas Kincannon. He had stolen it from Diana's pocket earlier in the day, figuring it would be required to convince the teacher to let him take Emily.

He could have used the old snatch-and-grab method, but it was too unpredictable, too messy. Yanking Emily off the street would have put him on the defensive, running from the cops. This approach took a little more work but would pay off in the end. He was going to steal the girl right out from under her teacher's nose, and she'd never know a kidnapping had occurred.

Ms. Patterson scanned the paper, then let out a sigh. "This is highly unorthodox, but I'll let you pick her up today because of the situation. If they're going to have you pick her up again, you need to get your name added to the list."

He nodded, folding the paper and returning it to his pocket. "I'll tell them, but I think this will be the only time."

Ms. Patterson turned back to the children. "Emily," she called out.

The girl turned her head, and the teacher gestured for her to walk over. "This is Mr. Banner. He's a friend of your uncle's, and he's going to take you home today."

She looked up at him with narrowed eyes. "Where's Grandma?"

"She had an accident," he said, crouching down to meet her eyes. "She'll be fine, but your mom and uncle wanted me to get you and take you to the hospital."

The little girl bit her lip, studying his face. "You know Uncle Thomas?"

He nodded. "Yes, I work with him."

"Can I see your badge?"

Hmm. She was smarter than she looked. "Sure." He reached into his pocket again and pulled it out. She held out her hand expectantly, so he placed it on her upturned palm. She stared at it, and he had the sudden uncomfortable feeling that she'd probably done the same with Thomas's badge countless times before. He knew it was a good fake, but would it fool her?

She passed it back to him without comment.

"Ready to go?" he asked, letting out the breath he'd been holding when she nodded.

They set off across the street, his heart pounding with adrenaline. He'd done it. He'd grabbed Kincannon's niece, right out from under the watchful eyes of her teacher in broad daylight. She'd even wanted to go with him, for God's sake! He felt like laughing in triumph, but he squashed the urge, knowing it would only ruin things now. There would be time for him to celebrate later.

He held open the passenger door for her, then walked around to the driver's side. Reaching into the backseat, he pulled forward a bag of food. "I thought you might be hungry," he said, passing her the Happy Meal.

She took it from him and mumbled, "Thanks."

"Your grandma is going to be okay," he said as he merged into traffic. He glanced over at her, noting the still-unopened bag of food on her lap. "Go ahead and eat," he urged. "It'll take a few minutes to get to the hospital, and you won't like the cafeteria food."

She unrolled the bag, then reached inside and pulled out the hamburger. She wrinkled her nose at it. "What's wrong?"

"I usually get chicken nuggets," she said.

He gritted his teeth. *Too damn bad.* "Sorry," he said. "I didn't know."

"It's okay," she replied, biting into the burger. "What happened to Grandma?" she asked quietly between bites.

"She fell down." It was true. She had fallen down, but it hadn't been an accident. "They're making sure she hasn't broken any bones." He didn't think she had, but who knew? Older people were just so fragile these days....

He hadn't meant for her to fall. He'd only wanted to talk to her, distract her enough to retrieve the piece of paper and then slip her something to make her sleep for a few hours. But she'd grown suspicious at his questions, said she was going to call Thomas. When he'd moved to take the phone away from her, she'd tripped over the rug and fallen to the floor, hitting her head on the counter in the process. The blow had knocked her out cold, which had suited him just fine. He'd hastily cleaned up the evidence of his presence, then grabbed the paper and left. Whoever found her later would assume she'd lost her footing, as there was no evidence of foul play. He really couldn't have planned it better.

"I broke my toe once," the girl volunteered, her words slurring slightly. "It hurt a lot."

"I bet it did," he said. Her head nodded forward and she jerked it up, struggling to stay awake. "Are you tired?"

"Uh-huh." The half-eaten burger fell to her lap as her hands relaxed.

"Just lay your head back and sleep. I'll wake you up when we get to the hospital."

After another head bob, she gave up and slumped against the door, her neck canted at an uncomfortable angle. Excellent. He'd put enough drug on the burger to choke an elephant, so she should be out for the next several hours.

He allowed himself to smile as he drove through the city, picturing the look of horror on Agent Kincannon's face when he revealed what he'd done. The man would do anything to get his niece back, of that Victor was certain.

He chuckled softly as he drove. Agent Kincannon and the rest of the Feds probably thought he'd run away, that they'd seen the last of him when his initial attempt to retrieve the documents and Dr. Fleming had been thwarted. Wouldn't they just scramble to catch up to him now? He was back in charge of the situation, just the way he liked it.

He looked over at the sleeping girl, who was now

snoring softly. So far, she hadn't been a problem. He'd just have to keep her drugged and out of his hair so he could work. There was a chance he'd have to hurt her before this was over, but he wasn't bothered by the possibility. Right now, she was more valuable to him alive, but that could change in an instant. Either way, he would use her to his advantage in this game he was playing.

"Checkmate," he whispered.

Chapter 7

Claire glanced up as Thomas closed his phone and tucked it into his pocket. She'd been trying to focus on the pages, but the low murmur of his voice in the background had distracted her. She hadn't been able to get back into the mental zone of total concentration yet, and she was forced to acknowledge that their earlier almost-kiss had rattled her more than she wanted to admit.

"Sorry about that," Thomas said with a sheepish smile. "It was my boss."

"Everything okay?" Claire kept her tone even, hoping he couldn't tell that she still felt shaken by what had almost transpired between them.

One shoulder lifted in an eloquent shrug. "He wanted an update."

"And you don't have one for him."

He shot her a quick grin that made her stomach flip. "Not yet. But I bet I will soon."

Ignoring his vote of confidence, Claire shook her head. "Was he upset?"

"Nah. Besides, he couldn't really hear me. I don't know what's going on at the office, but the place sounded like a zoo. I had to repeat myself several times. I think the old man needs to invest in a hearing aid."

Claire nodded absently, his words tugging at something in her brain. She turned them over in her mind, examining them from different angles, trying to identify what he had said that stuck out to her. Old man… office…zoo…

That was it! Zoo!

She shot bolt upright in the chair and reached for the papers, scrabbling like mad to gather them into a stack so she could read them one at a time.

"Um, Claire?" Thomas approached the table, concern in his voice, but she waved him away.

"Hush," she said urgently. If he distracted her now, she'd lose the thread, and then she'd never find it again.

Her eyes scanned the pages, cataloging the first word on every sheet before moving to the next. *Lion, zebra, hippopotamus*…each page began with a seemingly random animal, a pattern she had noticed before. But what did it mean?

Several years ago, she'd taken Ivan to the National Zoo during a break in their block of meetings. It had been a wonderful spring day, and walking around the exhibits had been a nice way to enjoy the weather and have a friendly chat. He'd mentioned a memory he had of his daughter. Long ago, he'd given her a book of animal stories as a Christmas gift. She'd fallen in love with the illustrations of the animals, and when he'd finally taken her to see them in real life, she'd insisted on bringing her book along.

"She was so excited," he'd said, recounting their trip. "She ran around to all the cages, comparing the real animals to the ones in her book."

The book had to be the key.

She booted up her laptop, heart racing as she waited for it to warm up. *C'mon, faster...*

With a few clicks, she was searching the internet for a Russian children's book on animals. It was a long shot, but it just might be the lead she needed.

There were hundreds of books, but she narrowed the search to ones that had been popular twenty years ago. That eliminated a lot, but there were still too many options to go through. Thinking fast, she typed in the animals that appeared on the pages, hoping to find out which book contained them all. Some of them were unusual, and it was her best shot at finding the book Ivan had given his daughter.

She held her breath as the search engine churned. After an endless second, the results appeared on the monitor. She grinned, exhaling in relief as she read. One book. And it had been digitized.

After that, it was child's play to decipher the code. The animal at the top of each page corresponded to a page in the book, which turned out to be a collection of stories about different animals. She quickly figured out that the number of pages for each animal's story corresponded to the letter she should pull from the notes. Since the lion's story was ten pages long, she took every tenth letter from that page of words, scribbling it down on a fresh sheet of paper.

She worked steadily until she'd translated all the pages, then leaned back to read what she'd discovered.

A list of names.

She read over them carefully, frowning as she recognized several men. Gregori Petrovich was a mobster who'd been in the news recently because he was a suspect in a series of political murders. Hakeem Anwar was a known al Qaeda operative. And Joshua Rollins had recently been convicted of an attempted pipe bomb attack on the D.C. Metro. Why had Ivan listed their names?

Claire stood, needing to move while she thought. They were connected, but how? Had Ivan just made a list of bad people, men who needed to be watched? Did he suspect them of wanting nuclear material? Had they approached him, wanting to buy spent fuel? Had he sold it to them?

That last thought made her freeze, halting her progress across the floor. What if this was a ledger of some kind? A balance sheet, so Ivan would know who he had sold to, how much they owed him. Insurance, so to speak. Surely Ivan had known these were dangerous men—he was smart enough not to trust them, to create some kind of guarantee that they wouldn't hurt him. A coded list of buyers would be incentive enough for them to leave him alone.

A movement from the direction of the table drew her eye. Thomas sat, his legs stretched out and his hands folded behind his head, watching her with a half smile on his lips. She didn't recall seeing him sit down, but apparently he'd been there the whole time.

"Can I talk now?" he asked, his tone teasing.

Claire felt her cheeks heat, remembering her earlier admonition. She hadn't exactly been polite. "Sorry about that," she said, tucking a strand of hair behind her ear. "I'd figured out the code, and I needed to focus to make sure I was right."

"I'd hate to be a distraction," he said. The look in his eyes belied the truth of his words, but he kept a straight face as he held out his hand. "May I see the translation?"

She passed the pages to him, waiting in silence as he scanned her work. She fought the urge to squirm, feeling a bit like a graduate student again, handing over her data for inspection. This time, though, she knew she was right. Her interpretation was sound. She just didn't know what it meant.

Thomas glanced up at her when he came to the end of the pages. "This is outstanding work," he said, a note of respect in his voice that made her want to puff out her chest a bit. "I knew you could do it."

Claire blinked back the unexpected sting of tears at his compliment. Only her father and Ivan had ever displayed such faith in her, an absolute confidence that she could do something and do it well. That Thomas had felt the same touched her on an emotional level and made it even more difficult to maintain a professional distance from him.

"Do you recognize any of these names?"

He returned his gaze to the papers, nodding slowly. "Some, yeah. These aren't nice people." He looked up at her, blue eyes intense as he studied her face. "Do you know them?"

Claire moved her shoulder in a jerky shrug. "Only by reputation. I certainly don't exchange Christmas cards with them, if that's what you're asking."

Thomas finished his second perusal of the papers, tapping them into order before turning back to her. Claire could tell by the look on his face that something was wrong—his expression was guarded, like he had bad news to share. He took a deep breath and she tensed, bracing herself for whatever he had to say.

"This...this doesn't look good for Ivan," he said quietly. "You know that, right?"

She dropped her eyes to the pages, nodding. Even she had to admit that this looked bad—the simplest explanation was that Ivan had created a list of clients, but a small part of her still refused to believe it.

There was a pregnant pause, as if Thomas had more to say. Apparently thinking better of it, he sighed quietly. "I need to call Harper, let him know you've figured it out."

Claire nodded. Of course.

"I'll be right back." He walked from the room, punching numbers on his phone as he went.

Feeling oddly drained, Claire walked to the window and stared at the afternoon sky, her thoughts a million miles away.

Oh, Ivan. What have you done?

Thomas snapped his phone shut, fingers tingling with excitement. This was quite possibly the break they needed to determine why Ivan Novikoff had been killed, why Claire—*Dr. Fleming*, he reminded himself—was now a target.

He leaned against the back of the couch, idly flipping through the pages. She was so damn smart. He'd been staring at the nonsense words for the past several hours, racking his brain to come up with the combination to unlock the code. He'd tried every permutation of the alphabet, had even looked up common ciphers in the hopes Ivan had used a historical or well-known puzzle. None of it had worked, and now it was obvious why.

He shook his head at Claire's accomplishment. How had she done that? How had she recalled a snippet from a conversation that had happened years ago, something Novikoff had probably mentioned without a second thought, and used it to decipher his files? It was amazing, the way her mind worked.

But…there was something about the whole thing that just felt *wrong*. He absently placed a hand over his stomach, the annoying churning of his gut a distraction that had him wishing for an antacid. If what Dr. Fleming had told him was true, Novikoff had only mentioned the book to her once, and in passing. Why, then, would he send her a file that required that particular book to decode?

Unless he hadn't meant for her to decode it after all. What if Novikoff had just wanted her to keep it safe for him until he could retrieve it? He ran a hand through his hair, then shuffled the pages back into a semblance of order. If Novikoff was involved in shady dealings— and that was looking increasingly likely—he wouldn't want his protégée to know about it. Even though he'd only known her for a few days, Thomas had no doubt that Claire—*Dr. Fleming*—would not hesitate to turn Ivan in. Surely Novikoff had known that as well.

He moved to stand in the doorway of the kitchen, hanging back a bit so he could watch Claire from the shadows cast by the afternoon light as it filtered through the trees. She was standing by the window, arms wrapped around her middle, staring into space with an absorbed look on her face. Her bruises were looking better, he noted, the healing pink slice on her cheek no longer a garish streak on her pale skin. Even so, his gut tightened at the image she presented—lost, alone, injured. How could Novikoff have used her like that? How could someone who had claimed to care about her put her in such danger?

More importantly, did she even know? Did she suspect Ivan had used her, had willingly set the dogs on her in a failed bid to escape? He heard the faint rustle of pages and looked down, surprised to find his fist tightly clenched around them. He exhaled, willing himself to relax, and opened his fist, smoothing the hopelessly wrinkled pages against his leg with his open palm. When he looked up, he saw she was watching him, a faint smile curving her lips.

"Everything all right?" she asked quietly.

He nodded, stepping into the kitchen and crossing over to the table to set the pages next to her notes. "Harper is thrilled with your work. He's sending James over now to pick up the pages so the team can get started tracking down the names. Hopefully, we'll know who's who and how they're connected to Dr.

Novikoff by the end of the day, or tomorrow morning at the latest."

She nodded, pressing her lips together in a pale line. "Good."

"Claire," he said, drawing a deep breath. "I think we need to consider the possibility that Ivan didn't mean for you to translate those pages."

She glanced up at him, her eyebrows pulling together as she regarded him with a quizzical expression. "What makes you say that?"

"Consider the odds," he said, running a hand through his hair. "What are the chances you would recall a remark he'd made in passing about an obscure children's book, and know to use that to decipher his code?"

She shrugged. "Lucky guess?" she offered. "I don't really have an explanation for it, other than to say I was cooped up inside with nothing else to focus on, so I had nothing better to do than relive every conversation I could remember."

"But how could Ivan know you would remember that specific conversation?" he pressed, wanting her to connect the dots on her own so he didn't have to spell it out for her. He did not want to be the guy who shattered her illusions about her erstwhile friend and mentor.

She tilted her head to the side, narrowing her eyes slightly. "Where are you going with this, Thomas?"

He looked down with a mental sigh. There was no hope for it—he was going to have to say it. "I think Dr. Novikoff knew he was in danger, and sent you those files for safekeeping until he could retrieve them later. I don't think he ever meant for you to translate them."

"But…" She swallowed hard, her gray eyes wide. "Why send them to me? Why not just hide them?"

He shook his head. "You were the safest bet. By sending the files to you, he got them out of the country, far away from himself and his family. Maybe he didn't think they'd come after you, but he took a huge risk with your safety by getting you involved." He gritted his teeth against the surge of anger tightening his gut at the thought of the dead scientist. Maybe he really hadn't known the gravity of the threat against him, but that was no excuse for involving Claire.

He wished Novikoff were standing in front of him, so he could reach out and shake the man, make him understand the consequences of what he'd done. But with the Russian scientist half a world away, and dead to boot, his ineffective rage had no target. He settled for tightening his fingers around the back of a chair, the wood smooth and cool under his hands.

Claire cleared her throat, and when she spoke again, her voice was wobbly. "Do you think Ivan knew they'd come after me?"

Yes. The word was on the tip of his tongue, but he couldn't say it. Novikoff was probably one of the bad guys, but maybe he really had cared for Claire in his own way. She'd certainly cared for him. It wasn't his place to decide what parts of their relationship had been real and what parts had been Ivan using her.

"I can't answer that," he replied, not meeting her eyes.

"That means yes," she whispered.

He looked up, but she had turned away from him,

returning her gaze to the scene outside. "Claire," he began, but she held up a hand to silence him.

He gave her space for a few endless moments, but when she made no move to turn around again, he walked the short distance to the window and stood behind her. If she noticed his presence, she didn't react.

"It's just," she said, then paused for a breath. "I thought I knew him, you know? I never dreamed he would do something like this."

He stayed silent, knowing he couldn't say anything to make the situation better for her. Besides, his thoughts were a jumble of contradictions and half-formed impressions, nothing he could coherently express, and certainly nothing that would comfort her. He wanted to haul her into his arms, press her against his chest and wrap himself around her. He needed to feel her against him, to know she was truly safe. Novikoff had gambled with her life, something Thomas would never understand, but he could make sure she came out unscathed. Physically, at least.

"It's okay," she said quietly. "You don't have to say anything."

"There's nothing I can say." She turned to face him then, and he clenched his hands into fists at his sides to keep from touching her. "There are no magic words I can use to make this easier on you, or to make things better. All I can do is tell you I'm sorry, but that's not nearly enough."

She gave him a sad smile. "It's a start," she whispered.

She leaned in, getting incrementally closer to him. Like a moth to a flame, he felt himself leaning forward as well, closing the distance between them until she rested her forehead against his shoulder. Her arms snaked around his waist while she pressed herself flush against his chest, and he gave in, wrapping his arms around her to anchor her in place.

The scent of lavender filled his nose when he dropped his head to her hair. He closed his eyes and breathed it in, savoring the warm smell of her. She felt so right pressed up against him, her round breasts firm against his chest, her hands clutching his back. The position was startlingly intimate, and he realized with a growing sense of alarm that another part of his anatomy had taken notice. Time to end this, before he embarrassed himself.

He reluctantly eased her away, putting a few inches of space between them. Her hands stayed on his back for a few heartbeats before she slid them off, running them down and over his hips before breaking contact. Her touch left a trail of heat on his skin, exacerbating his growing arousal.

Her eyes were liquid pools of silver, the lids half-drawn as she stared up at him. The warm afternoon light streamed in from the window, bathing her in a golden glow that made her appear lit from within. Her tongue flicked out, gliding across her lips in an echo of her earlier invitation, and heat pooled low in his belly.

Did he move? Did she? He wasn't sure, but suddenly his mouth was on hers, the silk of her lips sliding across his as he slanted his head to taste her. She sighed and pressed closer, eagerly returning his kisses as she reached up to grip his shoulders. He dipped his tongue inside her mouth, traced it teasingly along hers before pulling back and turning his head to adjust the angle of the kiss.

She let out a little moan, the sound rumbling through her and into him. Needing to take charge, he spun her around and backed her against the wall, reaching down to grab her legs and lift her up. She locked her ankles around his waist and he leaned forward, holding her against the wall with his weight pressed against her center. She arched her back, rocking against his arousal in a helpless rhythm, silently asking for more. He groaned, pulling his mouth away from hers to press openmouthed kisses against her neck. He kept one hand on her leg as the other skipped up her side to cup her breast. The firm swell fit his hand perfectly, her nipple peaking against the flat of his palm.

"Thomas..." she murmured.

"Hmm?" He kissed his way to the swell of her breasts, hitching her up higher on the wall to bring them to the level of his mouth.

"Thomas," she repeated again, this time more determinedly. She plunged her hands into his hair, tugging his head away from her skin.

He looked up, confused. "Yeah?"

"Your phone is ringing."

He frowned, trying to concentrate over the pounding of blood in his head and the sound of his harsh breathing. She was right—the faint electronic noise was insistent and jarring.

No, not again! With a sigh, he released Claire's legs to let her slide down, biting his lip to hold back a groan as she moved over sensitive areas. He stepped back, fished the phone out of his pocket and dropped his eyes so he wouldn't have to watch Claire tuck her shirt back into place and smooth her hair away from her face.

"Kincannon," he said, failing to keep the frustration out of his voice.

A soft laugh greeted his ears.

"Who is this?" he said, his patience running thin. Was Reynolds calling to give him a hard time? He pulled the phone from his ear to glance quickly at the display, but the number was unregistered. That was odd.

"This is Special Agent Kincannon," he said, tightening his grip on the phone. "I repeat, who is this?"

"Now, Thomas, is that any way to talk to me?" The voice was smooth and oily, even smug. Thomas remained silent as he tried to place it. He had heard it before, but where?

"Your neck is looking much better," the man continued. In a sudden, horrifying instant, the wheels clicked into place. Victor.

Thomas glanced up to see Claire standing by the window, watching him. He snaked out a hand to grab her arm, then yanked her away from the window. She let out a small sound of protest but didn't speak.

"Victor," he said, ignoring Claire's sharp intake of breath at the name. "Didn't think I'd hear from you again." He tugged Claire down the hall as he spoke, wanting to get her away from any windows or other points of entry. Did he have eyes on the house? How else would he know how the wound on his neck was healing?

There was a safe room off the main bedroom. It was small—no more than an alcove attached to the closet—but it was secure and he headed for it now, tugging an unresisting Claire behind him. Thankfully, she wasn't fighting him on this. He'd worked cases before where the civilians involved had resisted doing what they were told. It never ended well.

"Calling to turn yourself in?" He released Claire's arm to open the safe room door. She stepped inside, turning back to look at him with those gray eyes, now wide with alarm. He held a finger to his lips, and she nodded. Carefully, quietly, he shut the door.

"Not today, I don't think," Victor said airily, as if he hadn't a care in the world. "I was hoping to find out how Dr. Fleming is feeling."

Thomas slipped his gun free of its shoulder holster. "She's just fine," he replied, creeping from room to room, checking for an intrusion. He let Natalie sleep, knowing he couldn't wake her without a noisy explanation that he didn't have time for. "Never better, in fact." The house was empty, but Victor might be outside, watching them. Thomas paused in the kitchen, his hand hovering over the button that would trigger the silent alarm and bring backup.

"Did you just call to chat?"

"Yes and no." The man was infuriatingly calm, and Thomas had the distinct sense he was being played. But how?

"Just out of curiosity," he said, "how did you get my number?" He wanted to keep Victor talking, hoping he would give something away, let something slip that would reveal his location.

"Please," Victor scoffed. "Even you have to appreciate how easy that was for me. But you know—"

his voice changed, became even more smug and self-satisfied "—your number isn't the only thing I have that's yours."

Thomas froze as the words registered, the hair on the back of his neck rising as the implications sank in. "What do you mean?" he asked, very quietly.

"Claire's skin is so smooth, so flawless. Like porcelain," Victor mused, sounding distracted. "I was sorry I had to mark her like that. I didn't cut her too deeply though. She should heal. How is her cheek now?"

Thomas gripped the edge of the counter, keeping a firm hold on his temper. "It's fine," he said shortly. "What did you mean when you said you have something else of mine?"

"Tell her I'm sorry about it, will you?"

"What did you mean?" Thomas gritted out. A sense of clawing desperation was climbing up from his gut to wrap greasy tendrils around his throat, making it hard for him to speak.

"Never mind, I'll apologize to her myself," Victor went on, as if he hadn't heard. "I'll be seeing her soon enough."

"Like hell you will."

He laughed again, a soft, mocking sound. "Oh, but I will. And you're going to give her to me."

"What makes you so sure about that?"

"Because we're going to make a trade, Agent Kincannon. Tit for tat."

Thomas swallowed, trying to push down the rising tide of bile that burned his throat. "I'm listening."

"I figured as much." The teasing was gone from his voice, his tone now deadly serious. "Listen carefully,

Special Agent Kincannon," he said, placing a mocking emphasis on the title. "I have someone very close to you, someone you care about. You know, you really should be more careful with your loved ones," he chided, sounding disappointed.

"Who?" It came out as a strangled croak, the icy grip of fear tight around Thomas's heart.

"Now where's the fun in that?" Victor said. "I'll give you an hour to figure this out, Kincannon, and then I'll call you back with further instructions. Don't go too far."

Before Thomas could protest, Victor hung up, his mocking laugh a final punctuation to the call. Thomas dropped the phone to the counter, bracing his palms on the cold, smooth surface. Think, he had to think.

Did Victor really have a hostage, or was this just a ploy? He might be bluffing, trying to draw Claire out into the open again so he could take her. But what if Victor was telling the truth? Could he really take that chance?

Without thinking, his hand drifted back over to the button. First things first. Their position might be compromised, and he had to move Claire to another secure location. Then he could figure out if Victor was playing him. Either way, he couldn't do this alone.

He smashed his palm down. Time to call in reinforcements.

Claire breathed quietly, straining to hear over the pounding thrum of blood in her head. It was quiet, but she couldn't be sure if that was a good or bad thing. Where was Thomas? Was he all right? What if Victor had broken into the house and killed Thomas, and was even now sneaking from room to room, searching for her?

She wiped damp palms on her thighs, hating the thought of Thomas putting himself in danger, again, for her sake.

Her heart had skipped a beat when Thomas had said Victor's name. She had managed to shove thoughts of the assassin to the back of her mind while she worked on figuring out the code, but his sudden reappearance in her life shattered the illusion of security she had enjoyed. *I don't know why I'm surprised.* She shook her head. He was never going to just go away.

But why call Thomas now? What did it mean? Was he nearby, watching them? She shuddered at the thought of Victor's cold eyes seeing her earlier embrace with Thomas. If Victor had been watching them the whole time...

Don't think about it, she told herself firmly.

No matter where Victor was right now, she was probably still in danger. Thomas had spirited her away from the window quickly enough, wasting no time in getting her to the panic room. Was he just being extra cautious, or had Victor said something threatening?

She hated sitting in the dark, alone, with nothing but her swirling thoughts and nerves to keep her company. She couldn't tell how long she'd been in the cramped alcove, but her legs were starting to go numb from staying in the same position. It was too dark to see her watch, and with no light or sound cues, she had no idea how much time had passed since Thomas had stuffed her inside and left.

Slowly, carefully, she shifted position, wincing as the movement sent pins and needles tingling through her legs. Surely if something bad had happened, she would have heard yelling or the sounds of fighting or, God forbid, gunshots. She pressed her ear to the door, straining to pick up something, anything—any bump or noise that would give her a clue as to what was going on in the house.

Silence was her only reward.

She had two options: stay crouched in this small space, twiddling her thumbs and waiting for Thomas to come back and save her like some princess in the tower, or poke her head out and try to discover what exactly was happening. Option two might be slightly dangerous, especially since she had no idea what she would encounter, but she was tired of waiting. *I need to know what's happening.*

She raised her hand to the door, feeling along the panel for the knob. It twisted easily, and she gave a gentle push to open the door a crack, breathing out a soft sigh as it moved silently. The last thing she needed was a squeaky hinge giving her away.

It was dark in the closet, but she could see a rim of light under the door. She stood for a moment in the closet, waiting for her legs to regain normal feeling. It wouldn't do to walk into a dangerous situation with rubbery legs, that much she knew.

Leaning forward, she pressed her ear to the closet door. She heard muffled footsteps, the sound growing louder, then fainter, then louder again. Pacing, she realized. Someone out there was pacing back and forth.

Muted voices reached her then, deep, soothing tones punctuated by a harsher response.

Her curiosity piqued, Claire gently opened the closet door and crept across the room to the bedroom door. She took a step into the hall, pressing herself flat against the wall. She wanted to hear but was reluctant to stray too far from the relative safety of the closet alcove. If things went badly, she needed to be able to get back into the safe room quickly and without being detected.

"He's got Emily," Thomas said, his voice tight and strained. She heard footsteps again and realized Thomas was likely the one doing the pacing. *He* must mean Victor, but who was Emily?

"You can't know that for sure." That was James, calm and composed. Clearly, Thomas had called the other agent after speaking to Victor. Was he the only one here?

"I do know!" There was a loud thud, which Claire imagined was Thomas's fist hitting the wall. "My mother is lying injured in the hospital, and Jenny is sitting beside her right now. Emily is the only one unaccounted for—you know he's got her."

"And I know that there's nothing you can do about it right now," James pointed out. "Valdez is on his way. He's the best at working abductions."

"We've got to find her," Thomas interrupted, desperation and fear lacing his tone.

"We will," James said firmly. "But running off halfcocked isn't going to do anyone any good, least of all Emily."

There was silence from the other room. Although

she didn't know who Emily was, it was clear Thomas cared for her very much, and her heart ached for him and the despair she knew he was feeling. She took a step forward, intent on going to him, offering him comfort, but James's next words made her freeze.

"You know what he's going to want." It wasn't a question. She heard Thomas sigh before he replied.

"Yes. Claire."

"You'd do it, wouldn't you? Trade her for Emily?"

Another sigh. Then, quietly, "Yes."

Claire sucked in a breath, the word hitting her like a blow. She felt as though she'd been dunked in ice water, the shock of it making her numb. Her legs gave out and she slid helplessly down the wall, landing with a soft thump on the floor.

Thomas would betray her. He'd give her back to that monster, the man who was trying to kill her. *He wouldn't have to try very hard,* she thought, shaking her head. Thomas was apparently willing to hand her over on a silver platter.

How could I have been so wrong? She'd thought Thomas had feelings for her. His behavior at the hospital and again today had certainly seemed like that of a man who was interested in her. *Or just interested in getting into my pants.* Maybe that was it after all. He was attracted to her, but only wanted her for sex. *Figures.*

The realization stung, although she really should have anticipated it. Her own mother had seen her as a burden, not a daughter. Why would Thomas be any different? She certainly wasn't any less trouble now. He'd already been hurt trying to protect her, and the threat wasn't over yet. If he wasn't tired of dealing with her and her constant need for protection, he would be soon. Better to have a reality check now, before she let herself get any more attached to him.

"It won't come to that," she heard James say, as if he was trying to reassure Thomas. Like Thomas was the one who needed reassurance! *I'm being guarded by a man who wouldn't hesitate to hand me over to a professional killer.* What about the other agents? If this Emily was so important to Thomas, was she important to the rest of the team, as well? Was she safe at all?

"I hope not. Speaking of Claire, I need to get her. She's still in the hidden alcove." Panic had her standing up, moving quickly to get back to the closet. He couldn't find her, couldn't know that she had heard his conversation. Her heart pounded as she slipped into the alcove and drew the door shut behind her. She closed her eyes, forcing herself to breathe deeply and slowly. She had to appear normal, act like nothing had happened. She needed time to process what she'd heard, and she couldn't have Thomas suspecting her while she tried to figure out what to do next.

The closet door opened, and she heard Thomas move to stand in front of the alcove. "Claire?" he called out softly. "It's Thomas. Everything's all right. You can open the door now."

She took a deep breath, carefully arranged her features into a neutral expression and twisted the knob.

He looked the same, she thought with a bit of surprise. For some reason, she had expected the news of his intended betrayal to show on his face, but he studied her with an expression of calm assurance. There were faint lines of tension around his mouth and eyes, but they could easily be explained away by the stress of their situation.

"What happened?" She watched him carefully, wondering how he would respond, waiting to pick up any signs of deception.

He shrugged, dropping his eyes to the ground. "It was just Victor, calling to rattle us."

So he wasn't going to tell her. Disappointment formed a hard lump in her stomach. Despite his words to James, a small part of her had hoped she had misunderstood, that Thomas wouldn't betray her.

Now she realized the truth. She was nothing more than a pawn in this deadly game. And despite what her heart had desired, Thomas was nothing more than another person she couldn't trust.

Chapter 8

Special Agent Matt Valdez more than lived up to his reputation. He was a compact, wiry man, with dark brown hair and piercing black eyes that took in everything and everyone in a glance. Although he didn't speak much, he took command of the situation with a competence that should have been inspiring, organizing people and coordinating the response to Victor's call. As the specialist on child abductions, he was the bureau's go-to guy when a kid went missing, and he radiated authority and a calm reassurance that everything was under control. In short, he was ideally suited to run the recovery operation.

Thomas disliked him intensely.

How could he just *sit* there when Emily was gone? God only knew what Victor was doing to her. He was a psychopath of the first order, and capable of anything.

Was she hurt? Scared? Hungry? Cold? His stomach roiled as a sick, twisted thought entered his brain. Had the bastard *touched* her?

Thomas swallowed hard against the rising tide of bile burning its way up his chest, forcing his mind in another direction. He glanced over to see Valdez studying a map of the city, his gaze focused and intense even as he conversed with James. Their voices were a low buzz, a droning background noise that grated on Thomas's already raw nerves. He had to do something.

He pushed back from the table, the chair making a harsh sound as it scraped across the tile. James glanced up at the distraction, sending him a sympathetic smile. Thomas nodded at him, wending his way through the crush of bodies in the house—agents setting up phone taps, computers, extra guards. Staging things for when they got the signal to move.

If they ever did.

He sucked in a breath, his throat painfully tight. Air. He needed air.

He eyed the front door but thought better of it. If he started walking, he probably wouldn't stop. Besides, there were a few guys smoking outside, and he wasn't in the mood for company right now.

He stumbled down the hall, unseeing. Once, he'd thought Roger's death had been the worst thing that could happen to his family. Now he knew better.

"Find my baby," Jenny had said, her voice steely despite her tears, "or don't bother coming back."

His sister-in-law hated him, that much was clear. She hadn't even let him talk to Mom.

"She'll be fine," she said shortly, in response to his question. "No thanks to you."

He winced at the barb, but let it slide. He deserved that, and more.

"What happened?"

There was a pause, as if Jenny was debating whether or not to talk to him. "She told the police a man came to the apartment, said he worked with you." Her tone was accusing, as if Thomas had arranged the whole thing. "Next thing she remembers is waking up here."

"Will she be okay?"

Jenny sighed. "They think so. But you won't," she continued, her voice hardening, "if you don't find Emily." Then she hung up, the dial tone loud in his ear.

There was an empty bedroom at the end of the hall. Thomas headed for it, closing the door quietly but firmly. He leaned back against it, shut his eyes and rubbed his hands over his face.

They would find her. They had to—he simply couldn't consider the alternative. Tears pricked his eyelids at the thought of Emily in the company of that madman. She must be so frightened....

Worse was the fact that Victor had pretended to be his friend to gain access to Emily. Her teacher said he had flashed a badge and said he was a coworker. He hoped Emily knew the truth—that a real friend of his would never take her away from her family— but who could say? Maybe Victor was poisoning her mind, feeding her lies about why Thomas hadn't come for her yet, making her feel abandoned and unloved. It wouldn't be hard to make a kid who had lost her dad feel even more isolated.

God, Rog. I failed again.

"I'm so sorry," he whispered, knowing his brother couldn't hear him but needing to say the words.

"You love her, don't you?"

He jumped at the intrusion and hastily swiped his hands across his cheeks to rub the tears away. Claire was standing by the window, watching him with an expression of resigned sadness on her face.

"She means the world to me."

Something…was it anger?…flared in her gray eyes. She nodded once, pressing her lips together.

"You want to trade me for her." It wasn't a question; she spoke as if she was merely reciting a fact that was common knowledge. Had she overheard his earlier conversation with James? But how was that possible? She'd been in the alcove the whole time—hadn't she?

He looked away, not wanting to meet her eyes and the accusation he saw there. "It won't come to that."

She snorted, clearly not believing him. "Sure. Because everything else has been great so far."

"We will get her back," he said, anger making his voice louder than usual, "and we will do it without putting you in any more danger."

She stared at him for a moment, her expression flickering from hopeful to disbelieving to disappointed as she weighed his words. Finally, she shook her head. "She must be pretty special, huh?"

Emily's face flashed into his mind, her blond ponytail swinging and her legs pumping as she ran up the sidewalk, laughing with delight when she beat him to the door. He swallowed hard. "Yeah, she is."

Claire moved to walk past him but stopped before

she reached the door. "Just tell me one thing," she said, staring up into his face. "Why did we—" She gestured between them as she spoke. "Why did you kiss me out there if you've already got someone?"

His jaw dropped as her words sank in. "Are you telling me you think—"

She shook her head, cutting him off. "Never mind. It was a despicable thing for you to do, but it's none of my business. I hope you do find her."

He grabbed her arm when she moved to leave, holding her in place. "Wait just a minute—"

"No, you wait a minute!" She shoved at him, but he spun her around and backed her up against the wall, trapping her with his arms. She wriggled and twisted, trying to get free, so he leaned in, pinning her with the weight of his body. He'd been right earlier. She was angry, but he wasn't going to let her walk away. Not until they'd settled this.

"How dare you," she whispered, her eyes flashing as she glared up at him. "How could you kiss me like that when you already have a girlfriend? What kind of an asshole are you?"

"I don't have a girlfriend," he gritted out from between clenched teeth. "I wouldn't touch you if I did." He squeezed her arms for emphasis as he spoke.

"Then who—"

"She's my niece," he said, leaning in until his lips were a breath away from hers.

All the fight drained out of her as his words registered. She stared up at him, her mouth open in a perfect O of shock. "Your niece?" she repeated in a voice that cracked slightly.

He let out a breath. "Yes. Emily is Jenny's daughter. You remember Jenny from the hospital, right?"

Claire nodded mechanically, her head bobbing up and down like a puppet on a string. "Of course."

Thomas released her and took a step back, putting some much needed distance between them. He couldn't think when he was so close to her, touching her. His initial anger was quickly morphing into something hot and dangerous, an indescribable need he didn't understand but couldn't indulge right now.

Claire remained in place, leaning back against the wall, her face pale and her eyes wide as she regarded him. "How old is she?" she asked quietly.

He ran a hand through his hair, the gesture giving him something to do with his hands. "She's five."

Claire let out a sound that was a half sob, half moan. "Oh, God. She's just a baby." She met his gaze, her eyes pleading. "Are you sure Victor has her?"

He nodded once, not trusting his voice.

Claire shook her head, her hand coming up to cover her mouth. "Poor Jenny," she said softly. "She must be so worried."

"Angry, more like it," he said. "She wants to kill me, and I can't say I blame her."

The corner of her mouth lifted in a quick flash of a smile. "It's easier to be angry than worried. She knows it's not your fault though."

"Isn't it?" His words were no more than a whisper, but she heard them. She stepped away from the wall, coming forward to lay a tentative hand on his shoulder.

"No," she said firmly, her fingers curling into his shirt while she spoke. "Don't go down that road,

Thomas. This isn't your fault, and you won't be any good to Emily if you spend all your energy blaming yourself."

He shook his head, casting off her reassurances like a dog shaking off water. "It doesn't matter. Even if we do get her back—"

"When we get her back," she interrupted.

"—Jenny will still hate me for letting it happen," he finished, ignoring her.

Claire made an exasperated sound low in her throat. "Jenny strikes me as a reasonable person. Deep down, she knows this isn't your fault, and she's not going to blame you for it forever."

She didn't understand. Why should she? He hadn't told her about Roger's death, how it had nearly broken the family. Jenny and Emily were just starting to put their lives back together, and now this? It was a wonder his sister-in-law was still standing.

Thomas pulled away, too frustrated with her oh-so-reasonable tone to stand still. "Don't you get it? My family is falling apart, and I'm stuck here waiting like a damn helpless fool!"

She opened her mouth to respond, but he sliced the air with his hand, cutting her off. Then he told her— about Roger, about Emily's withdrawal, Jenny's depression. All of it. On one level, it felt good to get it all out there. He'd been carrying the weight of his worry for his family for so long, the burden had almost become a part of him. Just another feature like his red hair.

He hadn't really discussed it with anyone before. Certainly not with the guys at work. He preferred to keep his professional and personal lives separate, but sometimes, the division between the two grew thin. Every once in a while Thomas would catch James eyeing him thoughtfully, as if he was piecing together a puzzle. His friend had asked several times about his family, wanting to know how Thomas was doing in the wake of Roger's death. Thomas always brushed off the question, pretending everything was fine. It was easier that way.

He wasn't sure why he was telling Claire now. She couldn't do anything to help, and it was clear from the way her eyes were welling with tears that she felt bad about the situation. A detached part of his brain was telling him to shut up, but his mouth had hijacked the controls and was operating without a filter.

It was likely the stress of the situation, he figured, even as he spoke. After all, things couldn't get much worse. Claire already thought the worst of him, a fact that bothered him more than he cared to examine. Right now, he should be totally focused on getting Emily back, not worried about Claire's feelings for him.

Still, *this* was something he could fix. With her standing here in front of him, with nowhere to go, he could explain why he'd said the things he had. Why he was so willing to do absolutely anything to bring his niece home. Maybe she would understand, or maybe she wouldn't, but at least he would know he'd tried.

Claire was silent for several moments after he finished. "I lost my dad when I was eleven—older than Emily, but still young enough that I didn't really understand why. She's very lucky to have an uncle like you in her life."

Something about her tone made Thomas curious

to hear more. She sounded flat, almost detached, but there was an underlying hint of sadness that he didn't think was due solely to her grief.

"It must have been hard for you to lose your dad so young," he said, hoping she would take the bait and respond.

She laughed, a humorless sound that told him more about her past than any words. "You could say that."

"What happened?"

She was quiet for a moment, staring at the wall behind him with the unfocused gaze of memory. He could feel her withdraw as she retreated into her past, the silence stretching long and taut between them. It was all he could do not to touch her, to do something to jog her from her fugue, but he knew that if he startled her, she wouldn't talk about it with him.

And he found that he needed to know more about her.

The realization should have bothered him, but he was too strung out to care. Another time, another place, his feelings would have scared him. He hadn't been interested in a woman since Tanya had left, and the fact that he was so drawn to Claire should have been a warning sign that things were moving too fast. But he couldn't bring himself to stop. He knew better than most that life could turn on a dime, and he was determined to make the most of his.

Even if that meant letting go and falling in love again.

He reached up and gently ran his fingertips down Claire's arm, hoping the touch would bring her back. She blinked up at him, a soft pink spreading across her cheeks. "Sorry," she muttered, ducking her head. "I kind of spaced out there for a minute."

"Tell me about it?" He kept his voice soft, encouraging.

"There's not much to tell." She shrugged, trying to dismiss the question. "I was adopted. I found out after my dad died that my mother had gone along with the adoption to make him happy. She never thought of me as 'her' child, and once Dad was gone, she saw me as a burden—a reminder of the husband she'd lost. When she remarried and had a child of her own, I went from being tolerated to being outright hated. I moved out the day I graduated high school and haven't looked back."

Thomas felt his heart break for her and for the child she had been, grieving the loss of one parent while the other made her feel rejected and unloved.

"My God," he murmured, giving in to the impulse to pull her close and wrap his arms around her. "I can't imagine what that was like for you." In his line of work, he'd seen a lot of the horrible things people could do to each other, but no matter how many times he was exposed to it, he would never understand how a parent could treat a child so badly. More than that, he didn't want to understand it. That kind of behavior went against the laws of nature, and he hoped he never became desensitized to the point that he didn't turn away in disgust.

Claire relaxed against him, seeming to draw comfort from his embrace. He held her, wishing he could take away her unhappy memories, hating that she'd had such an awful childhood. She hid it well, but he could tell from the look in her eyes that it was painful for her to discuss her past. She rested her head against his chest, and the simple gesture of trust made his legs go weak. He was awed and honored that she had shared such personal recollections with him, and was overwhelmed by a feeling of tenderness, a desire to keep Claire safe. She'd experienced more than enough pain already.

She drew back slowly, and he relaxed his hold as she put space between them. She shook off her earlier sadness, and her eyes lost their soft, unfocused look as she returned to the present and tried to reestablish the boundaries between them.

Thomas watched her with a mixture of pride at her strength, and exasperation at her determination to keep him at arm's length. How long would it take before she no longer felt the need to put up a shield around him? Maybe someday she'd even tell him the rest of her tale. Her terse explanation had sketched a sad picture, but he knew the complete story lay in the things she hadn't said, in the silence between her words.

"I'm so sorry," she began, but then stopped, shaking her head.

"What is it?"

She looked down. "Sorry doesn't begin to cover it. You've already been through so much as a family. I don't know how you're able to stand here and be so calm about the whole thing."

He considered, if only for a heartbeat, rejecting her change of conversation. But no, if he pushed her to share more of herself now, she'd only shy away. If he wanted to earn her trust, he had to give her space.

He shrugged. "Trust me, on the inside, I'm anything but calm."

She laid her hand on his arm, the touch a warm, comforting weight. "I want to help." Her voice was firm, determined. She made it sound like a challenge, as if she knew he would argue with her.

She was right about that.

He shook his head, even as she jerked her chin up and placed her hands on her hips. He bit his lip to keep from smiling—he was at least four inches taller, but she was trying her best to look intimidating. He didn't have the heart to tell her it wasn't working.

"Absolutely not," he said flatly.

"But—"

"No. That's not what we do."

She crossed her arms over her chest and took a deep breath as if to calm herself. "You know Victor will trade Emily for me."

Thomas sighed. "Yes. But Valdez is in charge of the recovery operation, and there's no way he'd let that happen."

Her gaze grew considering while she mulled over his words. "Valdez, huh?" she muttered. Thomas could practically see the wheels turning in her head, and in that moment he was struck by the depth of her character. Not many people would willingly offer to go with an assassin who'd already made an attempt on their life, much less conspire to do so after their initial offer was turned down. Not Claire. She was bound and determined to help him get Emily back, even if it meant her life.

She would do it, he realized. She wasn't making an

empty offer, secure in the knowledge it would be turned down. She genuinely wanted to put herself in danger to save a little girl she'd never even met. Warmth blossomed in his chest as he watched her scheme and plan, and he was almost overcome by the urge to haul her close and kiss her, to stake his claim on her. For she was his now. No matter what happened, no matter how this went down, she would occupy a place in his heart for the rest of his life.

Claire glanced up and caught him staring at her. Some of what he was feeling must have shown on his face, because her eyes widened briefly in surprise before her gaze softened. Her mouth relaxed, and the lines of her forehead smoothed out as she sent him a small smile.

He held his arms out, wanting, needing, to touch her, to hold her against him. The fluttering sense of panic he felt whenever he thought of Emily was muted when Claire was touching him. He needed that now, to lose himself in the sensation of comfort she brought.

She stepped into his embrace, tucking her head under his chin like she was made for him. He would worry about his growing feelings, his increasing dependence on her later. For now, there was only Claire.

Claire pressed against Thomas, turning to rest her head against his chest. They were flush against each other, and yet it wasn't enough. She banded her arms around him, gripping him tightly. He was warm and solid and *real,* his presence a comforting buffer against the assaults of her memories.

Why had she told him about her past? She hadn't

spoken of it since she'd left Dena's house, not wanting to waste any more of her life on that woman. Bad enough she'd stolen her childhood—she wasn't going to let her ruin the rest of her life, as well.

But hasn't she?

She pushed aside the intrusive thought, not wanting to acknowledge the link between her adoptive mother and her avoidance of relationships. The idea that Dena's actions still affected her today left her feeling unsettled and restless.

She snuggled closer to Thomas, focusing on their embrace as a distraction. So she was cautious when it came to relationships. Who wasn't? That was just being smart. The papers were full of stories of women who had trusted the wrong person and been hurt or killed because of it. Claire was determined not to become another victim.

But Thomas won't hurt you.

That thought was harder to dismiss. She couldn't deny that he had protected her, even stepped into danger himself to keep her safe. The man didn't have an abusive bone in his body, yet she was still reluctant to let go and let herself feel, to put herself out there and hope he responded in kind.

We only just met, her rational side pointed out.

But her emotions didn't care. Her instincts had taken the measure of this man and judged him as excellent. Although she had only known him for a short amount of time, she couldn't deny that on one level, she felt she'd known him for years. There was something about him that made her feel safe, that had her lowering the resistance she held in place to keep the world at bay.

She was tired, so tired, of constantly being on guard all the time. It was a revelation to know that she could rest around him, could even share her burdens with him, and draw comfort and strength from his presence.

He had protected her once and nearly gotten killed for his troubles. Now, she wanted—no, she *needed*—to help him in any way possible. If that meant putting herself in harm's way to save his niece, so be it. Thomas had already been through so much, and he didn't deserve to lose what was left of his family.

They had to find Emily. The alternative didn't bear considering. She suppressed a shudder at the thought of Victor, her skin tingling with the memory of his hands on her. No child should have to be around such a monster.

It was clear Victor would trade the girl for her. The hard part would be convincing the FBI to go for it.

He'd have to take me somewhere, she mused as she swept her hand down Thomas's back in what she hoped was a comforting gesture. *He couldn't just kill me in front of the FBI.*

That would give them time to save her. Someone could tail them while Victor took her to his hideout, then sweep in and arrest the assassin before he had a chance to kill her. She had to admit that as far as plans went, it definitely needed a little work, but at least it was a starting point. Surely Agent Valdez would agree that an even exchange was the easiest, safest way to get Emily back.

Thomas stiffened, jerking her out of her thoughts. He pulled away and crossed to the door, yanking it open with a quick tug on the handle. He was halfway down the hall before she heard the noise that had caught his attention: his phone, ringing insistently in the kitchen under Agent Valdez's watchful eyes.

Claire made it to the kitchen a few steps after Thomas, just in time to see Agent Valdez slap his hand down over the ringing phone. Thomas made a low, dangerous sound deep in his throat, but the other man ignored the threatening glare Thomas sent his way.

"Keep him on the line," he said, his voice calm and even. "Agree to whatever he says. We'll go from there."

Thomas nodded impatiently, already reaching for the phone. Agent Valdez kept his hand in place for a few seconds longer, his gaze dark and intense. "Are you sure you can do this?"

"Yes!" Claire winced at his shouted reply. "Now give me the damn phone before he hangs up."

Valdez removed his hand to allow Thomas to grab the phone. He jabbed at the button, eyebrows drawn together in a frown, then pressed the phone to his ear.

"Kincannon."

Claire watched his hand clench into a fist, saw the lines of his arm sharpen into relief as his muscles tightened. Her fingers itched to trace over his skin, but she knew touching him would be an unwelcome distraction right now.

"Let me talk to her," he said, glancing quickly at Valdez, who gave an approving nod. The other man leaned over and pressed a button on the recording device on the counter. Claire flinched when Victor's voice flooded the room.

"Soon," he said, malice oozing from the word. She could almost *see* the satisfied expression on the assassin's face as he sat in his safe house, believing he had won. Rather than scaring her, his voice filled her with resolve. They would beat this monster, and she wanted to be a part of it.

"I'm ready to make an exchange," Victor continued, speaking as if he had all the time in the world. "Interested?"

Thomas's eyes flickered to Claire. She nodded, hoping he could see how determined she was.

"You know I am," he said quietly.

"Good. Tomorrow morning. The Armory. I assume you know where that is?"

Thomas swallowed hard. "I do."

"I'll bring the girl. You bring the woman and the papers. Six a.m."

"All right."

"And by the way," Victor continued, almost as an afterthought. "I don't need to tell you to leave your coworkers at home, do I, Agent Kincannon? I know they're listening in, recording me, trying to pinpoint my location." He laughed, a low rumble across the line. "It won't work, but I applaud your determination. Leave them out of this."

"You know I can't do that," Thomas fired back. "The minute you took my niece, you pulled the bureau into this."

Claire sucked in a breath. What was he doing? Valdez had told him to agree to everything. Why was Thomas arguing with this man? Apparently Valdez felt the same way, because he started gesturing fiercely, his movements silent but emphatic. Thomas caught sight of the other man and bit his lip, nodding in acknowledgment of his mistake.

"Call them off," Victor said, an edge creeping into his voice.

Valdez scowled and gesticulated again. Thomas held up a hand to placate him.

"All right," he replied, a muscle in his jaw starting to tic. "We'll come alone."

"See that you do," Victor said. "I would hate to have to hurt the girl. She's very fond of you, you know. Says nothing but good things about her uncle Tommy. Rather annoying, actually."

"If you touch one hair—" Thomas began, but cut himself off after a sharp jab from Valdez.

"Do go on, Agent Kincannon," Victor said, sounding amused. "I believe you were in the middle of threatening me?"

"Let me talk to her," Thomas said. "Please."

Victor sighed. "Fine. But only for a second."

There was a scuffling, scratchy sound while the phone was moved, then they heard Victor's voice, distant. "It's your uncle. Talk to him."

Claire leaned forward as a soft whimper came through the line. Then, "Uncle Thomas?" The words were hesitant but hopeful.

He squeezed his eyes shut, sucking in a deep breath. "Hi there, Emmycakes. How are you?"

"Cold," she replied. "Where are you?"

"I'm…" He trailed off, clearly fumbling for an answer. He looked to Claire, his eyes wide and lost. Not caring what his coworkers thought, she reached out to lay her hand on his arm, squeezing gently. He held her gaze for a few seconds longer, then gave a short nod. "I'm making sure your mom and grandma are okay, and then I'll come get you."

"When?" Her voice sounded small and teary, and Claire swallowed hard around the lump in her throat.

Thomas closed his eyes, clearly pained. "How does tomorrow morning sound?"

Emily was quiet for a moment, and Claire feared Victor had taken the phone away from her. Then she spoke again. "Okay."

"Good. Get some rest for me. Sweet dreams, baby."

More shuffling, then Victor was back. "Satisfied?"

"Thank you," Thomas said. Claire's heart ached at the hollow sound of his voice. Talking to Emily had been difficult for him, she knew; it was good to hear the little girl was unharmed, but now there was no way to deny or ignore the fact that Victor held her captive.

"Don't be late." Victor's parting words were followed by the click and drone of the dial tone, loud in the otherwise silent room. Thomas pushed a button on the phone, then stood still for a moment while he stared down at the device in his hand.

Claire saw the muscle in his jaw tighten, followed by a blur of motion as Thomas threw the phone across the room. It hit the wall with a loud crack, bits of broken plastic shrapnel flying everywhere.

When he slowly turned around to face the group, she could see he was not the same man he'd been when she first met him, not even the same man he'd been five minutes ago. Gone was the spark of humor in his eyes, the ever-present lift of the corner of his mouth, as if he was always on the verge of smiling. Now his expression was hard and cold, his features arranged in harsh lines and shadows. His eyes were bright with anger, and he turned that calculating gaze on Agent Valdez with an intensity that made Claire take a half step back.

"What's next?"

Chapter 9

It was all happening so fast.

Claire stood in the corner of the buzzing room, arms wrapped around her middle as she tried to stay out of the way. Agents moved about at a relentless pace, breaking off into groups, consulting maps, checking weapons. Everyone had a job to do, and they were going about it with grim-faced determination.

"Dr. Fleming."

She glanced over to see Agent Valdez gesturing her forward. He hadn't left his station in the middle of the kitchen, a location she'd come to think of as Command Central. Apparently, she wasn't the only one who felt that way—a steady stream of people had been milling around the agent, orbiting him as if he were the sun in this particular solar system.

The group made way for her as she approached.

Would he let her come along on the operation? She felt a small thrill in the pit of her stomach at the thought. It would be dangerous, she knew, but also necessary if they were to get Emily back safely. Tamping down the quivers of fear fluttering in her chest, she stopped in front of Valdez and waited for him to finish his phone conversation.

He disconnected and got right to the point.

"I need your clothes."

Claire blinked at him, stunned by the random statement. What was he talking about?

"Excuse me?"

"I need your clothes," he repeated, sweeping his eyes over her body while he spoke. Although she knew his assessment wasn't sexual, she felt her cheeks heat with a blush at his frank gaze.

"Why?" She swallowed hard, determined to ignore her schoolgirl reaction. For crying out loud, now was not the time to be shy!

"There's a chance Victor saw you today when he spoke to Agent Kincannon."

The reminder of just what she and Thomas had been doing before that phone call sent a fresh blush to her cheeks, and she glanced involuntarily at Thomas, who was standing off to the side, deep in conversation with James. If Valdez noticed she was lit up like a Christmas tree, he chose not to say anything.

He cleared his throat, dragging her attention away from that flame of red hair and the straight, taut lines of back and shoulders. "We will be sending someone with Agent Kincannon to retrieve both Emily and Victor, and she needs to look like you. Therefore, I need your clothes."

Agent Kincannon. Not Thomas. So there was a chance Valdez didn't know she and Thomas had been interrupted by that phone call. Either that, or he was pointedly ignoring facts that were of little relevance to the case at hand.

"I want to go."

"Absolutely not," he fired back, not even pausing to consider her words. "There is no way I'm sending a civilian—who is also a target—into this op."

"But—"

"No," he repeated, steel creeping into his voice. "Not an option. Now, please give me your clothes."

Claire raised an eyebrow as she regarded him. "Do you honestly think sending in a decoy is going to fool Victor? He may be a bad guy, but he's intelligent, and my guess is he already has something in place to trap Thom—Agent Kincannon."

"I know that," Valdez said, leaning forward. Claire resisted the urge to step back as the scent of stale coffee wafted over her face. She instinctively knew that if she gave an inch here, he'd take it as a sign of weakness.

"I've already dispatched a team to the Armory, to scout the site and set up a perimeter. They'll find and disable any booby traps Victor may have placed."

"I still think I should be there," she argued, knowing she was losing ground. "What if Victor won't give up Emily until he has me?"

"It's not going to get that far," Valdez said.

"But what if Victor doesn't bring Emily at all? What if he only tells Thomas where she is after I go with him?" He wasn't being logical. She had to make him see all the possibilities…

Valdez gave her a look that probably made his underlings quake with fear, but Claire refused to be intimidated. She was involved in this, damn it, whether he liked it or not. Victor was after her, and he had taken an innocent girl as a bargaining chip. It didn't get more personal than that.

After a few seconds, Valdez broke their impromptu staring contest. "Look," he said, letting out a sigh and stuffing his hands into his pockets. "This isn't my first rodeo, all right? I get that you're worried and that you want to help, but having you in the middle of things will do more harm than good. I've never lost a child before, and I'm not about to bust that record because you have a misguided sense of the contributions you can make to this op."

Stubborn man. She thought quickly, grasping for another line of argument to make him see reason.

"I just think we shouldn't antagonize Victor, that's all," she said, striving for a persuasive tone. "If he doesn't see me, he might hurt Emily."

"She's right."

They turned in unison as James joined the conversation. Claire felt a spurt of satisfaction knowing another agent agreed with her assessment, but she knew better than to gloat.

"Excuse me?" Valdez flushed at the interruption, clearly not accustomed to having his orders questioned.

"You know she's right," James continued, his tone reasonable. "For this op to have the greatest chance of success, she needs to go along. According to the boys in psych, Victor is hanging on by a very thin thread. It won't take much to push him over the edge, and we can't leave Emily's safety to something so risky. If Victor arrives in the morning to find Thomas with a decoy, there's no telling what he'll do to Emily. Do you really want that on your conscience?"

Valdez's gaze was dark with suppressed temper while he studied James. "You know I don't," he bit out, his jaw clenched so tight it was a wonder his teeth didn't break. "But you know as well as I do that we don't send untrained civilians into a hostage situation like this."

"She won't be going alone," James pointed out.

"Kincannon is not adequate protection."

Claire stiffened at his words, bristling on behalf of Thomas. How dare this man question Thomas's capabilities, especially after everything he'd done to keep her safe!

Valdez cut his eyes to her, apparently sensing her coming retort. "You're his asset, and that's his niece out there. If it comes down to a choice between the two of you, he won't be in a position to do the right thing."

"And what is that?"

Valdez looked away with a sigh. "Sometimes, hard choices have to be made. I don't think Kincannon is in a position to do that. Not on this op."

"That's why he won't be alone. Another agent will be in the car, one who is specifically tasked with looking out for Dr. Fleming."

"I suppose that would be you?" Valdez practically sneered at James, his disapproval loud and clear.

"No," James replied evenly. "One of your team. Someone you know and trust."

Valdez rocked back on his heels, considering. His eyes flicked to her, and Claire stood straight, trying to appear competent and unafraid. After a long moment, he sighed.

"Do you truly understand what you're asking?"

She nodded, trying not to seem too eager. "Yes. I want to go along tomorrow, to make sure Emily is returned safely."

"And you realize I cannot guarantee your safety?"

A frisson of fear rippled through her, but she ruthlessly tamped it down. "I know."

"But you want to go anyway?"

"I have to go," she told him, hoping he would understand. "If there is a chance my being there will help keep that little girl safe...I couldn't live with myself if something happened to her because I wasn't there."

Was that a flicker of respect in Valdez's gaze? Before she could decide, he turned away with a nod.

"Fine. You can go. But there will be an agent in the car with you, and you will do exactly as they say. Do I make myself clear?"

Claire nodded, nearly vibrating with excitement. "Yes. I won't be any trouble—I promise."

Valdez snorted. "Sure. Now go away before I change my mind."

She turned to James, mouthing a silent thank-you before stepping away. He gave her a slight nod in return.

This is really happening. The thought of seeing Victor again should have scared her, but it didn't, not really. Instead, a sense of nervous anticipation thrummed through her. She knew her part in this little drama would be insignificant, but she was happy to play it. If nothing else, she could make sure that Thomas came out of tomorrow's operation unscathed and reunited with his niece.

He kept surprising her, she realized as she retired to her bedroom, wanting to stay out of the way so she didn't give Valdez reason to reconsider her involvement. She sat on the bed, her thoughts drifting while she sorted through her memories of Thomas. Just when she thought she had him figured out, he did or said something that forced her to see him in a different light. He projected the image of the carefree, easygoing agent, but underneath that shell was a thoughtful, caring man.

Her heart had broken for him when he'd told her about his brother. He carried so much guilt over the loss it was a wonder he could stand. But in the short time she'd known him, Claire had come to understand that Thomas took on responsibility the way other people put on clothes in the morning. Telling him he wasn't to blame for Roger's death wasn't going to change the way he felt about it.

Having dealt with the loss of her father all those years ago, Claire could see that Thomas hadn't fully processed his brother's death. And it was no wonder— he'd jumped right in to help his niece and Jenny and his mother. He'd never taken the time to grieve on his own, to heal. She hoped that once this was all over, he would step back, let someone else carry the load for a bit. She could see, even if he didn't want to admit it, that he was very close to the breaking point, and if he didn't take care of himself, he was going to burn out before too long.

So she was glad to be going on the operation tomorrow, even though it meant she'd be in danger. She wanted to be there for Thomas, to make sure he got Emily back. More than that, she wanted to comfort him, to give him some measure of peace while they waited. She'd seen the way his eyes followed her in the crowd, knew he kept track of her wherever she went. While it was tempting to dismiss his actions as those of a competent bodyguard, there was a warmth in his gaze that couldn't be denied, and deep down, she knew he felt something for her. She could only hope that her presence tomorrow would help rather than hurt.

She'd never forgive herself if things went badly.

Thomas lay staring up at the ceiling, the blades of the fan giving him something to focus on while his mind whirled. His thoughts skipped and darted about, swirling like falling snow but always coming to rest on one topic.

Emily.

Despite his attitude, Valdez had come up with a solid plan. The only question was, would Victor fall for it?

His hands fisted into the comforter at the thought of the assassin, so smug, so self-assured. It would be a real pleasure to wipe that smirk off his face tomorrow morning.

He just hoped things didn't go to hell.

He'd nearly hit the roof when he'd found out Claire

would be tagging along tomorrow. His first instinct had been to refuse. She needed to be kept safe, and he couldn't protect her and focus on getting Emily back at the same time. Something would have to give, and he wasn't willing to put either one of them in more danger.

James had pulled him aside, explaining in calm, measured tones why Claire needed to go. His reasons were sound, and even now, Thomas couldn't really refute the man's logic. He still didn't like it though.

On the one hand, having Claire at the exchange would make Victor think he'd followed instructions. The assassin might be more willing to give up Emily if he thought he was really going to get Claire and the papers. That was a good thing.

On the other hand, things could turn quickly and Victor might not hesitate to shoot Claire and Emily, an act that would utterly destroy Thomas. The thought of losing them both made him want to vomit, but he couldn't deny the possibility. Even though Claire would be protected by an agent hiding in the car, he wasn't sure he'd be able to completely ignore her safety if things went south.

He rolled to his side, suddenly restless. The intellectual part of him knew he needed to sleep right now, save his energy so he'd be good for the operation tomorrow. But he was anxious to work, to be in the field scoping out the Armory site with the other guys on the team. He trusted them, no question about it, but he felt an ownership of this mission that he'd never experienced before. This was his niece, his family, his world on the line. He needed to be out there working, not twiddling his thumbs for the next few hours.

He slipped from bed, paced a few steps, then dropped to the floor for a round of push-ups. When his arms and shoulders began to burn, he flipped over to his back and started in on the crunches. The repetition was just the kind of familiar monotony he needed to bring him back down, keep him grounded so he didn't descend into an emotional tailspin.

He wasn't sure how long he moved, alternating between crunches and push-ups and back again to give his protesting muscles a break. When he finally stopped he spread out on the floor to stretch, his muscles twinging pleasantly and his mind finally, blessedly blank.

It could have been minutes or hours later when a soft rapping pulled him out of his mental white space. The noise was so faint he wasn't sure if it was a knock or the sounds of the house settling, but after a few seconds of silence, the tapping resumed, a bit louder this time.

He crossed to the door and pulled it open to find Claire standing on the other side, hand raised to knock again. She jumped a bit, obviously startled by his sudden appearance, and he hid a smile as a faint blush darkened her cheeks.

"Can I come in?" she whispered, darting a glance behind her as if she was afraid someone was watching.

He held the door open and stepped back in silent invitation. She gave him a small smile as she walked past, and he shut the door quietly behind her. Why was she here? And why was she being so secretive about it? The safe house was mostly empty at this time of night, with many of the agents out scouting the Armory site, setting up surveillance or resting. The ones who remained were occupied with planning in the kitchen, unconcerned with the goings-on in the back bedrooms of the house.

She stood in the middle of the room, facing away from him. The moonlight from the window lined her in silver, giving her an ethereal appearance like some ghostly apparition summoned from his dreams. He crossed to the bedside table and switched on the lamp, the muted glow allowing him to see her face but casting the rest of the room in shadows.

"Something on your mind?" he said quietly.

"I just…" She trailed off, then took a deep breath. "I'm scared for you. For tomorrow."

"Don't be," he said automatically. "We'll be fine."

She studied him a moment, her gray eyes appearing to look right through him. "How can you be so sure?"

How indeed? He thought he'd banished his doubts, but Claire's words started his gut churning with anticipation and adrenaline again. "It's a good plan," he said, moving past her to pace at the foot of the bed. "We're getting the team into position, scoping out the site. Everything is set."

"Do you really think Victor will fall for this?"

He stopped, looked her up and down as he considered her question. "I do." He started moving again, five steps forward, turn, five steps back. Repeat.

"I'll never forgive myself if this doesn't work."

Her words stunned him out of his pacing, and he turned to face her.

"It's not your responsibility," he said, struggling to keep his emotions in check. "This is my job—mine. Do you understand? My responsibility. I put myself in danger because I have to. I'm supposed to keep you safe. You can't control what happens tomorrow, and if anything goes wrong, you can damn sure believe it'll be because of something me or my team did, not you."

"So that's all I am to you? A job?"

He grabbed her hand as she spun around to leave. "Don't be ridiculous," he said, hauling her up against his chest. "You know I care about you."

She sighed and dropped her forehead to his shoulder. Her arms came up to wrap around his back and they stood there for a moment, holding each other.

"I'm sorry," she whispered. "I didn't come here to pick a fight. I'm just so worried, and I wanted to be by you before we leave in the morning."

He stroked his hand down the column of her hair, the silky softness flowing over his palm like water. "I'm sorry, too," he said. "I shouldn't have snapped at you."

"You're worried." She gave him a squeeze, spreading warmth through his chest. She held him a moment longer, then spoke again. "You should get some rest. Big day tomorrow." She pulled back and rose up on her tiptoes to press a soft kiss to his mouth.

The contact arced through him, setting all his nerve endings on fire. He gripped her shoulders when she moved away, and something in his gaze must have betrayed his need. She met his eyes for a beat, then kissed him again, her hands moving to hold his head in place as her tongue darted out to graze across his lips.

He groaned and opened his mouth, giving her the access she sought. She was wet and warm and willing, and he wanted nothing more than to lose himself in her, let her take away the stress and worry and anxiety about Emily, about Victor, about everything.

It felt so good to be holding her, touching her, and yet…there was a small corner of his brain telling him to stop. *Not like this,* the voice said, growing louder and louder until he couldn't ignore it anymore.

He pulled back, framing Claire's face with his hands. "We should slow down," he said in a voice too unsteady to be trusted.

She kissed his cheeks, his forehead, his nose. "Let me do this for you," she whispered, kissing his chin. "Let me help you tonight."

He swallowed hard. "Are you sure? If we go much further, I won't want to stop."

She ran her hands under his shirt and up his chest as she pressed her mouth to his, and he shivered, goose bumps fanning out across his skin in the wake of her touch.

"Who's asking you to?"

Chapter 10

Claire gasped when Thomas lifted her off her feet, holding her close as he walked them over to the bed. He laid her down with a gentleness that belied the tension she felt rolling off him and immediately covered her body with his own. She reached up to frame his face with her hands and pushed back a flaming lock of hair as she met his gaze. His blue eyes blazed with an intense need, a wordless desire fueled by desperation and hope. She pulled him down for another kiss, wanting to give him the comfort of her body so he would know he was not alone—not tonight, not ever again.

His kisses grew increasingly demanding while his hands roamed over her body, touching her everywhere, setting off sparks of sensation with each brush of fingers over skin. His mouth left hers so he could yank her nightgown over her head, and she fumbled with clumsy fingers at the waistband of his pants. She needed to feel him, to soothe him with her touch and help him find the release he sought.

He was having none of it. He reached down, bracketed her wrists with one hand and pulled her arms above her head, holding her in place. She was effectively trapped under him, totally at his mercy, and he took full advantage of it.

She bit back a soft cry as he nipped her with his teeth, then soothed away the sting with the warm rasp of his tongue. She tugged experimentally against his hold, but he tightened his grip, silently refusing to release her. Part of her recognized his need to be in control right now, so she acquiesced, letting him set the pace.

Her thoughts grew increasingly fragmented as he moved over her. Hands, teeth, tongue—he used them all to great effect, reducing her to mindless whimpers of pleasure. She arched against him, needing to feel him, needing to be filled by him. He chuckled softly at her wordless pleas, his breath warm against her breast. One hand trailed down and hooked under her knee, drawing her leg up along his body. She moved willingly, locking her ankles at the small of his back and urging him forward.

When he didn't move right away, she lifted her head to look at him. "What's wrong?"

His expression was one of pained disbelief, as if he couldn't comprehend what was happening. "I don't have a condom," he whispered, dropping his head to rest against her shoulder with a low groan. "I'm such an idiot."

Claire arched against him, using her legs to pull him back to her center. "I'm on the pill."

His head jerked up at that, hope shining in his gaze. "Really?"

"Really. Now are we going to do this or what?"

Thomas wasted no more time, entering her with a sharp thrust that made her gasp. He froze above her, his chest heaving with the force of his breathing. "Oh, God," he whispered reverently.

"Move, damn it," she bit out from between clenched teeth. He hesitated, so she rolled her hips against him, creating a weak friction that did nothing to satisfy her.

She had been content to let him take the lead earlier, but now she assumed control. She pulled her wrists free, placed her hands on his chest and shoved, forcing him to turn until he lay on his back. He let out a moan as she began to move, settling into a rhythmic pace that soon had them both gasping for breath.

He sat up, wrapping his arms around her. "Claire. I'm close. Are you?"

"Yes," she answered, biting down on his shoulder to trap the moan in her throat. "It's okay."

He touched her then, using the pad of his thumb to administer a few rasping strokes that short-circuited her brain and had her eyes rolling back in her head.

She must have cried out, because she heard him whisper "Hush" before capturing her mouth with his own. She realized in the dim recesses of her brain that he was back in charge, but as long as he kept touching her, she didn't care.

He didn't disappoint. A few more brushes with those clever fingers, and she was there, her whole conscious-

ness condensed to a single point of indescribable pleasure. She felt him move within her—one thrust, two,
and then he followed her into his own release.

They collapsed back onto the bed, a tangle of limbs
and sheets. She felt cold at the loss of him, but Thomas
quickly wrapped himself around her body, envelop-
ing her in warmth. "Claire," he murmured into her
hair, his voice soft with satisfaction and sleepiness.
"Thank you."

"Shh," she whispered back. "Rest now."

He gave a drowsy murmur of assent and she felt
him slip away, his breathing leveling out as he drifted
into unconsciousness. His arms were a heavy weight
keeping her in place, and she realized that even in his
sleep, he tried to protect her.

"Oh, Thomas." She sighed. "What have you done
to me?"

"Kincannon. Coombs. Check in."

Valdez's voice was tinny and close, making him
feel claustrophobic. Thomas fought the urge to touch
his ear, not wanting to give away the fact that he was
wired. Victor probably expected it, but still…better to
keep his cards as close to the chest as possible.

"Kincannon here. No activity so far. What do our
eyes up top say?"

There was a pause while his words were relayed,
then Valdez spoke again. "Nothing yet. Keep your eyes
open."

"Check. Kincannon out."

He heard a sigh from the seat next to him, and

turned to see Claire bouncing her leg in a rapid tattoo. "Nervous?"

Her leg stopped. "No."

He raised a brow, turned back to face the alley. "If you say so."

She let out another sigh. "I'm just not good at the waiting. I want something to happen."

"It will."

"How are you so calm right now?" She shifted in the seat, turning to face him. "It's your niece out there, and yet you seem very composed. How are you doing that?"

His thoughts flashed back to the night they had shared. The way Claire had touched him, given him release, made him feel it would all be okay.

Even though that feeling hadn't lasted.

"Experience," he heard himself say. "I've been doing this for a long time. If I let my emotions take control, I risk blowing the operation to hell."

"Still…" she said softly, her voice trailing off.

"Yeah," he murmured.

Truth was, he was wound so tightly it was a wonder he hadn't exploded yet. He was right on the edge, where one touch, one wrong word would set him off. The only thing that kept him in control was the knowledge that if he did let go, there would be no coming back.

Last night had helped. He'd let himself get caught up in the sensations of being with her—her softness and curves, her mouth, her touch. He could still feel her skin on his fingertips, her mouth on his chest, her hand wrapped around his—

He swallowed hard. Well.

He'd woken this morning feeling unusually rested,

an unfamiliar sensation that had taken him a moment to identify. He'd actually slept last night, miracle of miracles, and it was all thanks to the warm woman in his arms. He had turned his head to nuzzle the back of her neck, inhaling her sleepy, satisfied musk. She'd stirred briefly at the brush of his lips against her skin, then sunk back into sleep with a sigh.

He'd allowed himself a few minutes of peace, knowing that it wouldn't last. How could it? His family—his life—was never going to be the same again, and he needed to accept that. It was time to surrender this fantasy of the wife and the white picket fence. He needed to focus on putting what was left of his family back together, helping his mother and Emily heal, and repairing his shattered relationship with Jenny.

Besides, Claire deserved someone better. Someone who could focus on her, give her the support and attention she deserved. Someone who wouldn't use her to make himself feel better.

He should have sent her back to her room last night, or better yet, not even let her through the door. Now that he knew what it could be like with her, it was going to be that much harder to let her go.

Assuming she even wants you, he thought with a mental snort. He hadn't exactly been at his best last night. He couldn't blame her if their rough, no-frills encounter had failed to knock her socks off.

Before Emily had been taken, he'd entertained fantasies of taking Claire to his bed. How he'd go slow, touching her, tasting her everywhere. Making sure she was well and truly ravished. He'd make her understand how he felt about her, make her realize his feelings were real and serious.

It was hard to deny last night's encounter had fallen far short of the standards he'd imagined.

He wanted to talk to her, to apologize for his actions, but this wasn't the time. Once he had Emily back, and they weren't sitting in a car with a fellow agent lying down across the backseat, he could explain.

Another sigh from Claire brought him out of his reverie. "This is always the worst part," he told her, needing to fill the silence that had suddenly turned awkward.

"Does it ever get any easier?"

He shook his head. "Nope. But next time I'll bring a deck of cards."

That earned him a wry laugh. "No offense, but I hope there isn't a next time."

"You and me—"

"Heads up." Valdez's voice rang in his ear, causing his pulse rate to spike. He sat up a bit straighter behind the wheel, muscles tense and ready for whatever news he was about to hear. "I've got movement, coming from the north. Three blocks away."

"Can you see her? Can you tell if it's Emily?" His heart lodged in his throat, and he held his breath as he waited for Valdez to respond. *Please, please…*

"Still too far away…no, wait." Another pause. Thomas felt like screaming but kept silent, settling for gripping the steering wheel so hard his hands hurt. After a bit of crackling static, Valdez was back on the line. "Subject identified. The little girl is Emily."

The news should have made him happy, but Thomas

gripped the wheel even harder. "How does she look?" he asked, the words a strangled croak as he forced them past his paralyzed vocal cords.

"Doesn't appear to be injured," Valdez reported. "Look alive, team. They're approaching the meeting point. Let's keep her safe and bring her home unharmed."

There was a chorus of "Checks" as the various team members responded to Valdez's words, and Thomas felt something inside him loosen a bit at the audible reminder that he wasn't alone.

Thomas climbed out of the car and walked toward the front, eyes fixed on the intersection where Emily and Victor would soon appear. He heard another door slam and, a few seconds later, felt Claire standing behind him.

"You should get back in the car," he told her, not looking away from the street. "I don't want you out here when he arrives."

"I'm staying," she replied, her words quiet but determined. "No way am I leaving you out here to face him alone."

He turned to glance at her, anger and fear a potent combination in his gut. "Claire, get back in the—"

"Here they come," Valdez reported.

Thomas sucked in a breath as Emily appeared at the intersection. She was about fifty yards away, but she appeared to be fine. She was walking normally, and he didn't see any obvious wounds. Her face split into a wide grin when she saw him, and she broke away from the man by her side to run forward. His heart caught in his throat, but Victor made no move to stop her.

"Uncle Thomas!" He crouched down to meet her, and she flung herself into his arms.

"Hey, baby," he said, his voice shaky. He quickly ran his hands over her body, checking for injuries or devices. Why hadn't Victor tried to stop her?

"I missed you!"

She was clean. He scooped her up and headed for the car, ignoring Victor. Let the team mop up here. He was taking her to the hospital. "I missed you, too."

He opened the door and deposited her on the seat. She balked at the sight of the agent crouched in the back, but Natalie sent her a quick grin and told her she was playing hide-and-seek. "Help me hide?" she asked.

Emily nodded, sinking down next to Natalie.

Thomas kept one eye on the man standing in the street while Claire climbed into the car. Now that he had Emily back, there was no way he was going to hand over Claire. But Victor made no attempt to come closer. *Why isn't he moving?*

Ignoring the churning in his gut, he climbed into the driver's seat. "I've got her. We're on our way to the hospital."

"Roger that," Valdez responded. "We'll take it from here."

Thomas glanced in the rearview mirror as he sped away, a hot spurt of satisfaction spreading through his chest when he saw Victor with his hands up high in the air, the members of the team approaching with their guns trained on him. *Got you, you monster.*

"All right, baby," he said, shifting his gaze to Emily. His heart warmed at the sight of her, the knowledge she was safe and whole mixing with his adrenaline to leave him feeling light-headed and giddy. "Let's get you back to your mom."

Victor raised his head from the high-powered scope attached to his sniper rifle, cursing under his breath. He hadn't expected them to bring the woman. She was supposed to stay behind, vulnerable and alone in the safe house. Kincannon's niece should have been the perfect distraction, an easy way to misdirect the focus of the FBI. Instead, the idiots had brought her along.

As if he'd really show up this morning.

He watched in detached interest while the little girl ran to Kincannon, leaving her escort behind. Another mistake. His finger caressed the trigger when he sighted the man's head in his scope. He was supposed to keep her by his side the whole time, drag out the process. Not let her go at the first tug of her hand.

Served him right for using a drunkard to do the job.

He could end the man's life right now. He really should, if only to punish him for his mistake. But that would draw attention to his location, and then the FBI would know he was nearby. He still held the element of surprise, and he wasn't about to give up that advantage any time soon.

Kincannon's car shot away with a squeal of tires. Evidently, he wasn't sticking around for the cleanup.

It was time for him to go as well. He hummed softly as he disassembled and packed up the rifle. Plan A hadn't worked out like he'd wanted, but there was always plan B. He could hear the faint shouts of the FBI agents as they took down the man in the alley. With so many of them here, the safe house had to be deserted, especially since Dr. Fleming was with Kincannon. He'd simply slip inside and hide.

She had to come back sometime. No way would the FBI let her go home when they discovered he was still at large. No, they'd return her to the safe house in a bid to keep her protected.

Delivering her straight into his arms.

Chapter 11

They had done it.

They'd gotten Emily back, and Claire hadn't had to see Victor. It had been so easy, so simple, she almost couldn't believe it.

After spending yesterday afternoon imagining a multitude of possible outcomes, Claire had gone into this morning's operation feeling more than a little keyed up. The comfort and release of last night had faded with the rising of the sun, and her stomach had been twisted up in knots as the meeting time approached. She'd nearly fainted when Valdez had announced Victor was near, and it was only her concern for Thomas that had given her the strength to stand next to him when Emily and Victor had appeared.

She glanced at him, wanting to reach over to touch his leg but reluctant to distract him. His attention was split between the road and the rearview mirror, his grip on the wheel tight enough to turn his knuckles white. He'd been tense all morning, something she'd attributed to the stress of the operation. But now that they had Emily back, doubts were starting to creep in.

Did he regret sleeping with her? Maybe she had come on too strong, pushed him too hard. She'd wanted to comfort him, to offer him support, but perhaps he thought less of her this morning for having used her body to do it. He didn't seem to mind last night, though, she thought, a prickle of irritation flaring to life.

"Almost there," he murmured, though whether to himself or to her, she couldn't be sure.

Will you get a grip? She pushed away her irrational worries and focused on the hospital that had just come into view. They would reunite Emily with her mother, get her checked out and then they could regroup and celebrate the fact that Victor was out of their lives. There would be time for her to explore her growing feelings for Thomas later, when everything had settled down again.

He pulled up to the front entrance and left the car running while he collected Emily from the backseat. "Nat, can you deal with the car?"

Without waiting for an answer, he set off. Claire scrambled to keep up, not wanting to get left behind.

She caught up to him at the elevator. He offered her a tight smile as they ascended, then jumped off and strode down the hall when they reached the sixth floor. Claire hurried after him, no match for his long-legged stride.

She turned the corner just in time to see Emily race

into her mother's arms. "Mom!" she cried, wrapping her small body around Jenny's frame.

Jenny clutched her daughter in a fierce grip, her face buried in Emily's hair. Claire slowed as she approached, not wanting to interrupt their moment. She came to a stop a few feet away from Thomas, who was watching the reunion with an odd expression that looked like a combination of longing and relief. A tall, blonde woman with delicate, graceful features stood by Jenny, wearing a benevolent smile as she watched the pair.

"Not so hard, Mommy," Emily said, wriggling a bit to loosen her mother's grip. "You're squeezing me too tight."

"Sorry, baby," Jenny murmured, rubbing her hand along Emily's back.

After a long moment, Jenny leaned back from Emily. Running her palm over the girl's hair, she offered her a watery smile. "Why don't we go see Grandma?" she asked, rising to her feet and pushing open the door of the room behind her. As Emily walked inside, Jenny turned back to face Thomas, gratitude shining in her eyes. *Thank you,* she mouthed.

Thomas nodded, his shoulders relaxing as he watched his sister-in-law and his niece disappear.

Claire took a step forward, wanting to lay a hand on his arm. Her limbs were rubbery in the aftermath of the morning's adrenaline rush, and she could only imagine how Thomas felt. Now that Emily was safe and his family reunited, he had to feel a powerful sense of relief.

We did it, she thought, effervescent bubbles of joy rising up her chest. *We beat him.*

She opened her mouth to speak, but before she could form the words, the tall blonde woman strolled up to Thomas and kissed him.

Not just a friendly peck on the cheek either. She stood on tiptoes and pressed her mouth fully against Thomas's. Her hands moved from his shoulders to his head, threading through the fiery strands of hair to hold him in place as she licked and sucked his bottom lip. Thomas did nothing to stop her, made no move to break her embrace or end the kiss. Claire stood there, trapped, shock and rage keeping her frozen while the kiss went on for an endless moment.

But the worst part of all was the expression on Thomas's face when the woman finally pulled away.

His eyes were glazed with lust as he stared down at her, and his tongue darted out to catch the last of her taste on his lips. The blonde murmured something to him, but Claire didn't stick around to watch his response. She turned away and quickly walked down the hall, blinking back tears as she moved.

Idiot! She'd been a classic fool. No wonder Thomas hadn't waited for her as he'd practically run through the hospital. He'd wanted to get here, to celebrate Emily's safe return with whoever this woman was. And if that was the way they celebrated in public, she could only imagine how they'd celebrate once they were alone.

The thought of Thomas's hands on that woman, touching her tall, slender body the same way he'd touched her last night…she shook her head, trying to dismiss the painful images.

*I don't have a girlfriend. I wouldn't touch you if I did.
You know I care about you.*

His words echoed in her mind, mocking.

Maybe he didn't consider the blonde to be his girl-friend. But if that kiss was any indication, something was going on between them. Now his earlier tension, his withdrawal, made perfect sense. He had used her last night, and now that he was back with his "friend," he no longer needed her warm body.

She almost laughed at her naïveté. God, she'd actually thought she'd been helping him last night! In re-ality, she'd been nothing more than a fun diversion, a way to pass the time until morning arrived. She sucked in a breath as she waited for the elevator. How could she have been so stupid?

She'd wanted to believe they had something in com-mon—the pain of losing someone you loved. She'd dropped her guard, letting him into her heart and body in an effort to connect with him. She had ached for him and the guilt he so clearly felt over his brother's death. Unless it was a ruse to win sympathy with the ladies. He probably told that sob story to all the girls, and she was just the latest in a long line to fall for it.

She shook her head, blinking back tears. Once again, she had made a mistake, opening her heart to the wrong person.

The doors opened with a faint ding, and she plowed ahead, nearly careening into Natalie.

"Oh! I'm sorry," the woman said. She peered at Claire's face, her eyes narrowing as she looked her over. "Everything okay?"

Claire sniffed, nodding. "Yes. Everything is fine.

Can you please take me back to the safe house? I'd like to collect my things. Agent Kincannon has some things to take care of here, so he asked me to ask you to drive."

"Sure." Natalie stepped back into the elevator, pulling the keys out of her pocket. "You sure you're all right? You look like you've been crying."

Claire tried to smile at the other woman. "It was just so wonderful, seeing Emily reunited with her mother. I got a little teary."

Natalie seemed to buy the excuse. "I can imagine. We got lucky today. Things could have gone a lot worse."

Claire nodded her agreement, but her heart cried out its denial. All her illusions concerning Thomas, her fledgling hopes that this might be the start of something between them, feelings that she hadn't dared to voice, even to herself—they were all gone, destroyed in a single instant.

Things didn't get much worse than that.

What the hell?

Thomas stared down at Tanya, trying to figure out when he'd dropped into this alternate reality. She'd pressed herself against his chest and was gazing adoringly up at him, her hand stroking the hair at the nape of his neck as she whispered words of love.

Maybe he was asleep. The past few days had been rough; it was possible he was hallucinating, or that this was just a bad dream. He blinked to clear his vision. Nope. Still Tanya.

Moving carefully, he placed his hands on her shoulders and steadily pushed her away. A flicker of hurt danced across her face at the separation, but she didn't try to touch him again.

Oh man, this was going to be so awkward.

Raising his hand, Thomas wiped her kiss from his mouth, his mind whirling. It was true, then. Jenny had been dropping hints, saying that Tanya was back in town and wanted to see him, that she still had feelings for him. He hadn't acknowledged the news, thinking Jenny had only brought it up out of a sense of nostalgia. After all, he and Tanya had spent a lot of time with Jenny and Roger. It was only natural Jenny would long for those happier days, especially in the midst of her grief.

Never in his wildest imaginings had he thought he would see Tanya again, and he certainly had no interest in picking up where they had left off.

"What the hell do you think you're doing?"

Tanya smiled up at him, unperturbed by the harshness of his words. "It's so good to see you again, Tommy," she purred, reaching up to run her fingers down his chest. He stepped back, repulsed by her touch. When had that happened? Only a few short years ago, he had welcomed her hands on him. Not anymore.

"The feeling isn't mutual."

She stuck out her bottom lip in a little moue that she probably thought was sexy, but it only made her appear ridiculous. *Claire would never look at me like that....*

"Now, Tommy, is that any way to greet an old friend?"

"We're not friends."

"I know I made a mistake, but I was hoping you'd forgiven me for my little indiscretion."

Thomas stared down at her, torn between the desire to laugh in her face or turn and walk away. He wanted nothing to do with her. He'd written her off after she'd cheated on him and moved to Chicago. He'd long since gotten over her and the time they'd spent together. No way was he going to take her back now, when he'd finally found someone he was interested in.

He wanted nothing more than to walk past her, but he needed to make sure she understood that there was no future for them. The last thing he wanted was for Tanya to hang around in some misguided attempt to win him back.

"There's nothing to forgive, Tanya. I'm over it."

Her face broke into a wide smile, and he realized she had misinterpreted his words. "There is nothing between us," he hastened to add.

"But there could be," she said, cocking her head to the right and lowering her lashes. "We were good together." She stepped forward, her voice a murmur meant for his ears only. "We could be again. I still…" She blinked and swallowed hard, playing her part to the hilt. "I still love you."

Oh, she was good. She was turning in an Oscar-worthy performance, that much was certain. In another time, under different circumstances, he might have been affected by her words, her air of injured vulnerability. But he'd been burned by her before, and now that he'd met Claire, he understood that what he'd had with Tanya had never been real. The time he'd spent with Claire, brief though it was, had given him a glimpse of what a true partnership could be, what a relationship should be like.

Life was too short—and too precious—to settle for anything less.

"No."

She stopped, a flash of anger sparking in her eyes before she smothered it with another smile. *There you are,* he thought. *That's the real Tanya.*

"You're just stressed," she said indulgently, the way she might talk to a child who'd requested a cookie. "That's why you're being so unreasonable. It's your job. Once you finish this case, you'll be able to focus on us again, why we should be together."

She lifted her hand to touch his chest, but he brushed it away before she could make contact. He didn't want Tanya to erase the lingering feel of Claire's touch on his skin. Bad enough that she'd kissed him already—he wasn't going to let her take any more liberties.

"Why are you here?"

She blinked up at him, apparently taken aback by the question. "Wh-what?"

"You heard me."

Tanya took a half step back, confusion and anger warring for control of her features. "I'm here for you," she said slowly. "For us."

"There is no 'us.' There never will be. If you've returned to hang around my family out of some desperate attempt to win me back, it's not going to happen. You should just leave now, before Jenny comes to rely on you as a friend again. I won't let you hurt her."

"Tommy—"

"And don't call me that," he snapped.

She lifted a perfectly arched eyebrow. "Roger used to call you that all the time. You were fine with it."

"Times change. I have. And you no longer have the right to use a nickname with me." It grated on his nerves, the way she threw the childish name around like he was some kind of pet. It was a name his mother had used when he was a kid, but she hadn't called him that in years. His brother, on the other hand, had continued to call him Tommy, but usually only when he was trying to underscore the age difference between them. It hadn't bothered him before, but now that Roger was gone, he felt a little zing of pain every time he heard the name, like someone was pushing hard on a fresh bruise.

She pressed her lips together, then deliberately pasted on a smile and tried again. "Thomas," she said, stressing his name ever so slightly. "I think if you consider what I'm offering, you'll find that it's really for the best. For both of us."

Was she this delusional when we were together? It was possible, but he doubted it. She'd always been determined, but she'd never before seemed so out of touch with reality. She must be truly desperate to win him back to so willfully ignore his words.

He shook his head, recognizing a lost cause. He didn't have time to stand here and argue with her or to explain in very small words why he was never going to want her back. He needed to check on his mom and make sure Emily was truly okay. And where was Claire? Had she gone into his mom's hospital room when he wasn't looking? He took a step toward the door, being careful not to brush Tanya as he moved past her.

"It's her, isn't it? That little blonde bitch who was with you when you showed up."

That stopped him in his tracks. He turned slowly, his temper straining to be free of the leash he held with a viselike grip. "What did you say?"

Either Tanya didn't realize her mistake or she didn't care. She plunged ahead, spewing bile and hatred with every word. "I saw the way she looked at you, like a teenager swooning over a movie star poster in her bedroom." She smiled maliciously. "She has quite the crush on you, Thomas. Pathetic, really. She doesn't stand a chance."

There's no competition. He stared down at her, his anger giving way to pity as he registered the desperation lurking behind her eyes.

"What happened to you, Tanya?" he said softly. "You've changed."

Her shoulders dropped when she looked down. "We've all changed." She fiddled with the cuffs of her shirt, deliberately folding and pleating them until they were arranged just so. She was clearly hiding something, but what?

"Life in Chicago didn't agree with you?"

She smiled thinly. "You could say that. I learned the hard way that Jeremy wasn't one of the good guys."

His brain kicked into overdrive, flashing a series of ugly images through his mind. Blood, bruises, the sickening thud of fists meeting flesh as a woman cried out in pain. James's wife, Kelly, had been abused by a former boyfriend, and she'd told him a few stories about that time in her life, making it all too easy for him to imagine what she'd been through.

He swallowed hard, suddenly seeing Tanya's advances in a new light. Had she been abused? Had she come back to D.C. to try to find a safe place again?

"Did he hurt you?" If she needed help, he was happy to put her in touch with people who could get her set up with a safe place to stay. He had a friend in D.C. who practiced family law. He could probably help expedite a restraining order, if it came to that. Although Thomas had no intention of becoming personally involved with her, he wasn't such a coldhearted bastard that he'd leave a woman in distress hung out to dry.

She looked up, and her eyes widened when she saw his expression. "Not like you're thinking. He didn't beat me up or anything."

The tension drained out of him at her words. "Then what happened?"

Tanya sighed, the corners of her mouth turning down. "I made the mistake of falling in love with him."

"That doesn't sound so bad."

"Yes, well. He didn't feel the same about me. I'd picked up my life, moved halfway across the country to be with him, and then found out he was only interested in a casual fling. He cheated on me almost from the beginning."

"I'm sorry," he replied automatically. And he was surprised to discover that he truly meant it. The residual anger he'd felt toward her had faded over the past few days, bleached to nothingness by the light of Claire's presence in his life. The realization made him feel less weighed down somehow, as if a burden he didn't know he'd been carrying had been lifted from his heart.

Tanya waved her hand in dismissal. "It's fine. I mean, can you believe him? Cheating on me like that?" She gestured to herself as she spoke, a beauty queen pointing out her best features. "It's his loss, really. He can't possibly expect to find someone better than me. He was lucky I was even with him in the first place!"

Thomas blinked, biting his cheek to choke back the laugh that was bubbling in his throat. The woman had pluck, he'd give her that. Although her perspective was amazingly twisted, he couldn't bring himself to point out the irony of her situation.

He glanced around, searching for Claire. *God, please don't let her have seen that kiss*. Even though it meant nothing to him, if she saw it out of context, she'd likely think he and Tanya were an item. He winced at the thought, recalling their earlier discussion in the safe house, when she'd assumed Emily was his girl-friend. That had been a simple misunderstanding, eas-ily cleared up. This…this was something else entirely and would require a longer explanation. They hadn't had a chance to talk about his past relationship with Tanya yet, and while he wasn't trying to hide any-thing from her, he hoped she hadn't seen this twisted little reunion.

"Thomas?"

He turned to find Jenny standing in the doorway of his mother's hospital room. She looked from him to Tanya, her glance questioning. Had she known what Tanya was planning?

"Are you coming in? Mom's awake and asking to see you."

"Yes," he replied shortly, starting for the door.

"Thomas," Tanya called after him. He stopped, mentally bracing himself for whatever she was about to say.

"I'll see you later." Her tone was casual, almost subdued. She sounded like a friend saying goodbye—no innuendos or hidden promises that they'd talk again. Maybe he really had gotten through to her, and she would move on with her life. "I'm going to grab a cup of coffee and let you guys have a few moments to yourselves as a family."

"Thanks," he said, appreciating the gesture for the peace offering it was. The maelstrom of emotions whirling inside him calmed somewhat, now that this little drama had been resolved. Emily was safe, Mom was recovering and Tanya seemed to understand they didn't have a future together. Now, he just had to find Claire, confess his feelings and hope that she liked him enough to overlook his shortcomings.

He approached Jenny, who hadn't moved from the door. "Is Claire inside?"

Jenny frowned at him, shaking her head. "The woman you're protecting? No, she's not here. Why, should she be?"

Chapter 12

Thomas felt the bottom drop out of his stomach at Jenny's words. "What do you mean she's not here?" he said, enunciating carefully in a bid to keep the words from tumbling out in an incomprehensible jumble of sounds. "She was with me in the elevator when I brought Emily up."

Jenny shrugged. "I didn't see her. I only had eyes for my baby girl."

Oh, God. Oh, no. If Claire wasn't in his mom's room, then she had stayed in the hall. And if she'd stayed in the hall…

He uttered a low, fierce curse. Jenny's mouth turned down in disapproval, and she moved quickly to shut the door, lest his words be overheard by his mother or niece. Normally, he would have found her prudishness amusing, but he didn't have time to deal with her offended sensibilities right now.

"Tell Mom I had to go back to work. An emergency came up."

"Thomas," she began, her unhappiness coming through loud and clear.

"I'll be back soon," he said, already heading for the elevator. He reached for his phone, blinking at it in mild surprise when it started to ring in his hand. He debated not answering it, but Valdez might have an important update for him.

"We've got a problem."

Tell me something I don't know. He'd thought things were under control back at the Armory, but now with Valdez's words, he wasn't so sure. "What's wrong?"

"The guy we picked up? It wasn't Victor."

Goose bumps rose on his skin, and he instinctively looked back at the door to his mother's hospital room. Hadn't they been through enough? How was it possible that this nightmare wasn't over yet?

"Kincannon? You still there?"

Thomas shook his head. "Yes, I'm here. What do you mean, it wasn't Victor? Who was it?"

"Some guy he hired. Picked him up off the street, gave him five hundred dollars to take a walk. Has Emily said anything about it?"

"No. I haven't had a chance to ask her about it yet. We just got her to the hospital a few minutes ago."

"We need to talk to her. He may have said something to her, or she may have seen something that will tell us what he plans to do next."

"I'll ask her about it."

Valdez didn't respond right away, which triggered alarm bells in Thomas's head. "Actually, I'm going to send someone to the hospital to talk to Emily. You're too close to the situation."

Thomas tightened his grip on the phone. "You think I can't get my niece to answer questions about her experience?"

"I'm sure you can," Valdez said, his voice taking on a soothing tone that only grated on Thomas's already frayed nerves. "I just want someone there who has a little more experience talking to kids."

"Fine," he bit out, knowing the other man was right.

"I already briefed Natalie on the situation with Victor. She's en route to the safe house with Dr. Fleming, where they'll stay until we figure out Victor's next move."

Thomas felt he'd been punched in the gut. So Claire had left. That confirmed his worst suspicions. The only reason she would have gone without telling him was if she'd seen the kiss. He'd been a fool to think otherwise.

At least she was safe, he told himself. Natalie was a good agent, and she'd protect Claire until he could get to her. Assuming Claire ever wanted to see him again.

He shook his head, frustration building inside him, making his chest feel too small. The situation with Tanya could not have come at a worse time. He needed to go to Claire, to explain that she was the only one he cared about, the only one he had feelings for, but he didn't have the luxury of time. With Victor still on the loose, he needed to make sure she and his family were safe. There would be time for conversation later, once the danger had passed.

Thomas wasn't stupid enough to think Victor had just given up. He'd taken Emily to use as a bargaining chip, and the only reason he'd let her go was because it suited his purposes. But just what did he have planned? It was no secret Victor wanted Claire and Ivan's decoded pages. But by letting Emily go, he'd lost the advantage. Unless…

Had Emily been a diversion? What if Victor had lured them to the Armory with the promise of delivering the little girl, knowing Thomas and the rest of the team would jump at the chance to get her back? He would know where they were, would know that the team would be tied up for hours making sure Emily was okay and interviewing the man he'd sent in his stead. Everyone would be gone, leaving the safe house empty and undefended. The perfect opportunity for Victor to break in and hide, lying in wait for them to return.

His stomach twisted, a rush of adrenaline leaving a bitter taste in his mouth. He had to trust Natalie. As much as he wanted to run to Claire, to see for himself that she was safe, he couldn't leave his family unprotected until he had more information.

Besides, what if that was just what Victor wanted? Maybe he was watching him even now. Victor had to know Thomas would head straight for the hospital with Emily. Maybe his plan was to follow him to the safe house. Running off half-cocked would only feed into his twisted plans, something Thomas refused to do.

Hopefully Emily could shed some light on the situation. He doubted Victor had been careless enough to reveal anything to the girl, but she was a smart cookie and she may have picked up something without even realizing it. He just hoped the agents Valdez sent would be able to question her without traumatizing her.

"How long until the agents get here?" he asked. As soon as he knew his family was protected, he could focus completely on Claire.

"They should be arriving in a few minutes," Valdez replied.

Thomas spied two no-nonsense women striding toward him, their determined gait and polished appearance practically screaming federal agent.

"Let me guess," he said, wanting to verify their identity before running off. "Two women? One brunette, one blonde?"

"Yes," Valdez confirmed. "Tyler and Matthews. They're very good."

"Glad to hear it," Thomas replied absently, his mind already jumping ahead to the next problem. If Natalie was taking Claire back to the safe house, she had the car. He eyed the women as they drew near, hoping they'd be willing to help out a fellow agent.

"Got to go. Keep me posted." He hung up before Valdez could respond and walked forward to introduce himself, pasting on a smile he didn't feel. As his grandmother used to tell him, "You catch more flies with honey."

Time to turn on the charm.

Natalie pushed the button to shut the garage door, unlocking the car only after she saw that they were sealed in. She waited until Claire joined her by the driver's side before walking to the house door.

"You know the drill by now," she said with a small smile. "Let me go first."

Claire nodded, hanging back until Natalie had checked the kitchen and small dining room. The other woman waved her in and headed down the left hall to clear the den. Her phone rang as she walked, and she pulled it from her belt, frowning at the display.

"It's Thomas," she said, concern lacing her voice. Claire gritted her teeth against the flip of her stomach at the mention of his name. He was a jerk, a cad and she'd do well to remember it.

"I hope nothing's wrong with his niece," Natalie said as she continued down the hall, her fingers working to answer the phone. "Natalie here—"

She broke off abruptly, and Claire heard a solid thud. Then Natalie screamed out, "Claire, run!"

Claire froze for a split second, uncertain. She couldn't go back into the garage; the doors were down, locking her in. The front door was too far away. The bedroom, and its panic alcove, was her only option. In the split second it took her to make the decision, a loud bang sounded from the den.

Oh, God. Oh god oh god oh god. Blinking hard to clear the tears from her eyes, she sucked in a shallow breath and ran for the bedroom off the right hallway, trying desperately to keep her movements quiet. Had Victor sent someone else for her? Or had he somehow escaped the FBI and found her?

"Claire." She jerked as Victor called to her, his voice floating from somewhere behind her. How was he here? Why wasn't he in custody? "Come out, come out, wherever you are." The monster was cheerful, his taunts delivered in the singsong rhythm of a child's rhyme.

Claire hunched her shoulders, defending herself from the slap of his voice. It didn't matter how he'd found her. All that mattered was that he was here, in the house, playing with her the way a cat toyed with an injured mouse. After what seemed like an eternity, she reached the bedroom door, forcing herself to slow down as she slipped through. Once inside, she dashed for the closet. The sound of footsteps in the hall made her heart stop, and she sucked in a breath when she heard Victor enter the second bedroom.

She pulled the closet door shut behind her and wrenched open the door to the secret alcove. She dove in and pulled the door shut as she heard Victor enter the bedroom. With shaking fingers, she flipped the lock and pressed herself to the back of the alcove.

"Claire," he said, drawing her name out as he searched. "This is getting boring. Why don't you come out so we can talk? I'm not going to hurt you, I promise."

Yeah, right. He opened the closet door, and she pressed her fist to her mouth, biting down hard. A thin strip of light outlined the door of the alcove when Victor turned on the light, and he chuckled, the low sound giving her chills.

"Clever girl," he said, amusement lacing his tone. "But of course, that's one of the reasons I like you so much. You're not one of those whimpering, sniveling women. You have a brain, and you actually use it." His voice came closer, and Claire curled up in the corner, trying to get as far away from him as possible. The door separated them—for now. What if he tried to kick it in? She had no idea how sturdy it was, or how long it would take for him to break through.

A thin scratching sound broke the silence, making her shudder. She had the sudden, vivid image of Victor running his knife along the wood of the door, and she shook her head, trying to dislodge the disturbing picture.

"We're equals, you and I," he said, tapping his fingers on the door. "I know you're scared, but you don't have to be. You're too interesting to destroy."

Claire felt wetness on her hands and realized she was crying. She hastily wiped her cheeks dry, trying to keep her breathing as shallow as possible. Why wouldn't he just *go away?*

"I have to be honest with you though, my employer wants you gone. They think you can implicate them in this business. But…" Victor lowered his voice, his tone turning confessional. "I think they're being short-sighted. A woman like you would be an amazing asset. Once their tempers cool, they'll understand, and they'll agree that I did the right thing by keeping you alive. You don't have to worry, *milaya*—I'll protect you from them."

Claire flinched at the perversion of Ivan's endearment, burying her head in her arms in a bid to block out Victor's words. He chattered on, describing his plans for them—where they would go, the beautiful things he was going to give her. The pride in his voice made him sound like a new husband describing the perfect honeymoon trip to his bride.

Oh my God, he's insane. She'd known he was dangerous, but the cold, calculated nature of his actions had made her assume he was rational. Hearing the elaborate, twisted fantasy he'd constructed turned her blood to ice. There was no telling what he'd do to her, all in the name of "love."

After a few moments, he fell silent. Claire held her breath, straining to hear any sounds of movement. Was he still out there, or had he left? He wouldn't go far, she knew, but just having more distance between them would make her feel so much better.

Her hopes crashed back to earth when he spoke again. "Claire," he said, his voice taking on an edge. "You are making things more difficult than they have to be. Will you come out? I swear on my mother's grave I won't harm you."

Claire shook her head. Even though he couldn't see her response, the need to refuse him was so great she couldn't stay still. Apparently her silence was answer enough, for he sighed loudly.

"Very well." He sounded dejected. "I had hoped it wouldn't come to this, but I see now that you require additional persuasion. So be it."

He did move then, and Claire exhaled silently when she heard him step away from the door. "You will come to me, Claire," he said, his voice cold. "Just remember I tried to make it easy for you. What happens next is your fault."

She heard him shut the bedroom door and let her head fall back to rest against the wall. Then the shaking started. She shivered violently, unable to control her limbs as they vibrated with an intensity that was almost painful. She sucked in deep, heaving breaths, no longer worried about staying silent. Victor knew where she was, so what was the point?

After an eternity, she stopped quivering long enough to dry her face. It didn't help. Tears continued to leak from her eyes, tracking down her cheeks to drip off her chin. She pressed her sleeves to her eyes but gave up after a moment. She had bigger things to worry about right now.

It was unlikely Natalie had managed to send a distress call. Victor had been all too willing to chat through the door, which meant he wasn't worried about backup arriving. Still, she clung to the hope that Thomas had heard the shot and called for help. Even though it was unlikely, the thought that a SWAT team was about to storm the house made her feel less alone.

It's up to me, she realized, sniffling. She had no idea if she'd get cell service in this alcove, but she had to try. She stretched out her legs and patted her pockets, searching for the familiar bulge of her phone. Her heart dropped as she realized her pockets were empty. Fighting to control her breathing, she checked again. Nothing.

With a sickening lurch, she imagined her phone tucked into the pouch on the side of her purse, the memory as clear as a photograph. She'd dropped the bag on the table upon entering the house, not thinking she should hang on to it. She was safe here, after all.

A quiet sob escaped as the true magnitude of her situation sank in. She was trapped in this alcove, with a psychopathic murderer lying in wait. She had no phone, no way of contacting the outside world. No means of protecting herself.

She was alone.

Chapter 13

Thomas tightened his grip on the phone, hardly daring to breathe. Something was terribly wrong.

Natalie had answered, but she'd been cut off in midsentence. Now she wasn't responding to his calls. Neither was Claire.

Pressing hard on the accelerator, he wove through traffic as he made his way out of the city. Keeping one eye on his phone, he redialed Natalie's number.

Maybe she just dropped the phone, his rational mind said, looking for an innocent excuse for her lack of contact. He'd done it any number of times. If it hit the ground at the right angle the battery popped out, and it took several minutes to put it back together and reboot the damn thing. That was the most logical explanation. She wasn't picking up right now, but that didn't necessarily mean Victor had found them.

His gut told his brain to shut the hell up.

He would give her one more try, and then he was calling in the rest of the team....

The phone buzzed in his hand, Natalie's number popping up on the display. He nearly shouted with relief.

"Natalie? What happened? Why didn't you answer your phone?"

"Agent Kincannon, so good to hear your voice."

Thomas felt his heart stall in his chest at the sound of Victor's voice. His gut turned to water as realization sank in. He was calling from Natalie's phone, which could only mean one thing.

"What have you done with her?"

"Nothing," Victor said. "Yet."

Thomas swallowed around the lump in his throat. The thought of Claire in the clutches of this madman tore him up inside. She had to be terrified, and given the fact that Victor had cut her earlier, he didn't doubt the assassin would be quick to hurt her again.

"What do you want?" His body screamed at him to move, but he was coming up on a sea of brake lights and he couldn't go any faster.

"I want you, Agent Kincannon," Victor replied, his tone implying that this should be obvious. "I am not accustomed to people walking away from an encounter with me, and you will not be the first."

This was about preserving his macabre record? Insane. This man had assaulted a woman, kidnapped a child and was even now holding Claire hostage, all because of some ego-driven quest? Thomas felt an oddly serene calm settle over him as a sense of resolve filled his chest, chasing away the anger and fear for Claire.

"I repeat, what do you want?"

"I want you to face me, man-to-man. For the last time." The challenge was unmistakable, the other man's conceit coming through loud and clear.

"Where and when?"

There was a pause, as if Victor had expected more resistance, or perhaps threats. Too bad. Thomas wasn't about to waste words, or to give Victor even a hint of what was to come.

"The safe house," the other man finally said. "Bring the papers. And I don't need to tell you to come alone, do I? I've already killed your friend, the woman agent, but I still have Claire. She's very lovely, you know." His voice dropped to a confessional tone that made Thomas's stomach twist. "All that smooth, pretty skin over soft curves. It would be a shame to hurt her."

"I suggest you don't," Thomas replied evenly. "If she dies, you have no bargaining chip."

Victor laughed, a low, soft chuckle that slithered across the connection. "Oh, Agent Kincannon, how naive you are. The human body can take so much punishment before giving out. And I know just what buttons to push. Trust me," he finished, a smile evident in his tone. "I can make her scream."

Thomas gritted his teeth, determined not to rise to the bait. If Victor knew how much he really cared for Claire, the man wouldn't hesitate to punish her to get to him. Bad enough she was being held hostage now, but for her to be tortured as part of some sick vendetta? He'd never forgive himself.

"I'm coming," he said, ignoring the other man's taunts. He hung up the phone before Victor could respond—a small, but satisfying, victory. With careful, controlled movements, he slipped the phone back into his jacket and ran a hand through his hair.

He toyed with the idea of calling Valdez but dismissed it. The other agent would want to set up a plan of attack, to deploy backup. An understandable response, but one that would only put Claire in more danger. Victor was rash, deadly and crazy, but he wasn't stupid. He'd know right away if an operation was being set up outside the safe house, and Thomas wasn't willing to risk Claire's safety. No, he had to do this alone.

The thought of walking into this situation solo and blind should have worried him. It didn't. Rather than feeling nervous, Thomas felt a sense of determined anticipation. This was going to end today. One way or another, Victor would no longer be a threat to the people he loved.

Even if it killed him.

He hadn't come back.

She had no idea how long it had been, but after leaving the room, Victor hadn't returned. Claire wasn't naive enough to think he'd left completely, but as the minutes passed with no sign of him, she had begun to relax a bit.

She shifted now, attempting to find a better position. The alcove wasn't very big, and it wasn't designed for comfort. She'd been huddled for so long her muscles protested the movement with sharp twinges that shot down her legs as she uncurled. Wincing, she stretched what she could, rubbing her thighs to help ease the tension that had held her in its grip.

The panic that had overwhelmed her earlier was now a manageable thing, something she felt she could control, at least for a time. Like a lion on a leash, she knew it was only a matter of time before it broke free again, but she was determined to make the most of this interlude while she could.

Out of habit, she closed her eyes as she thought through her options. There weren't many to speak of. The lack of a phone meant she couldn't dial out for help. She pictured the rooms of the house, trying to recall the closest phone to her…probably the one in the den. She would have to risk leaving the alcove and sneaking through the hall to get to it, and even then, she couldn't be sure Victor hadn't cut the lines.

No, she decided, venturing out for a phone was not a chance worth taking. Besides, she had no desire to see what Victor had done to Natalie. She wanted to remember the woman as she had been—friendly and full of life—not as another of Victor's victims.

Her only alternative was to try to escape through a window. The bedroom had one, a smallish square above the bed. It wasn't huge, but given her determination, she could squeeze through, provided she could move the bars currently covering the glass. It would be tight though, and she knew the sound of breaking glass would draw Victor. Just the thought of him finding her hanging half-out the window was enough to make her shudder. No, the window was not an option.

That left running for the door. The riskiest plan, and the most likely to get her caught. She had no way of knowing exactly where Victor was right now. He could be parked outside the bedroom door like a cat watching a mouse hole, just waiting for her to leave the alcove in a bid for freedom. *But,* said the voice of reason in her head, *he could also be distracted, off doing something else.* It was entirely possible the assassin was sitting in the kitchen drinking a beer, with no view of the front door. *I could get out....*

Claire focused all her attention on the sounds, or lack thereof, coming from the bedroom. Still silent. Still no sign that anyone was nearby. Should she take the chance? Even if she didn't make it out, it would be better to know what was going on. Anything was better than sitting in this claustrophobic prison, feeling the space shrinking down on her as the silence grew heavy and pressing.

Taking a deep breath, she raised a shaking hand to the lock on the small door. It was now or never. This would either be the smartest thing she'd ever done, or the dumbest. *I hope I live long enough to figure out which one.*

The knob of the sliding lock was cool to the touch and fit perfectly in the curve of her palm. Carefully, so carefully, she pushed it gently to the side, holding her breath in anticipation of the telltale screech that never came.

Now all she had to do was push the door open. Just one firm shove, and she'd be able to crawl out of the alcove. That's all it would take.

So why wasn't she moving? Her hand was on the knob, all she had to do was push, but she couldn't make herself do it. *Stop stalling,* she chided, swallowing hard against the growing lump in her throat. Yes, Victor was still out there, but better to face him in the open than to stay cowering in this alcove. For all she knew, he was preparing to burn down the house around her. If she had to die, she wasn't going to do it locked in a tiny room, huddling in fear.

Her mind made up, she took a deep, fortifying breath and moved....

What was that?

She paused, pressing her ear to the door. Muffled, indistinct sounds were her only reward, but something didn't feel right. The house had been so unnaturally still that these faint stirrings set off alarm bells in her head.

Moving quickly, she slid the latch back into place and scooted back until she hit the wall farthest from the door, cursing silently at this change in circumstances.

Her window of opportunity had closed. He was coming back.

Chapter 14

This definitely wasn't one of his better plans.

The trouble was, he didn't really have time to come up with anything else. With the clock ticking, and Claire at the mercy of that madman, Thomas didn't have the luxury of developing a foolproof strategy. He had to wing it, which left a lot of room for error. A fact he was doing his best to ignore at the moment.

This had to work. The alternative was unacceptable.

He parked several blocks away from the safe house, in front of an empty lot at the end of the street. The closest neighborhood was about five hundred yards away, and the intervening land had a neglected, lonely feel, the broken bottles and decaying plastic bags tangled in the tall weeds a testament to the general lack of interest in this property.

It was perfect.

After a quick glance around confirmed no one had noticed his arrival, Thomas casually removed a crowbar and bolt cutters from the trunk and stepped over to the storm drain. A few quick tugs, and he slid the manhole cover to the side. With a final look around, he slipped through the opening and dropped into the sewer below.

The air was dank and musty, the smell of stale mildew so strong he could practically chew it. And no wonder—in the beam of his flashlight, he could see the walls were no longer concrete but a fuzzy, wet green that seemed to breathe around him.

"Nice mold," he muttered, moving carefully so as not to brush against it. No telling what that stuff was, and the last thing he needed was to poison himself on this harebrained rescue mission. There was no backup, no cavalry riding to the rescue. If he succumbed to some kind of toxic swamp thing down here in the storm drain, Claire was doomed.

He played his flashlight across the walls, searching for the opening he knew was there. His heart kicked into his throat when he encountered nothing but glossy, unbroken green. Where the hell was the door?

Was he in the wrong place? He had checked the plans twice, but the screen on his phone was so damn tiny it was possible he'd misread them in his excitement. *I really should have been a better Boy Scout....*

He circled again, slower this time, playing the light across the walls in a methodical sweep. He was rewarded with a flicker on the right wall, and he stepped closer. The light illuminated a faded metal sign that was barely legible in the gloom: *City of Reston, Fairfax Water Authority. Restricted Access.*

About a foot lower he found the padlock, right where it should be. It was tarnished but not rusted through, a sign that the bureau did occasionally perform maintenance checks.

Hopefully that means the tunnel is still functional, he thought as he made short work of the padlock. After all, why bother to lock a door that led nowhere? Maybe, just maybe, they would get out of this alive after all.

He used the crowbar to scrape most of the green stuff off the handle. There was still too much left for his liking, but this was no time to be squeamish. He just hoped the slimy residue didn't interfere with his grip. The door looked heavy and imposing, and he was going to have to put some effort into yanking it open.

Before he could test it out, his phone buzzed insistently in his pocket. It was Valdez. Thomas frowned. Was Emily okay?

"Kincannon." He spoke quietly, unsure of how well sound carried in the tunnels. Even though he was a few blocks away from the safe house, he didn't want to take any chances.

Valdez didn't waste time with preliminaries. "Natalie isn't answering her phone. Neither is Dr. Fleming. I'm sending a team out there now. How are things on your end?"

Thomas cursed silently, his mind racing. Victor wouldn't hesitate to kill Claire if a team of agents stormed the safe house, but he had to admit, the idea of reinforcements was comforting. How could he make this work to his advantage?

"Kincannon? You still there?"

"Yeah." There was no help for it—he was going to have to share his plan with Valdez, and trust that the other man would do the right thing. "Here's the deal. Victor called me. He's got Claire. He wants me to come alone."

Valdez released a rapid stream of Spanish, his tone leaving no doubt as to his meaning. Thomas bit back a grin. "When this is over I'm going to make you teach me what you just said. Jenny gets pissed at me when I swear in front of Emily."

"Tell me you are not being an idiot right now," Valdez said, ignoring his request.

Thomas shrugged. "Not an idiot, no," he said. "Maybe a little reckless though."

"Let me get this straight," Valdez said. "Natalie is dead, and you're walking into a trap. Is that about right?"

"I have to."

"You can't save her if you're dead!"

"I don't plan on dying." That was true, but then again, neither had Natalie.

"Pendejo," muttered Valdez. "Where are you?"

Thomas hesitated, then shrugged. Even if Valdez did know where he was, it would take time to get agents to his location. "In the storm drain a few blocks south of the house."

He could hear the sound of fingers on a keyboard. Valdez let out a hum of satisfaction. "You are planning on using the escape tunnel?"

"Seemed like the best strategy to me."

"It's not bad," the other man said, grudging admiration in his tone. "Better than a frontal assault, I'll grant you that."

"Gee, thanks," Thomas replied. "Now if we're done here, I have to go. Time's running out."

"I can't let you do this alone," Valdez said, a thread of steel in his voice.

"I'd love some help," Thomas replied, his patience running thin. "But not if you're going to get in my way. The longer we sit here gabbing, the less time I have to find Claire and get her out of the house. I can't let you send in a team of agents to storm the gates, because Victor will expect that and he'll kill her. That's a chance I'm not willing to take. So if I have to go in there alone and sacrifice myself to keep her safe, then that's the price I'll pay."

There was a beat of silence as Valdez absorbed his words. "This isn't just an operation to you, is it?"

"Not even close."

The other man sighed, a heavy gust across the line. "You have *cojones,* I'll give you that. But I wonder if they're bigger than your brain? Do you have a plan B?"

Thomas gritted his teeth at the question. In point of fact, he didn't have a plan B. He had some half-baked ideas floating around, but nothing so coherent as to be mistaken for a plan. "Not exactly," he said carefully.

"This is where I come in, then." He could *hear* the smile in Valdez's voice, smug and satisfied. Biting back a reflexive retort, Thomas listened to the other man as he outlined his idea. It was a long shot, but it just might work. Best of all, it was so crazy, so outside the realm of normal siege tactics, there was no way Victor could anticipate it. He'd be caught completely by surprise, a thought Thomas relished. It was about time Victor was one step behind.

"That's actually a good plan," he said, unable to keep the shock from his voice. If Valdez noticed, he didn't waste time commenting on it.

"Let's hope so," he said. "We should be there in fifteen minutes. Can you stay alive that long?"

Thomas glanced at his watch. "I have to move now. Any way you can push it?"

"I'll try. Just don't do anything stupid, okay?"

Thomas huffed out a laugh. "Yeah. I'll get right on that."

"Keep your phone on. If he moves you, we can track it."

"Roger that. And, Valdez?"

"Yeah?"

"Thanks."

There was a soft chuckle. "Saying thank you doesn't get you off my list, Kincannon."

Thomas felt his lips twitch in response. "It's a start." He ended the call with a soft click and tucked the phone away, then turned and faced the door. It took surprisingly little effort to pry it open, and the overall dampness of the environment kept the hinges from squealing too loudly.

He stepped through to find the escape tunnel, created soon after the house had been built in the eighties, blessedly dry, if a little on the dirty side. Cobwebs decorated the wall, and he had the distinct impression rats probably used the area as a hangout. Tamping down a reflexive shiver, Thomas rubbed his hand dry on his slacks and started down the hall, gun in one hand, flashlight in the other. It was unlikely Victor knew about the escape tunnel, but he wasn't going to take any chances.

He moved carefully, fighting the urge to run. He hated leaving Claire alone with Victor any longer than necessary, but running into the situation blind was a surefire way to get killed. Caution also made him step lightly. It was unlikely that sound from the tunnel carried into the house, but his whole plan would go up in smoke if Victor caught wind of his approach.

After a few agonizingly slow moments, he reached the end of the escape tunnel. Dusty metal rungs protruded from the wall, leading up to a large square. Based on the plans he'd studied, he should come up in the pantry of the kitchen. It was a low-risk entry point, considering the fact that the door to the pantry was nearly always shut. The lack of light outlining the door led Thomas to believe it was shut now, meaning Victor wouldn't see him come up.

On the other hand, who knew how long it had been since anyone had tried to open the escape hatch? If the hinges groaned, or if some fool had set groceries on top of the door, the noise would be a dead giveaway. The pantry was roomy, but there was no other exit. If Victor found him, he'd be a sitting duck.

But on the bright side, he wouldn't live long enough to really regret his mistake.

A quick glance at his watch confirmed he was running out of time. Not only was Victor's deadline approaching but Valdez had set wheels in motion after their conversation. While he appreciated the backup, some primitive, testosterone-fueled part of him wanted to be the one to rescue Claire, to be her knight in shining armor.

He forced himself to wait a few moments, focusing on the door above and the absolute lack of sounds coming from the house. What he wouldn't give for a wire-cam right now! He comforted himself with the fact that a camera would have taken too long to set up. Besides, if this entry was compromised, he didn't exactly have another option.

Here we go. Tucking the flashlight in his pocket and his gun in the waistband of his pants, Thomas stepped onto the ladder. He only needed to stand on the first rung to touch the door. Steepling his fingers against the smooth wood, he gave it a tentative shove. It moved easily, rising gently and then falling back into place.

Wanting leverage, he moved up a rung. This time he pushed steadily, the door lifting until he used his hand to steady it in the vertical position. He waited in the tunnel a beat, then slowly peeked through the opening, searching for an ambush that wasn't there. Satisfied he was alone, he quickly climbed into the pantry and drew his gun.

There was a low hum as the heater switched on, but otherwise, the house was silent. Now that he was inside, the lack of movement was unnatural—the stillness a palpable *thing* that raised the hairs on the back of his neck. The place felt abandoned and lonely, and he felt a sudden clench of fear low in his belly. Had Victor taken Claire somewhere else? Was this whole thing just another setup?

Moving quickly but cautiously, Thomas left the pantry and stepped into the kitchen, leading with his gun.

A quick scan confirmed the room was empty, so he moved forward into the dining room. Claire's purse sat on the table, her cell phone poking out from a pocket, blinking insistently in the late-afternoon sunlight. *No wonder she hadn't answered...*

He approached the living room, his stomach dropping as the smell of death hit him. *Am I too late?* He stepped through the door, the sight hitting him like a punch to the gut. Blood was everywhere—splattered on the walls and ceiling, soaking the carpet. His eyes jumped from one spot to another, flitting around the room as he searched for the telltale gleam of golden hair in the gore. Nothing. She wasn't there.

Relief washed over him, followed swiftly by the sharp stab of guilt. Natalie—a good agent, with a family and people who loved her—had died. He shouldn't be happy that Claire wasn't here. He should mourn Natalie's death. And he would—just as soon as he took down Victor.

Thomas knelt next to the fallen agent, hesitating a moment before patting her down with quick, efficient movements. It felt wrong, disrespectful in a way, but dead people didn't need weapons, and he wanted to be prepared.

Her service weapons were missing, but he found a small piece in an ankle holster. It wasn't much, but it was better than nothing.

With a final pat on Natalie's shoulder, Thomas rose, silently vowing revenge. *I won't let him get away with this,* he promised.

He started down the hall that led to the bedrooms, anxiety mounting with each step. Where was Claire?

Why hadn't Victor shown himself? Was he hiding, waiting for Thomas to come to him? For what purpose? He couldn't shake the feeling he was missing something, but he didn't have time to stop and think about it. Phase two of this crazy scheme was going to happen any minute now, and he needed to make sure Claire wasn't hiding under a bed somewhere.

The first bedroom was clear, with no sign of occupancy. He spared a glance at the bed, where only hours before he had woken with Claire in his arms. Desperation clawed his gut, eating him from the inside out. Where the hell was she? Only one room left to check.

Empty.

He stood in the doorway surveying the room, refusing to believe his eyes. No. She couldn't be gone. He refused to believe he'd failed to protect another person he cared about. He blinked hard, but the reality didn't change. She wasn't here.

He pushed down the scream that stuck in his throat, denying himself the satisfaction of releasing it. There would be time for that later. He turned to leave, but his gaze snagged on the closet door. It was ajar, a sliver of light escaping to slice across the floor. That was odd....

His heart kicked up as he approached the door. He had stashed Claire in the panic alcove once before, so she knew it was a safe place to go. Did she get there in time?

Gun at the ready, he entered the closet. The door to the alcove was shut, fueling his growing hope. He crouched down and leaned in close, his heart in his throat. *Please, please, please...*

"Claire?"

* * *

She sucked in a breath, hardly daring to believe her ears. *Was that—?*

No, it couldn't be. Her mind was simply playing tricks on her. She was so desperate for help, her panicked brain had conjured up Thomas's voice. And despite what she'd seen at the hospital, what she now knew to be true, her traitorous heart leaped at the sound of his voice, imagined or not. She closed her eyes against the sudden prick of tears, hating the weaknesses that kept her trapped in this alcove, in love with a man who would never love her back.

"Claire? Are you in there? It's Thomas."

She lifted her head at the muffled voice. Okay, that was definitely real. Someone was in the closet, someone who knew about the safe room. Someone who sounded a lot like Thomas.

"Thomas?"

There was a soft thud against the door, as if her visitor had laid his hand against it. "I'm here."

Her breath rushed out in a strangled sob that might have been his name.

"Claire, open the door. We need to get out of here."

She slid the latch open before he'd finished speaking, stifling a cry of joy at the sight of him, kneeling in front of the alcove. He reached for her as she fisted her hands in his shirt, pulling herself against his broad, wonderfully solid chest. She plastered herself to him, wanting to crawl inside his embrace, never wanting to let him go again. He was really here. He had come for her; she wasn't alone any longer.

Then she caught a whiff of the cloying, musky perfume saturating his shirt, and she leaned back, putting some much-needed distance between their bodies. *He's not really mine.*

He cupped her face with one hand. "Now is not the time," he whispered urgently. "But don't believe everything you see. It's only you, Claire."

He pressed something small and cold to her palm. She curled her fingers around it, realizing with a small shock that he'd given her a gun. "I don't know how—" she protested, but he cut her off.

"You shouldn't need it, but just in case. You only have to point and shoot." He squeezed her shoulder at her nod. "That's my girl. Keep it down by your side while we move."

"Where are we going?" she whispered, wincing when she took a step. Her muscles, having adjusted to the cramped conditions in the alcove, protested her sudden change of position. Pins and needles shot down her legs, making her wobble a bit. Thomas noticed her difficulty and slipped his arm around her, drawing her close to his side while they moved through the bedroom.

"There's an escape tunnel in the kitchen. That's our goal. If something happens—"

"What do you mean, if something happens? What could go wrong?"

His mouth tightened at her question, sending a spike of dread through her belly. She had assumed that Victor was gone, but if Thomas was worried, then maybe that wasn't the case. Swallowing hard, she forced herself to ask, "Is Victor still here?"

Thomas shifted his gaze to the door, as if he couldn't

bear to look at her. His reaction made her stomach flip-flop. She screwed her eyes shut and focused on her breathing, counting so loudly in her head she almost missed his soft answer.

"I don't know."

Great. Just great. Thomas hadn't found him in the house, which meant he was still out there somewhere. Oh sure, Thomas would get her out of this situation, but what about the next time? And the next? Until Victor was arrested and put in jail, he was free to find her, free to terrorize her until he succeeded in kidnapping her, or until she died.

Was it only a few moments ago that she'd thought this ordeal was over with? When she'd opened the door to the alcove and seen Thomas in front of her, so strong and reassuring? She'd felt so safe with his arms around her, like nothing bad could ever happen again.

She shook her head, cursing herself for being a naive fool. This wasn't some movie, where the good guys always won. This was a nightmare, one she would never get to wake up from as long as that monster was still out there.

"Claire?" Thomas's voice broke into her thoughts. She opened her eyes to find him watching her, a concerned look on his face. "I know this is a lot to deal with, but we have to move, now."

She nodded woodenly, accepting his orders without question. What did it matter, at this point? Victor was only going to find her again. This would never end.

Thomas gave her arm another squeeze. "I will find him, Claire. I will find him, and I'll make sure he doesn't hurt you or anyone else ever again." His blue eyes burned with a fierce gleam as he spoke, almost scorching her with the force of his determination. Her heart melted a bit at the sight. He looked like such a warrior, ready to ride into battle. She wanted to believe him, she truly did, but it was just too much to ask. She settled for a nod and a lopsided smile, which had him frowning in response.

"Stay behind me, okay?" He tucked her hand into the waistband of his pants, anchoring her in place. "Don't let go."

With that, he turned and stepped into the hallway. She followed, crouching in the shelter of his shoulders, focusing hard to keep from stepping on his heels as he walked. The last thing she wanted to do was trip him as he guided her down the hall.

"Almost there," he whispered, then froze as he stepped into the living room. Claire stopped, too, but when he didn't move again, she risked a glance around his body to see into the room. It appeared empty. Why had he stopped?

Slowly straightening up, she lifted her head to ask that very question, only to see the answer for herself. Victor stood flush against the wall, his arm extended with his gun pointing directly at Thomas's head. The bastard had been lying in wait the whole time.

"So glad you could join us, Agent Kincannon," he said solicitously. "Claire was quite upset at the thought of leaving without saying goodbye."

Son of a bitch!

He knew it had seemed too easy. He'd been so focused on finding Claire he hadn't stopped to really search the house, to verify that Victor was gone. It was a costly mistake, one that he was now going to pay for.

"Drop your gun," the man instructed.

Gritting his teeth, Thomas did as he asked. At least Claire still had a weapon. If she could even use it. She was holding on to his pants with a death grip, and she seemed frozen in place. Shock, probably. No telling what Victor had said to her while she huddled in the small panic room. No, he couldn't count on her to shoot him, but maybe she could give him the gun....

He casually reached back with his right hand, hoping she would catch the gesture and hand it over.

Unfortunately, Victor wasn't stupid. Before Thomas could so much as wiggle his fingers to get her attention, the assassin jerked him forward and around, swinging him into the living room and away from Claire.

"Much better," he said with a smile, keeping the gun trained at his chest while he moved to stand in front of Claire. "I don't like you so close to her."

Thomas tried to catch Claire's eye, but she stood unblinking in the hallway. He could tell by the glazed look in her eyes that she wasn't registering what was happening in front of her. Maybe that was for the best. She'd already been traumatized enough.

"So what's your plan now, Victor? Are you just going to shoot me and run?" Not his best suggestion, but he wanted to stall, to keep the other man talking until Valdez's plan kicked in. It should only take a few more minutes....

Victor shrugged. "Yes. But before I go, I wanted to tell you what a sweet little girl your niece is. Emily and I had so much fun together. Has she told you about it?"

Thomas took a step forward, his hands curving in anticipation of wrapping around Victor's neck as rage, white-hot and blinding, pumped through him.

Victor laughed and raised the gun, his eyes widening when Thomas didn't stop. "If you attack me," he yelled, backing up a step, "I will pay her a visit when I'm done with you. Your sister-in-law, too. And your mother."

That brought Thomas up short, his chest heaving like he'd finished a marathon. Victor didn't know that backup was on the way—if Thomas got killed now, there would be nothing to keep the assassin here. Better to wait until he had numbers on his side. Then he could kill the man. Slowly.

"You're sick," he spit, his arms shaking with unspent anger.

"Hardly," Victor drawled, his voice calm now that he was back in control. Or so he thought.

"I'm simply a man who takes advantage of every resource," he continued, stepping forward again. "You have too many weaknesses, Agent Kincannon. It makes you an easy target."

Thomas opened his mouth to reply just as a flash of movement caught his attention. Claire stepped forward, her gaze focused on Victor's back, her eyes full of fear and determination.

"Oh yeah?" Thomas replied, hoping Victor hadn't heard her move. "Then why did it take you so long to kill me?"

Claire raised her arm, the gun wobbling as she took aim. Thomas fought to keep his expression neutral. If she missed, he was going to get hit, and then it was game over. Although, if he had to die today, better to be shot by the woman he loved than by a psychopathic killer.

Victor sneered and took a small step forward just as Claire pulled the trigger. His body jerked when the bullet entered his back, but he didn't go down. He turned to face her while she fired again, lifting his arm to aim his own gun at her. Seeing his chance, Thomas reacted on instinct, lunging forward and tackling him as Claire fired for the third time.

Victor struggled, thrashing under him with a surprising amount of force for a man with two bullets in him. Thomas elbowed him in the nose and fought for the gun Victor still held in his hand. He had to get that weapon before Victor got a shot off.

He yanked hard on Victor's arm, pulling it back until his elbow gave with a sickening pop. The man screamed but didn't stop fighting, twisting and rolling in an effort to dislodge Thomas. Thomas brought up his knee, planting it in Victor's back and pushing, trying to get some leverage over the other man while he worked to pry his fingers off the gun.

A loud boom split the air, and Victor jerked underneath him. A second boom, and the man lay still, his muscles slack. Confused, disoriented, Thomas turned to try to find the direction of the sound.

Claire stood off to the side, his gun in her hands, her arms locked as she kept the gun pointed at Victor. Tears streamed down her face while she stared at the man, and after an endless moment, she lowered her arms. The gun slid from her hand, dropping to the floor with a thud he felt in his knees, and she reached up to wipe her nose. He saw her lips move when she looked at him, and realized with a sense of shock that he couldn't hear her.

He shook his head, reaching up to rub his ear. He started to move off of Victor's limp body but lurched at a sudden dizzy spell. His arm shot out just in time, his hand on the wall the only thing keeping him from doing a face-plant on the floor. He tried to push off, but his body wouldn't respond. He sagged forward until he hit the wall, the wallpaper blessedly cool against his heated cheek.

Hands grabbed at him, tugged him back. He opened heavy eyelids to see Claire kneeling over him, a look of abject terror on her face.

"Don't worry, he's dead," he mumbled. He tried to reach up to cup her cheek, but his arm wouldn't cooperate. Her tears fell on his face, hot droplets that soaked into his skin until he felt he was drowning. With a sigh, he closed his eyes and let the water take him away.

Chapter 15

Claire couldn't take her eyes off Thomas, lying so still on the gurney. The flame of his hair was muted by the darker red of his blood, a red that coated her own hands in a sticky, drying mess.

"Please," she begged, stepping forward in an attempt to get closer to him. If she could just touch him, let him know she was here, that she was sorry...

Jenny stepped in front of her, cutting off her access and her view of the E.R. doctors working to cut the clothes off Thomas.

"Stay out of the way," she snapped, her hands tightening painfully on Claire's arms.

"Please, just let me see him. I need to talk to him." She craned her head, trying to see around Jenny, but the other woman mirrored her movements, blocking her at every turn.

"No, you don't. You need to stay away from him and let the doctors do their job." Jenny punctuated her words with a little shake. "They can't work on him if you're in the way. You need to leave, now."

She felt the air stir and turned her head to see the woman from earlier, the one Thomas had kissed, dash toward the gurney.

Claire choked back a protest when another set of hands grabbed her, taking her shoulders and steering her away. But not before she saw *her* lean over the gurney to whisper something to Thomas. He smiled at her, his hand coming up to cup her cheek before falling back down to the bed as his eyes drifted shut.

Don't believe everything you see. It's only you.

Yeah, right. Fool me once, shame on you. Fool me twice...

"Come on, Dr. Fleming. Let's wait outside."

It took her a moment to register who held her. Valdez. She stared up into sympathetic brown eyes. "We need to get you cleaned up."

She glanced down, registering her appearance for the first time. Blood soaked her clothes and stained her skin, making her look like a deranged ax murderer. "Oh my God," she murmured, pulling the soaked shirt away from her body.

"It's not that bad," Valdez assured her as he led her from the room. Once in the hall, he removed his blue FBI jacket and draped it around her shoulders, zipping up the front to hide the worst of the carnage. "Nothing a quick shower and a change of clothes won't fix."

"I shot him," she murmured while he guided her down the hall. "I can't believe I shot him."

"You did a good job, Doctor," Valdez replied, his tone low and fierce. "Victor Banner was a bad guy who deserved to die. I'm sorry you had to be the one to kill him, but I'm not sorry he's dead."

Claire shook her head. "No, I shot Thomas."

Valdez stopped, one eyebrow raised as he regarded her. "Are you sure?"

"Yes," she whispered. "Victor didn't fire his gun. I was the only one who pulled a trigger tonight."

Valdez shook his head slowly. "I don't want to dismiss what you're saying, but I can tell you from experience that shootings can be very chaotic. Is it possible you're mistaken? Perhaps Banner did get a shot off before you hit him."

"Maybe," Claire said, knowing she was correct but not wanting to argue the point.

"I'm going to take you back to headquarters, where you'll be debriefed. There's an evidence team at the house now, and once their report is in, we'll know once and for all who shot whom. In the meantime—" he started walking toward the elevator again, his grip on her arm solid but gentle "—try to put it out of your mind. Nothing good will come from you worrying about it now."

She nodded, knowing he was right but unable to turn off her thoughts.

In the past forty-eight hours, she'd gone from having a normal, if slightly boring, life to this waking nightmare. Ivan was dead. She'd been stabbed, chased, battered and bruised, and she'd fired a gun for the first time in her life, killing an international assassin and badly wounding the man she was on her way to falling in love with.

Except he didn't want her, and never would.

Thomas had his own family, his own life and she had no place in it.

It was like the situation with her mother all over again, except her mother had never lied to her about her feelings, or lack thereof.

It's only you.

I don't have a girlfriend.

Over and over, his words raced through her mind, haunting her. Why had he said those things to her? What had he gained by lying to her?

She nearly snorted. He'd gotten a roll in the sack, but she wasn't so conceited as to believe he'd been desperate for her company. Whoever she was, his mystery girlfriend was a beautiful woman and, given the way she'd kissed him, quite passionate. No, it was unlikely Thomas was feeling lonely.

But maybe he was one of those men who liked variety. She shuddered at the implications of that thought. Although she was on the pill, they hadn't used any other form of protection. Aside from her broken heart, what else had she taken away from their encounter?

How could she have been so stupid? Looking back on it, she could see why she'd fallen for him. Ivan's death had brought her grief over the loss of her father to the front of her mind, and after learning about Thomas's brother, she'd wanted to connect with someone who understood the pain of losing a loved one. She'd let her emotions cloud her judgment and her interactions with Thomas, and now she was paying the price.

Her feeling of betrayal was further complicated by the deep disappointment she felt at the thought of Thomas. He'd seemed like such a nice person, a stand-up guy who had put his own safety at risk to protect her. She just couldn't reconcile the Thomas who'd saved her from Victor with the Thomas who'd slept with her and then very publicly kissed his girlfriend a few hours later.

Although by now she should really understand how complex people could be. She'd thought she'd known Ivan, too, but she couldn't argue that the evidence suggested he'd been involved in shady dealings. It was just another example of her spectacular failure in judgment. If she couldn't be trusted to see the complicated facets of a dear friend, why should she see them in someone she barely knew?

Lesson learned, she thought, as Agent Valdez ushered her into the car. *You played with fire, and you got burned.*

It was time for her to move on.

Three weeks later

Claire closed her eyes and lifted her hands to her head, rubbing her temples in a vain attempt to soothe the ache that was her constant companion of late. There was just so much to do and not enough hours in the day.

With a sigh, she returned to her computer and the half-finished email on her monitor: Therefore, we recommend increased security and heightened restrictions for access to all nuclear materials, regardless of quantity...

In the weeks following Victor's death, her workload had exploded. Ivan's papers had been sifted through by her Russian counterparts, and thanks to the packet he'd sent her, a clear picture had emerged: Ivan Novikoff was not selling nuclear fuel on the black market, but he was quietly investigating individuals and groups who had expressed an interest in obtaining those materials. His records had been thorough and meticulous, and unfortunately, they'd also been his undoing. When the Russian mob had gotten wind of his off-the-books investigation, they'd moved quickly to eliminate the threat.

Fortunately, Ivan had been quicker. Realizing the danger he was in, he'd shipped off the most incriminating documents, unwittingly exposing her to the danger as well.

While Claire was relieved to know that her friend was innocent, she wished he'd gone about his search differently. Not for the first time, she wondered if he would still be alive if he'd only involved the authorities. *I wish he would have told me. I could have saved him.* How, she didn't know, but she couldn't help but feel that if Ivan had let her in on his thoughts, she could have done something to protect him. It was one more stone of guilt to add to her already heavy burden.

She glanced out the window, hoping for a distraction to redirect her thoughts. It was overcast and gray, a perfect complement to her mood. She watched as pedestrians hurried along the sidewalk, umbrellas tucked under their arms in preparation for the threatening rain. A woman in a silver raincoat flitted past, artfully dodging the slower walkers who ambled along. Claire watched her move, envying her energy as she slipped through the crowd like a darting minnow.

A splash of color caught her eye, and she focused on the small red maple planted in the square across the street. It was beautiful, the leaves a jumbled combination of reds and oranges and golds, glowing like a living flame in stark contrast to the colorless day. The vibrant splash of colors made her think of Thomas, and she felt a flutter in her belly as she pictured his face.

Had the bruises faded yet? Was he being a good patient? She snorted, a smile playing at the corners of her mouth. Not likely. He was so stubborn, so determined—he probably wasn't resting or sitting still for very long, which would only prolong his recovery.

She shook her head, wondering for the millionth time when she'd forget about him. Wasn't it enough that he'd used her? Why did she have to keep being reminded of him every day? Her brain recognized it was time to move on, but her heart, that weak organ, hadn't gotten the message. She found herself thinking of him at least a dozen times a day, wondering if he was okay, if Emily was doing better. It was pathetic, really, the way she ached for a family and a connection that had never been real.

She turned back to her computer, the blinking cursor mocking her. Maybe one day, she wouldn't think of him every time she closed her eyes, wouldn't picture those blue, blue eyes and red hair. The curve of his mouth when he gave her that sexy grin she loved. The way he rubbed his chin when he was deep in thought, or the way his hair felt against her skin.

Yeah, right.

Just thinking about him made her pulse pick up, her traitorous body desperate to see him again. To *feel* him again. They had fit so perfectly together, almost as if they were made for each other. She'd never experienced that with anyone before, even though it had turned out to be a lie. She had the sinking feeling she never would again.

But what was that saying? Better to have loved and lost? Something like that. Cold comfort at a time like this, though.

Shaking her head, she placed her fingers on the keyboard, determined to get back to work. She'd wasted enough time mourning the loss of a relationship that had never been. Time to focus on the things that were still a part of her life.

"Do you ever take a break?"

Claire jumped at the unexpected question, her hand flying to her throat too late to stifle her startled squeak. She glanced up to find Thomas standing in the doorway, his gaze serious as he took in her office.

"What are you doing here?" Her question came out in a rush of breath, but she didn't trust herself to speak again. Instead, she ran her gaze over him, drinking in the sight.

He looked surprisingly good for a man who had been shot in the head. His hair had been shaved for the surgery, but it was growing back quickly, a red-gold fuzz that looked wonderfully soft. She wanted to rub her palm over the top of his head to let the strands tickle her skin but settled for clenching her fist instead.

His cheekbones were a bit more prominent, a testament to the fact that he'd spent the past few weeks recovering from a major injury. He wasn't gaunt, but she could tell he'd lost a few pounds. It didn't detract from the width of his shoulders or his height, which were still as imposing as ever. If anything, this new, leaner appearance gave him the look of a jungle cat: eerily still, but coiled and ready to spring.

And with his blue eyes fixed on her, cold and assessing, she had the sinking suspicion she was the prey.

"I'm here on official business," he replied, moving into the office with a casual grace. "I wanted you to know that the FBI's investigation has formally concluded, and you are no longer thought to be at risk."

Claire raised her brow at his statement. "What happened?"

Thomas shrugged, as if the matter was of little consequence. "The Russians are cleaning house. The list of names you translated has resulted in a lot of arrests, and with so many of the players behind bars, you're no longer a target."

She swallowed, trying to ignore the flutter of fear in her stomach. "What about the people who hired Victor?"

If the name of her would-be assassin bothered him, he didn't show it. "Victor was hired by a man with connections to the Russian mob," he said, sounding almost bored. "From what we can tell, he was trying to make a name for himself within the organization, and to prove his chops he was tasked with getting the list from Dr. Novikoff. You were never supposed to be a target."

"But I was."

He nodded in acknowledgment. "He was an eager beaver who overstepped his bounds."

She didn't miss his choice of words. "Was?"

"If it makes you feel any better, the man is dead. Not only did he cost them Victor, one of their best hired guns, but his actions drew attention to the mob, something they don't tolerate. The Russian mob doesn't take kindly to failure."

She quickly slammed the door on the mental images *that* statement evoked. "How can you be sure they won't come after me again?"

"As I said before, you were never a target. Furthermore, the Bratva aren't interested in triggering an international incident. They're too busy trying to mitigate the damage from Dr. Novikoff's list."

"I see."

"As long as you stay away from the Russian investigation, you'll be fine. But should you have any further need of the bureau, don't hesitate to call."

His tone was professional and detached, and it set her teeth on edge. After everything that had happened, everything he'd done to her, he was just going to dismiss her without so much as an apology?

"You're back to work already?"

He didn't answer right away. A muscle in his jaw twitched, and he glanced down briefly before meeting her eyes again. "Not officially. But I wanted to deliver this message in person."

Of course he did. Why waste an opportunity to twist the knife a bit more?

Claire nodded, trying to keep her anger and pain from showing on her face. She wouldn't give him the satisfaction of knowing he still had the power to touch her that way.

They stared at each other for a moment, the silence growing louder as they faced off. Finally, she cleared her throat. "Well, it seems like your message has been delivered."

"Yeah," he said quietly. "Sure looks that way."

"Was there anything else?" *Go. Please just leave so I can cry in private.*

Thomas shook his head. "No." He turned and took a step toward the door, then whirled back around. "Actually, yes, there is something else."

He marched forward, not stopping until he hit the edge of her desk. Claire leaned away, her heart pounding furiously. His face had reddened, and from the set of his mouth, she could tell he was gearing up for a fight. She met his glare with one of her own. If he wanted to have words, that was fine by her. She had things to say as well.

"Why did you leave the hospital?"

Claire blinked, taken aback by his question. She never would have guessed her motivation for leaving was unclear, but perhaps he needed things spelled out.

"Let's see," she began, deliberately keeping her voice level in a bid to stay calm. "I had to run to keep up with you that day, only to arrive just in time for a front-row seat to making out with your girlfriend, whoever she is. Mind you, this was after we had slept together, and after, I might add, you had told me that you weren't seeing anyone. To say I was upset would be a huge understatement, and I had to leave before I did something stupid."

He waved his hand dismissively, as if her explanation was meaningless. "I'm not talking about when we brought Emily back. I'm talking about after I got shot. Why did you leave?"

She frowned up at him. "What do you mean? I didn't see you in the hospital after you were shot."

Thomas stared at her as if she'd sprouted a second head. "Yes, you did," he said. "I was lying there on the gurney, and I heard your voice. You were asking to see me. Then you stood next to me and leaned over, and I reached up to touch your face, and I said—" He broke off and looked away, the tips of his ears turning pink.

Oh my God. Was it possible?

Claire reviewed her memories of that awful moment, seeing the encounter in a new, sickening light. If Thomas was telling the truth, he'd thought he was talking to her, not to that other woman. He'd meant to caress *her* face, whisper to *her*. She'd misinterpreted the whole thing.

Her stomach dropped as the images she recalled started to assemble into a new picture.

"I never saw you in the hospital," she said slowly, her anger toward the mystery woman building anew. "Jenny wouldn't let me near you. She said I needed to give the doctors room to work."

Her words hung between them for a long moment.

"Then who—" Recognition dawned in his eyes, and his face went slack. "Tanya," he whispered.

Claire felt a hot spike of jealousy at the other woman's name, but she held her temper in check. "Yes. I saw her lean over you, watched you reach up and say something to her. I was standing against the wall, just before Valdez escorted me out."

"So you never knew." His whole demeanor changed, going from tense and brooding to relaxed and light, as if someone had flipped a switch inside him. He grinned down at her. "You never knew," he repeated, his voice rising with excitement.

"I don't know why you're so happy about that," Claire snapped, her irritation with Jenny and the other woman still fresh.

Thomas sobered, but the corners of his mouth twitched. "I've been angry with you this whole time, over something that wasn't your fault. You have no idea the things I'd come up with to explain your behavior, and it's a relief to finally know the real reason behind your silence. I thought you just didn't care about me, but now I know the truth—you didn't know how I feel about you."

"I'm glad we cleared that little mystery up," she said. "But I'm still angry, and I'm afraid I can't turn my emotions off as quickly as you do."

"What do you mean?"

"I'm talking about the other woman. Tanya." At the mention of her name, Thomas's face fell. Claire continued, "I have to be honest with you, I have no idea what to make of the two of you. You tell me one thing, I see another. I don't know what to believe anymore."

"Tanya is no longer an issue," he said quietly, looking down. His refusal to meet her eyes only added fuel to her already blazing temper.

"Oh, really? And does she know that? Because it

seems to me she's under the impression the two of you are an item."

When Thomas didn't respond, Claire shook her head. "I'm not interested in a competition. And I'll be damned before I'll share."

He did look at her then, his blue eyes sparking. "No one's asking you to share."

Claire raised a brow. "No? You sure about that?"

"Tanya and I dated, a few years ago. Then she left me."

"She left you?" Claire echoed, at a loss. What kind of woman would leave a man like him?

Thomas pressed his lips together in an expression of distaste. "To be more specific, she cheated on me. Packed up her stuff and moved to Chicago. She came back to D.C. a few months ago, started hanging out with Jenny again." He looked down, shaking his head. "Seems the guy she left me for cheated on her, and she was hoping to pick up where we'd left off."

"I see."

"That day in the hospital—it was the first time I'd seen her in years. She came on strong in the hopes that I'd take her back. But I told her there was no chance. That I'd found someone else."

Claire's heart thumped at his words, a tingle starting low in her belly as she met his gaze. "Oh?"

Thomas nodded. "But there's something I need to know. Why didn't you trust me? I know you were upset by what you saw between me and Tanya, but I told you multiple times that I wasn't involved with anyone. Why didn't you believe me?"

Now it was her turn to look away. "It was too hard," she said, feeling ashamed. "I wanted so desperately to believe you, but what I saw…" She trailed off, shaking her head. "I couldn't reconcile your words with the actions."

"I see." His voice was flat, expressionless, and she had the vague sense that she'd disappointed him somehow.

"Can you blame me?" she asked, feeling defensive. "I didn't really know you. My friend was dead, I had been attacked and I was feeling vulnerable. I slept with you, and the next day I'm treated to the vision of you locked in a passionate embrace with another woman."

He opened his mouth, but she held up a hand to forestall his response.

"I know now that wasn't your fault, but at the time, I had no idea. Then when I see you again, you tell me there is no one else, but your actions at the hospital say something different. And yes, I see now that it was all a misunderstanding, but I had no way of knowing that. All I could see was that I had opened up to you and shared myself with you. I thought we had a connection, but you didn't seem to feel the same way. Is it any wonder I was hurt and angry?"

"No." He ran a hand over his head, a faint rasping sound accompanying the gesture. "When you put it that way, it makes perfect sense."

He sank into one of the chairs across from her desk, and they fell into silence, each lost in their own thoughts. Finally, Thomas spoke again.

"God, given the way you must have felt, it's a wonder you even spoke to me when I pulled you from the alcove."

Claire raised a brow. "If you recall, I *did* shoot you in the head," she said coolly.

He shot her a cocky grin as he rubbed the side of his head with his fingertips. "Are you saying that was my punishment?"

"No." She shook her head, all teasing gone. "I'm so sorry. I never wanted to hurt you. I was so scared, but I knew I had to do something." She broke off to wipe her eyes, rubbing away the tears that had formed at the memory of that horrible day.

"It's okay." His voice was soothing as he leaned across the desk and took one of her hands in his own. "You did great. Besides," he added, his grin returning, "I'd rather get shot by you than him any day."

Claire huffed out a laugh. "That's what Valdez said."

"Oh, yeah?"

She nodded. "When the forensics report came back, it proved that I had been the one to shoot you. Valdez hadn't believed me when I told him, but he couldn't argue with the data. I felt horrible about it, and I started crying. Not pretty, delicate crying either, but huge, wet sobs that made me sound like I was choking on bagpipes. Valdez's eyes got really big, and he pushed a box of tissues over. When that didn't help, he sat next to me and started to pat my back." She pantomimed the awkward motion of his exaggerated gestures, which made Thomas laugh. "He told me it wasn't my fault, and that it was okay. Then he said he was sure you wouldn't mind, because it was better that you were shot by me rather than Victor." She made a face at the memory.

"I'm not quite sure why that is, since you would get hurt either way, but whatever."

He gently squeezed her hand. "I knew if Victor fired, he wouldn't miss. With you, I at least had a chance of not getting hit."

Claire stared at their joined hands for a long moment. When she looked up, Thomas was watching her, a small smile on his face. She smiled in return, feeling curiously light.

"So where do we go from here?"

She didn't miss the "we" in his question, and she felt her chest grow warm, as if a candle had been lit in her heart.

"I'm not sure," she said. And she truly wasn't. Now that she knew Thomas didn't have any feelings for Tanya, all her insecurities had melted away. She could allow herself to believe that they had a chance, that things might really work out between them. "Why don't we start with you telling me what you said in the hospital?"

Thomas looked down and took a deep breath before wetting his lips with the tip of his tongue. *He's nervous,* she realized with a small start. She laid her free hand over their joined ones, squeezing gently to offer reassurance. The corner of his mouth curled up when he met her eyes.

"I love you," he said. "I know we haven't known each other for very long, but I love you. I love how smart you are, how caring, the way you put yourself in danger to help save Emily...the way you make me laugh, even when I don't want to. The way you reached out to me, comforting me when you knew I was hurting. All of it."

Claire didn't try to stop the tears, not wanting to release his hand to wipe her face. She gripped him tightly, holding on to him like a lifeline.

"I know you probably don't feel the same way about me, but I was hoping you'd at least give me—give us—a chance."

She nodded enthusiastically, a wide grin splitting her face. She opened her mouth to speak, but he held up his hand.

"Before you answer, you need to know that I'm part of a package deal. My mom, Jenny, Emily...they're a big part of my life."

"I wouldn't have you any other way," Claire said, speaking around the lump in her throat. "Besides, I haven't had a family in years. It will be nice to feel like I belong."

He tugged on her hand, pulling her close until she was forced to sit on his lap. She felt his warm breath in her hair as he whispered to her.

"You will always belong with me."

She closed her eyes, breathing in the scent of him— soap, starch and an underlying musk that was just *Thomas*. She began to relax, the worry and tension leaving her muscles as her body recognized his and surrendered to the knowledge that she was truly safe.

"I love you," she whispered, knowing she should say it louder but unable to summon the energy to raise her voice.

He responded by tightening his hold, his lips brushing across her forehead in a gentle kiss.

"I know," he murmured.

"We're quite the pair, aren't we?"

She heard the smile in his voice as he stroked her back with a gentle hand. "The perfect team."

* * * * *

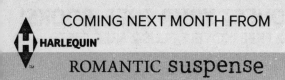

REQUEST YOUR FREE BOOKS!
2 FREE NOVELS PLUS 2 FREE GIFTS!

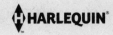

ROMANTIC suspense

Sparked by danger, fueled by passion

YES! Please send me 2 FREE Harlequin® Romantic Suspense novels and my 2 FREE gifts (gifts are worth about $10). After receiving them, if I don't wish to receive any more books, I can return the shipping statement marked "cancel." If I don't cancel, I will receive 4 brand-new novels every month and be billed just $4.74 per book in the U.S. or $5.24 per book in Canada. That's a savings of at least 14% off the cover price! It's quite a bargain! Shipping and handling is just 50¢ per book in the U.S. and 75¢ per book in Canada.* I understand that accepting the 2 free books and gifts places me under no obligation to buy anything. I can always return a shipment and cancel at any time. Even if I never buy another book, the two free books and gifts are mine to keep forever.

240/340 HDN F45N

Name   (PLEASE PRINT)

Address   Apt. #

City   State/Prov.   Zip/Postal Code

Signature (if under 18, a parent or guardian must sign)

Mail to the Harlequin® Reader Service:

IN U.S.A.: P.O. Box 1867, Buffalo, NY 14240-1867
IN CANADA: P.O. Box 609, Fort Erie, Ontario L2A 5X3

Want to try two free books from another line?
Call 1-800-873-8635 or visit www.ReaderService.com.

* Terms and prices subject to change without notice. Prices do not include applicable taxes. Sales tax applicable in N.Y. Canadian residents will be charged applicable taxes. Offer not valid in Quebec. This offer is limited to one order per household. Not valid for current subscribers to Harlequin Romantic Suspense books. All orders subject to credit approval. Credit or debit balances in a customer's account(s) may be offset by any other outstanding balance owed by or to the customer. Please allow 4 to 6 weeks for delivery. Offer available while quantities last.

Your Privacy—The Harlequin® Reader Service is committed to protecting your privacy. Our Privacy Policy is available online at www.ReaderService.com or upon request from the Harlequin Reader Service.

We make a portion of our mailing list available to reputable third parties that offer products we believe may interest you. If you prefer that we not exchange your name with third parties, or if you wish to clarify or modify your communication preferences, please visit us at www.ReaderService.com/consumerschoice or write to us at Harlequin Reader Service Preference Service, P.O. Box 9062, Buffalo, NY 14269. Include your complete name and address.

HRS13R

SPECIAL EXCERPT FROM

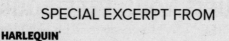
HARLEQUIN®

ROMANTIC suspense

When Josh Patterson, Marine Corps sniper, is sent on an
op to rescue a woman kidnapped from her charity nursing
work deep in the Amazon jungle, he gets more than he
was prepared for in the brave Aly Landon.

Read on for a sneak peek of

JAGUAR NIGHT

by Lindsay McKenna, part of the
COURSE OF ACTION: THE RESCUE
anthology coming September 2014 from
Harlequin® Romantic Suspense.

Glancing at her, he saw that she had gone even more ashen.
She kept touching her neck. Damn. He turned, kneeling
down. Taking her hand away, he rasped, "Let me." She nodded, allowing him to examine the larynx area of her throat.
When he pressed a little too much, she winced. But she
didn't pull away. Aly trusted him. He dropped his hands to
his knees, studying her.

"You've got some cartilage damage to your larynx. It has
to be hurting you."

Aly nodded, feeling stricken. "I'm slowing us down. I'm
having trouble breathing because that area's swollen."

"You're doing damn good, Aly. Stop cutting yourself
down."

She frowned. "Are they still coming?"

"They will. Being in the stream for an hour will buy us some good time." He glanced down at her soaked leather boots. "How are your feet holding up?"

"Okay."

He cupped her uninjured cheek, smiling into her eyes. "Who taught you never to speak up for yourself, Angel?"

Josh closed his eyes. Aly was a trouper, and she did have heart. A huge, giving heart with no thought or regard for herself or her own suffering. He leaned down, pressing a kiss to her brow, and whispered, "We're going to get out of this," he rasped, tucking some strands behind her ear.

He watched Aly's eyes slowly open, saw the tiredness in them coupled with desire. Josh had no idea what the hell was going on between them except that it was. Now he had a personal reason to get Aly to safety. Because, general's daughter be damned, he wanted to know this courageous woman a lot better.

Don't miss
COURSE OF ACTION: THE RESCUE
by Lindsay McKenna and Merline Lovelace,
coming September 2014 from
Harlequin® Romantic Suspense.

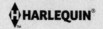

ROMANTIC suspense

UNDERCOVER IN COPPER LAKE
by **Marilyn Pappano**

A past he'd rather forget, a future he secretly longs for...

DEA informant Sean Holigan never imagined he'd return to Copper Lake and revisit the ghosts of his past. But bad memories aren't the only thing waiting for him. With their mother in jail, Sean's nieces are in the care of their foster mother, Sophy Marchand. Years and miles haven't erased Sean's high school memories of the young, studious Sophy, but she certainly has grown up. Beautiful and benevolent, Sophy represents a life, and love, Sean longs for—and one of three lives he must protect. Targeted by ruthless killers, Sophy and the girls depend on Sean... almost as badly as he depends on them.

Look for UNDERCOVER IN COPPER LAKE
by Marilyn Pappano in September 2014.

Available wherever books and ebooks are sold.

Heart-racing romance, high-stakes suspense!

www.Harlequin.com

HRS27886

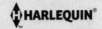

ROMANTIC suspense

ONE SECRET NIGHT
by Jennifer Morey

*The morning after brings dangerous consequences in Jennifer Morey's next **Ivy Avengers** romance.*

After stumbling into the cross fire of a black ops mission, Autumn Ivy is saved by a dark, sexy hero—and swept away for a night to remember. Weeks later, she discovers her secret lover is soon to be a secret daddy, but what's more shocking is when Autumn tracks her mystery man right into the path of a killer.

Part of a famous Hollywood family, Autumn comes with paparazzi who threaten Raith De Matteis's hidden identity. But it's Autumn's news that puts the lone-wolf agent in jeopardy. Now more than his client is at risk.
This time it's his woman...and his baby.

Look for ONE SECRET NIGHT
by Jennifer Morey in September 2014.

The ***Ivy Avengers:*** The children of a famous movie director and Hollywood heavyweight, the Ivy heirs live anything but a charmed life when danger always follows them

Available wherever books and ebooks are sold.

Heart-racing romance, high-stakes suspense!

www.Harlequin.com

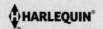

ROMANTIC suspense

WHEN NO ONE IS WATCHING
by Natalie Charles

*The red-hot passion between them isn't exactly
an open-and-shut case...*

To find her missing sister and an attacker she can't
remember, criminal profiler Mia Perez teams up with
gorgeous Boston P.D. lieutenant Gray Bartlett. Their prime
suspect: a psychotic serial killer. But when Mia's prints are
found on the gun used in recent murders, Gray doesn't
know what to think. Is the brainy beauty he's falling
for being framed?

Mia finds herself incredibly attracted to the hero risking his
life and career to protect her. Yet she keeps a deadly secret
of her past from Gray. Now she needs more than his desire—
she needs him to prove her innocence, find her sister...
and keep her alive.

Look for WHEN NO ONE IS WATCHING
by Natalie Charles in September 2014.

Available wherever books and ebooks are sold.

Heart-racing romance, high-stakes suspense!

www.Harlequin.com

HRS27888